FIRST COMES THUNDER

By

S. L. Sandmann

Publishing Services provided by Paper Raven Books LLC
Printed in the United States of America
First Printing, 2024

Paperback ISBN 979-8-9900662-0-5
Hardback ISBN 979-8-9900662-1-2

ONE

KYA KNEW ALL THE SIGNS OF A BREWING thunderstorm. The too-perfect day with the gorgeous red sunrise and no wind—a miracle in Wyoming, really. But it always led to the most devastating of storms. So why didn't she see this one coming?

It was the perfect day. Utterly perfect… her look was perfect. The graduation cap didn't, by some divine intervention, make her look like her hair was plastered down. She delivered her valedictorian speech perfectly, even if she couldn't remember what she'd said. She hadn't tripped in her heels. Her afterparty was epic. And she'd made enough money from gifts to survive her first semester of college. Definitely a perfect day.

But as she approached the fire pit outside of her friend Mitch's house, who was magnanimously hosting the senior party, she felt anything but perfect. After wiping her sweaty palms on her old worn jeans, Kya double-checked her hair and took a deep breath. She mentally checked her expression and tucked her hands into her pockets to stop the trembling. It was essential to look calm and confident. She always said yes and remained calm, cheerful, and helpful, no matter what else she had going on. That's what everyone expected of her… perfection.

And usually, that wasn't hard to do. Kya liked being the responsible and reliable good girl. But tonight, she was literally acting against herself. Her stomach rolled.

She had promised Mitch she would attend their final party as high schoolers. She hadn't gone to any of the others. The killing of brain cells and turning oneself into an idiot just to be cool simply wasn't her scene. But this was her last day of high school. She had to participate in at least one act of stupidity before entering the real world, right? Besides, Mitch really wanted her to go. He was her friend. And it was a tradition in their small town of Upton, Wyoming. At least that's what she kept telling herself.

Upton was on the very edge of the Black Hills, covered with pine and cedar trees, grey shale, and red gravel roads. Heck, the majority of the streets in town were like that. Prairie and sagebrush stretched to the south and west. The largest building was the high school. This tiny town thrived on traditions. It lived and breathed high school sports, and graduation was the highlight of the year. Every year, there was a party of extreme proportions that went down somewhere in the trees which surrounded the northeast half of town.

Kya only knew of these escapades from rumor and reputation. She pushed her nerves and fears out of her head and focused on the present. She concentrated on the emotion she could feel buzzing under her skin, making her twitchy. It was what she knew she should feel—excitement. Graduation! Finally, she was a graduate. This chapter was ending, and she would be able to move on from this place. Move forward with her plans… if she could get her parents on board with her. They wanted her to pursue a "legit" career. Something like business, or accounting, or law. Kya shuddered at the thought. How could she make them understand?

There she went again, drifting from the present and back to her responsible self. She gave herself a mental slap. That was a worry for another night. She was here to celebrate!

But this was so outside her normal that Kya couldn't shake the nerves. There was a tickle of fear lingering in the back of her mind. From what she'd heard, anything, absolutely anything, could happen.

Her mother had supplied her with a bottle of Apple Pucker. It might seem odd for a mother to hand her underaged daughter alcohol. However, when you considered the alternative, it was much safer.

They had gone over the rules before she'd left the house. If you drink, don't drive. Stay alert. Don't put yourself in a compromising position, i.e., drinking to excess or being alone with someone untrustworthy. Don't accept drinks from anyone if it's open (hence the Apple Pucker clenched in her hands). And finally, call. No matter what, call.

"Kya, I know you're responsible," her mother said, as she handed her the green bottle of alcohol. "But please be careful. I'm going to leave my phone on when I go to bed. Call when you're done. I will come get you."

"But you have to be up at four for work in the morning." Kya had replied.

"I don't want you getting in a vehicle with someone who's been drinking."

"I won't. I could walk home. It's not that far. That way, you don't have to get up."

"I'm okay with that. Just please be careful."

Kya had hugged her mom and gotten in Mitch's car.

Mitch now walked ahead of Kya, parting the crowd like Moses. He was the biggest guy in her class at six foot two and weighing in at 220 pounds. The only reason she knew exact numbers was because he was a wrestler. The guy was built like a boulder with legs. He had broad shoulders and a barrel chest. Many people saw him as overweight or fat, but after they watched him pick an opponent off the mat and toss them over his head to the ground, they quickly lost that idea. He was a pillar of muscle.

Kya followed in his wake as everyone moved out of his way. She was always anxious in a crowd, like she was wearing too-tight clothing, feeling uncomfortable and exposed. The gathered crowd stared at her like she was an alien. It only cemented her feeling out of place.

Mitch led her to a log near the fire where his family sat eating dinner and drinking beer. He said his hellos and made polite introductions while Kya kept a death grip around the Apple Pucker bottle. She already knew his immediate family, but right after the extended family was introduced, she quickly forgot their names. Not that they would remember Kya's anyway. As they stood around the fire outside, cars began to file in. More and more kids showed up, and not all of them were seniors. After a good majority arrived, the drinking began.

Settling next to Mitch on a log, she kept quiet and partook in one of her favorite activities—people watching. But when Mitch crushed his first can of beer against his head, she jumped so high she nearly fell backwards off the log. This was so not her scene.

"You going to drink that stuff you've got there or keep holding it till it's piss warm?" Mitch asked her, bumping her shoulder with his elbow.

"Uh." Kya looked down at her hands. "I need a cup, I guess."

"There should be some by the ice cooler on the table next to the porch."

"Okay." Kya levered herself off the low log and headed over to where Mitch had indicated. By the time Kya found a cup to use for her Apple Pucker, there were so many people there she had to elbow her way back toward Mitch.

She found her spot on the log around the fire again and sat down, but Mitch had disappeared. Kya looked down into the acid-green liquid in her cup and swirled it. She wasn't entirely sure about this. Hanging out was fine and dandy, but adding alcohol to the mix was a whole new territory where she had never trod before. She had drunk, yes, but not to excess, and only if her parents let her, so it was pretty much just a sip here and there. She had never been around her classmates when they were drinking. Alcohol did weird things to people.

Kya remembered a time when her dad's family had gotten together, and alcohol was flowing. She had been too young at the time and had been sequestered to the basement with the other kids. They kept sneaking up the stairs to watch the escapades of the inebriated adults. Kya had not been impressed. Her aunt had started the whole assemblage of adults in on a leg wrestling competition. It was absolutely ridiculous to watch full-grown adults act dumber than school kids. They had finished the night off with chair hurdling.

Since then, Kya never really had any interest in experimenting with alcohol. Especially when she got to witness the aftereffects on all the adults the next morning.

Kya kept to herself and studied the maze of trailer houses that was Mitch's home. She knew one of them straight across from her held a pool table. The one to her left was their main house. There was one more behind those, but she wasn't sure what that was. And there was another back in the trees behind where she sat as well, and Kya had never been near that one. All this was situated on some land off a gravel road to the north of town in the dense trees. Kya's own house was about two more miles farther north. Her family lived on forty acres in a large log home.

She let her gaze drift through the crowd, trying to find Mitch, or maybe Rachel. Her other bestie was angsty, a bit opinionated, and mouthy. But she was always completely genuine. The Rachel you saw was the real Rachel. She didn't bother faking it or holding up pleasantries. Kya smiled; she was the best.

Rachel and she had not made any official plans for the

evening, bearing on the fact that Rachel firmly believed Kya would chicken out and not go to the party. And lo, here she was at the party, seemingly alone.

Kya had never really had many friends. In elementary school, she'd had a small girl group made up of Rachel and Trish, who was currently strutting around the firepit wearing high heels. In middle school, their group had grown to include nearly every girl in their class, and some from the grade above. So, a total of maybe ten of them, because there were only six girls in her class. But when they entered high school, it all changed. Suddenly, Kya always seemed to be on the outside. She drifted to the edges of social life because she didn't play sports, so that sequestered her, and her group of friends became muscly Mitch and riotous Rachel.

Scanning the crowd, she searched for them, but with no luck. It appeared she had been ditched. Maybe she should call her mom to come get her. But it was ten o'clock already. Her parents would be in bed.

They both worked in the coal mines. Her dad had worked there her whole life. Her mom didn't start till Kya was old enough to watch her little brother, and he was pretty much taking care of himself. Her mom took the job in the pit, operating equipment, to help make ends meet. Her dad worked in the plant, running the machinery system that crushed, stored, and shipped out the mined coal. They worked twelve-hour shifts and had an hour bus commute, rotating nights and days. It made for very long shifts and exhausted parents.

And consequently, it put a lot of responsibility on Kya

from a young age. She had to make sure her little brother, Tucker, got up in the morning and made it home in the evening. She cooked dinner most nights and did a lot of the cleaning. Anything to help out. She wasn't going to wake her parents up if at all possible. It was the little things that mattered and seemed to help the most.

Kya looked back down into her cup full of green liquid in her hands. Finally, she took a sip. It tasted like tangy tart sour apples and burst on her tongue. So delicious and sweet. She sipped some more.

As she sat on the log sipping her beverage, the sun set over the trees before her. Below the darkening indigo sky, the forest around the fire was thrown into inky darkness. The fire's light made the shadows even blacker.

Glancing over the flames, Kya scanned the crowd. One of her classmates fell into some older guy's lap. That dude graduated like four years ago. Why was he at a high school party? He draped his arms around the girl's waist and leaned into her ear. There were people talking in small groups, all with a beverage in their hands. Some guy peed on a tree about ten yards away, while holding a cigarette in one hand. Apparently, it was too far of a walk to get out of view of everyone. Disgusted, Kya moved on with her perusal. Her gaze landed on a couple sitting across the fire from her. They were wrapped in a blanket, not talking, just looking cozy. Their hands were laced together, and his thumb rubbed circles on the back of her hand. They looked so calm and happy.

That was one thing Kya had always wanted, to find her

perfect match. A guy who would make her feel as sappy as all the romance movies out there. Kya had never even been kissed yet. My gosh, she was lame. It wasn't as if she hadn't had any prospects. She'd never even been asked out, except for Mitch that one time, and he didn't count. Kya chalked it up to being in a small town. The pickings were slim. She honestly wasn't interested in anyone in that way, yet. Sure, she knew Mitch liked her much more than just a friend. He had admitted as much to her in junior high. He had written it all down on paper. But she had turned Mitch down. She didn't think of him that way. Still didn't.

And yet they had remained close friends to this day. She couldn't remember when they became friends. She wasn't really sure why they were friends. They had nothing in common. He was a wrestling, scraping-by slacker who liked to "hang out" and do stupid stuff. She was a no-sports, all-academic, straight-A student who spent her free time with her family, or behind her camera. But for some reason, he could make her laugh.

A tall head bobbed out of one trailer. And, sure enough, Mitch lumbered to her side. But as he sat next to her, the log rolled beneath his weight, throwing Kya off balance. Flailing backwards, sticky green liquid flew from her cup and drenched her hand and her pants. Great. Now not only would she smell like campfire, cigarettes, and alcohol, but apples, too.

"Sorry." Mitch wiped at her leg, attempting to clean her up.

"Dude, it's fine. Just leave it." Kya pushed his hand away.

She tipped her cup up, but it was empty. She sighed and tossed the plastic thing into the fire. The heat consumed it, curling it into itself, and sizzling out into nothing but ash.

"So, where did you disappear to?" Kya asked.

"Aw, just hanging out here and there. Talking to people. Drinkin' beer." Mitch raised his can.

How many has he had? But the thought fled when he pulled out a cigarette and lit it. Suddenly, a plume of smoke filled her face, and her lungs convulsed.

Coughing and eyes burning, she glared at Mitch, who took another deep drag on the foul stick of death. The end of the cancer stick glowed red as it burned down at least a half an inch. She pulled her nose inside her old t-shirt when he exhaled, as a cloud of smog billowed through the air.

"Since when do you smoke?"

"What? Oh, just when I drink," he replied, taking another drag, burning the stick to the quick. He tossed the butt into the fire. "There, no more icky smoke for Princess Kya."

Kya rolled her eyes and thought back to all the times Mitch had gone to parties which involved drinking. "What about your wrestling scholarship?"

"Like a cigarette can touch these muscles." He flexed his bicep, sliding the sleeve of his t-shirt up. "Besides, it's not like I do it all the time."

Kya pursed her lips into a thin line and tipped her head in a slow nod.

"So, you ready to have some fun this summer?" Mitch threw his arm over her shoulders. The weight of it was comforting in that he always seemed to have his arm over her shoulders. He often used her much smaller stature as a sort of leaning pole.

He leaned into Kya, turning slightly to look her in the eye.

"Yes!" Kya smiled despite the horrendous nicotine smell that clung to him. "We're gonna go to the lake, right?"

"Definitely! Like I would miss a chance to see you in a bikini." He bumped into Kya playfully. She knew the comment was only meant in a joking manner, but she also knew that there was truth under it as well. She wasn't stupid. Mitch liked her. He made far too many sexual innuendoes disguised as jokes when she was around. She had to admit that his jokes were funny, but behind every joke was truth.

"So, are parties all that you dreamed they would be?"

"All that and more," Kya said with a raise of her eyebrows. And, oddly enough, she was having fun. It beat sitting at home watching her brother play video games.

"I figured as much. I seriously thought you'd back out at the last minute. This really isn't your scene, is it?"

Did everyone assume she would chicken out? "No, but I'm still having fun. It's a new experience, and that in itself is intriguing."

"And she's off with the big words. No wonder you were valedictorian."

"Are you kidding me? I wasn't even trying for it. And I only beat Trish out by .05."

"You should have seen her face while you were giving your speech. She was filleting you with her eyes." Mitch's eyes got big and overly dramatic.

Kya laughed, "I've never seen anyone hate so much."

"I think that's what makes it better. You weren't trying for it, and you still beat her."

"You better help watch my back. She's here tonight, so I may end up with a pop tab in the eye."

"Oooh, nice graphic." Mitch downed the rest of his beer and popped open another one. Kya had no clue where he had them stashed. They seemed to appear out of thin air like there was a magical beer fairy.

"I aim to please. But what about you and your all-star wrestling butt?"

"Oh, whatever, all I do is mindlessly toss other men to the ground by groping them."

Kya giggled, "You said grope."

"Well it's true." Mitch leaned forward. "That is exactly what I do. Unlike you who actually achieved upgrades in mental capacities." Mitch's face was inches from Kya's. She couldn't move away due to the iron bar across her shoulders.

"What am I, a character in a video game? You've received 100 gold coins! You can now upgrade your mental capacity to 40 percent!" Kya mocked.

Mitch chuckled, "You'd think it was something like that, the way you pick up on shit." He leaned even closer.

The rumble of a very large engine wrapping up RPMs blasted through the lull of the party-goers' chitchat. A horn started honking about halfway down the driveway clear into the parking area. Mitch pulled away to see who was coming. The engine cut, and a tall lanky guy jumped out of the jacked-up truck.

"What's up, bitches!" Connor yelled, lifting an already open beer in the air.

"Holy shit! Fuck, man. Didn't think you would come!" Mitch jumped up to greet his friend.

"What? Of course I came!"

"Don't you have an interview tomorrow?"

"Interview, schminterview, I just graduated high school, and I'm getting fucked up!" The gathered crowed cheered.

Connor was definitely the life of the party. What was a quiet night of gathered teens suddenly turned into a flash mob. He propped open the doors of his truck and cranked the radio. When Garth Brooks started belting "Friends in Low Places," so did everyone else. Kya laughed and joined in, listening to the totally drunken and off-key chorus of voices. And then by some shot of fate, right after that song, Nitty Gritty Dirt Band came on with "Fishing in the Dark!" By that point, no one was actually singing anymore. They were merely screaming at the top of their lungs. As the song ended, the crowd was in stitches, all laughing for various reasons.

"All right, this calls for some shotguns!" Mitch called as he smashed another beer can against his head.

Kya, fascinated because she had no idea what they meant, stood to watch, but her head spun ever so slightly. The feeling was not welcomed. She quickly realized it was an alcohol buzz. No more drinks for her tonight. The tipsy feeling was awful. She had no control over her own body. It seemed unwilling or slow to follow the commands she was giving it. As she walked, she concentrated on making it look like she wasn't feeling it. Straight line, up right, right and left, one foot in front of the other. Her head swam. She hated the sensation.

Kya realized in that moment, all this time she'd wondered about parties, she hadn't missed anything.

She made her way over on unsteady legs, which she forced to appear steady, to the group of guys. Mitch, Connor, and three other guys all picked up an unopened can of beer. They broke the tabs off of their empties and curled them into the crook of their fingers. They wedged the sharp edge of the tabs into the bottom edge of the full can, quickly covering the hole with their thumbs.

"Ready?" Connor called. The others nodded. They placed the hole they'd made to their mouths and cracked open the tab on the top. They all chugged the rush of liquid down. It spilled out the corners of their mouths and down their chins. Mitch finished first with a loud belch, followed by Connor, then the other three.

Kya stood near the group.

"Another!" Connor shouted, and they all grabbed another beer.

"You want one?" Mitch held a can out to her.

"Uh, no."

After the third shotgun, one guy lost it all back onto the ground. Mitch slapped the guy's back as he walked by, staring straight at Kya. Mitch walked without an ounce of drunken clumsiness. Physically, it was difficult to tell Mitch was drunk. But there was no way someone could drink as much as him and not be feeling an effect.

"Would you like to dance?" He offered his meaty hand to Kya.

Kya looked around the crowd. Three girls were grinding on each other. There was the blanket couple swaying to the music… None of these dance styles matched the song that was playing.

"Uhhh." Kya shrugged. "Why not!"

By the look on Mitch's face, you'd have thought she'd given him a thousand dollars. He dragged her over to the other side of the fire and placed his hands on her waist. She dropped hers over his shoulders. She could smell the beer and cigarettes on him as he swayed back and forth. Kya screwed up her face, trying to figure out what beat he was on. She kept listening and trying to match him. She finally discovered that he wasn't on any beat. He was just moving. He stepped on her toe twice, and her knees kept bending directly into his.

"Okay, what song are you listening to? 'Cuz it obviously isn't the same one I'm hearing."

"Fuck, I can't hear at this point. I'm just moving."

Kya couldn't help but laugh. *What had she gotten herself into?*

Suddenly, someone shoved Mitch from behind, causing him to barrel into Kya. His arms wrapped around her instinctively. Behind him, some junior dweeb was laid out flat on the ground.

The kid managed to push himself up. "Sorry, dude," he slurred.

Mitch flipped around so fast Kya stumbled in his wake.

"What the fuck! You son-of-a-bitch!" Mitch fisted the kid's shirt collar in one hand. "You interrupted our dance," Mitch said in a deadly voice. His fingers curled into a fist.

She could see the fear in the kid's eyes. He seemed unable to string two words together as it washed over him.

Mitch pulled back his fist for a death-blow punch that was sure to knock the kid out or possibly kill him.

Kya jumped forward, grabbing a hold of Mitch's punching arm.

"Mitch! Mitch, stop!" she shouted. His eyes never even shifted off the kid's face. He shoved Kya to the side with his shoulder like he was twitching away from an annoying insect, which she did not appreciate. Instinctively, she shoved herself between Mitch and the kid, a feat considering how close Mitch was holding him, and laid her palms on Mitch's chest. Shoving hard, she threw him off balance, and his grip tore free from the kid's shirt.

Kya got in Mitch's face and slipped into her bossy, older sister voice. "Hey, weren't we dancing?"

"That punk kid got in my way! He needs to learn respect," Mitch bellowed.

"Yeah, well, he probably will in the morning when all the alcohol he's had comes back to haunt him… Let karma do the dirty work," Kya stated directly in his face.

Connor pushed his way through the crowd toward them. He did not look pleased. His brows were lowered over his eyes. A muscle popped in his jaw, and his lips were set into a thin sneer. As he got closer, Kya noticed that his anger was aimed at Mitch.

He looked Kya in the eye, and she realized that he wasn't drunk. He turned his glare back to Mitch, then back to her, and mouthed the words, 'Are you alright?'

Kya nodded with the smallest tilt of her chin so Mitch would not see. He got upset when she and Connor 'teamed up against him,' as Mitch would say.

Kya looked back into Mitch's eyes. Murder seemed to boil in their depths.

Finally, he turned his attention to her, and the rage drained from his features.

She thought quickly. What usually distracted Mitch best was taking care of her.

"Hey." She got in his face again, so he had no choice but to focus on her. "I could use some water. I'm sorta feeling the alcohol."

Mitch scoffed. "Lightweight."

"Overgrown caveman," Kya snarked back.

"I suppose you want your fancy-pants bottled water? Can't just drink tap?"

"Nope, bottled only," Kya said with a vigorous shake of her head.

"Pampered princess," Mitch quipped.

"Neanderthal."

Connor and he walked off toward the raft of coolers lined up by the porch and began digging through them.

Mitch's shirt stretched tight over his large muscled back as he dug through the coolers for water. Kya realized her buzz was gone now, but at least his search for water had distracted him away from his violent nature. Besides, the water wasn't a complete lie. She was really parched.

He returned and handed her a bottle. She downed half its contents in one gulp.

"Enjoy that water. I had to hunt to find it. Most of the beverages here are alcohol-based. Go figure."

"Oh, don't worry. I am." Kya looked through the crowd once again. "Hey, have you seen Rachel anywhere?"

"No, and good riddance to that trollop."

"Hey, watch who you're calling names, you Sasquatch," Kya accused. "And she's not a trollop."

"Whatever." Mitch turned away.

"Yo! Connor, have you seen Rachel?" Kya shouted to him across the fire pit.

"No! Haven't seen her," Connor shouted back.

"Hey, you know what?" Mitch gripped her arm and turned her to face him. "Why don't we go in and watch a movie?" His grip tightened as he commandeered her into the house. As they kicked their shoes off at the entrance, she glanced back at Connor. He shrugged one shoulder and looked back at her with an expression of concern and skepticism.

Mitch kneeled in front of the stack of movies on the floor in his room. Kya claimed a seat on the bed.

"Help me pick a movie." He began reading off titles to her, then lifted a beer to his mouth and took a long swig before smashing the empty can in his hand. Again, she marveled at how many he'd had. By her count, he was somewhere around seven or eight, but she knew he had

had much more than that. Kya removed the cap from her water and sipped it.

Mitch scanned his collection of DVDs until he came across the perfect movie for the night, one with lots of toga parties, drinking, and all-around funniness. Mitch snatched her hand and squeezed it tight. She winced slightly from his grip. Her hand looked like a child's compared to his.

"You are my best friend, you know that, right?" he asked.

Kya smiled at him. "Of course."

After putting the movie in the player, he sat next to her on the bed.

As the movie began to play, neither of them moved. An awkward tension filled the room. She'd watched movies with Mitch countless times before, but this night, it felt very different.

Kya's nerves were charged. She prayed what she suspected was about to happen wasn't going to happen.

"Kya," Mitch began, and he took her hand in his, "I want to be more than friends. And I'm running out of time. Once you go off to college, I may never see you again. And I'm not keen on sharing you. Can't even dance with you without being interrupted. You're all I want. All I'll ever want."

"Mitch…" Kya sighed. It was awful breaking up with someone you weren't even dating.

"Kya, please. How do you know we wouldn't be great together? You've never tried."

"Because, Mitch, I just don't feel that way for you." Kya patted the back of his hand holding hers.

"Why not? We're best friends. We do nearly everything together."

"I don't know why, but I don't like you that way."

"Kya, what makes you think there will ever be another guy? No one else here but me likes you."

Kya would never admit it out loud, but that did seem to be true. "This is a very small town. There are billions of other people out there. I still have college to get through, too."

"There's no one for you out there. You're mine!" Mitch growled.

"Mitch, we'll still be friends. I'm sorry, but I don't feel the same way." Kya tried to pull her hand from his. His grip tightened, and the fragile bones ground together. Cold fear settled in her stomach.

Kya hadn't realized he still harbored crazy-intense feelings for her. He'd never acted upon them… until now.

She recalled Mitch's rage when the kid had pushed him, and how he'd swatted her away like a fly. She looked at his large hand wrapped around hers. His fingers bit into her skin. Terror raced down her spine, and she was suddenly very aware of how alone they really were. And in his bedroom to boot.

"Mitch, I… I just want to go home." She couldn't meet his eyes. "It's late, and I'm tired…"

His other hand reached up and gripped her chin roughly. He lifted his hand and squeezed tighter, forcing her to her feet. Tears welled out of her eyes.

"Just kiss me, Kya, and you'll see," Mitch whispered.

Before she could cry out, he smashed his mouth to hers

so hard she tasted blood. The hand that was ripping her fingers off moved up her arm, attempting to bring her closer. Kya struggled against him, trying to escape. With one arm firmly in his grip and the other pinned between them, her struggles were futile. He pulled at her arm, and the shoulder joint popped. She had to break his hold before her arm was removed from its socket. It was difficult to breathe. His mouth crushed against hers. He pulled her tighter to him.

Kya panicked. She screamed into his mouth, and her knees dropped out from beneath her. The sudden weight surprised Mitch, and he released her, catching her under the arms before she hit the floor. That same crazed look of desperation was back, souring his face.

Kya tried to back away from him, but his arms were locked around her. However, this time, she was ready to fight. She pulled her arm up from his awkward hold and smashed her elbow into his nose. He released her then, and Kya turned, scrambling away from him to get out of the room, but he snagged the shoulder of her shirt.

"I'm sorry," he said.

"Let go," she growled. She could smell the alcohol and cigarettes bleed out of his pores. The stench wafted out of his mouth and engulfed her in a cloud of noxious fumes that made her gag. A small line of blood ran from his nose.

His grey eyes darkened, and his desperation grew angry. The rage was back in his eyes. He was very strong. The seams of her old t-shirt were ripping. She had worn old clothes, just in case something happened, like having someone throw up on her. Never had she imagined that someone she called a friend would rip her shirt off her.

His hand pulled back and smacked her across the face. She could feel the skin tear on her lip. Jerking away, her shirt ripped, and Mitch released the fabric. Kya swung around and dashed for the door.

As she passed through the living room holding her tattered top in place, Connor called her name, but she didn't stop. She was minutely aware of everyone in the front room staring open-mouthed at her. Kya didn't care anymore. She just wanted out. She took off running out the front door, forgetting her shoes. Her bare feet hit the metal front steps. The gravel of the driveway stabbed into her bare feet and slowed her progress.

Everyone outside turned to look at her. She felt Mitch's presence behind her as the eyes on her shifted to a spot behind her. She needed to move faster.

Too late. His fingers brushed her shoulder, curling around the only thing they could hold on to, which was the tattered remnants of her shirt.

Kya turned and twisted to free herself from the shredded fabric. She planned to fight dirty and kick him where it was sure to knock him down, but she stumbled backwards into one of the logs surrounding the campfire. The log pressed into the back of her calf. Kya's stomach dropped to her toes as the sensation of falling claimed her.

There was nothing she could do to stop the trajectory of her fall. Instinctively, her hands went out behind her to catch herself. Her left hand sank into the ash inside the fire pit. An ear-splitting scream ripped from her lungs as pieces of burning tinder rolled over her fingers and surrounded her hand, burying it in the smoldering embers at the base of the fire. In an instant, the white-hot coals at the bottom of the pine bough fire melted away the flesh of her palm. She jerked her hand free and rolled to her side. Dragging her legs over the log which tripped her, she lay on the ground in a shaking ball with her burned hand cradled to her chest. Her breaths came in short gasps. Her eyes screwed shut against the pain.

Her mind kept screaming at her to move! Move now! Move faster! But time seemed to be moving in slow motion.

In a distant fog, she could hear Mitch saying her name repeatedly. Tears streaked across her face as she gritted her teeth with a groan, determined not to scream again. She rolled to her good hand, scrambled to her feet, and sprinted away from the crowd toward the forest that surrounded the trailer house. Behind her, Mitch's voice called her name. It spurred her forward. Barefoot and half naked, she ran into the darkness.

TWO

The painful throb in her hand rendered her feet numb to the rough terrain as she climbed a hill. But once she reached the top, her legs gave out. Wrapping her arms around her chest, careful of her scorched hand, she crouched on her heels. Rocking back and forth, a tight sob escaped her sore mouth. Her lungs ached as she tried to catch her breath, and her heart slammed against her chest, as though it would break through her ribs to escape the overwhelming pain.

Tipping her head back, she gazed at the heavens. The pale glow of the moon was eerie, yet peaceful, as it shone on the sagebrush-covered hillock, casting shadows. It was calm and mysterious and hinted at magic. Something her world seemed to be lacking at the moment.

Dragging in a ragged breath, Kya shivered. She couldn't stay here. What if he came looking for her? She stood on shaking legs and looked back at the house.

It sat in a small clearing of pine trees. From the top of the hill, she could see the fire in the pit outside the door of the house. The crowd of her classmates surrounding it were washed in its orange glow.

She couldn't hear what they were saying, and she didn't want to.

Stumbling toward the road, she tottered with her hands loose at her chest. The chilly night wind seemed to slice her skin as if it were blowing shards of glass. It was odd to be shirtless with only her bra covering her. The rough ground wore on the soles of her bare feet. She couldn't muster the energy to care. It felt exactly like she did… rough and dirty.

Once on the road, she turned toward home. Kya stayed in the bar ditch because the gravel of the road was much worse on her feet, and she preferred the shale. If a car came, she would see its light before it saw her and attempt to dive into the trees first. Then she realized it was after midnight and no one was going to see her. After she had walked about a mile, she dropped her arms to her sides. The blood rushed down, and her burned hand throbbed heavily. She pulled it back up to her chest. Her hands shook uncontrollably, and her body felt hypothermic.

Kya was so consumed she was beyond noticing anything, but when a vehicle topped the hill she had just crossed, a shot of fear ran cold down her spine and clenched her stomach. She knew she should head for the trees. It was probably Mitch coming after her. She was moving too slow, in a daze. The car would see her. But she didn't have the energy to move fast enough. Shaking severely, she simply stayed in the ditch, praying it wasn't him. She wrapped her arms around her chest, too tired to truly care about her state of undress.

What if it was Mitch looking for her? The thought shot a

fresh chill of fear through her body. Her heart galloped, and her hands trembled. Her muscles tightened, ready to sprint.

The vehicle passed her. It was a pickup. *Not Mitch.* It put the skids on and started to back up. Kya continued her trudging, ignoring her fears, tired and worn out. It seemed the only action she had left in her was to walk. The truck pulled up next to her and traveled along with her.

The window rolled down, and a voice spoke to her from inside. "You need a ride?"

"No, I can walk." She was amazed she found her voice, even if it didn't sound like her.

"Are you sure? It's kind of chilly, and it would save your feet." The voice was male. She shuddered slightly. She could feel the goose bumps prickling her arms in the cool night air. It was not cold enough to require a jacket, but a shirt would be essential. She didn't respond. The engine roared, and the truck took off. She relaxed, thinking he was leaving. Then it stopped a little way ahead of her. The driver's side door opened, and a guy about her age, maybe a few years older, got out.

Kya stopped, wondering about his intentions. He hesitated and raised his hands in a reassuring, I-mean-no-harm motion. Then he pushed forward with a determined stride.

She dropped her gaze to the ground. In her peripheral vision, she watched his boots progress forward until they came to a stop a few feet from her. Lifting her gaze, she watched as he wrapped his fingers around the bottom of his shirt, pulled it over his head, and offered it to her.

Tears ran down her face and splashed on the ground. In order to take it from him, she'd have to expose herself to him.

He said, "Shit. Sorry."

She peeked up and saw him place his hand over his eyes and dangle the shirt from his fingers. As soon as she snatched it from his fingers, he turned around and kept his back to her.

Kya pulled her burned hand gingerly through the sleeve, then yanked her arms the rest of the way through and slipped it over her head. It was big, but it covered her at least. And it was warm.

"Thanks," she said.

He turned around. The first thing she noticed was his kind face with a strong jaw and a soft smile.

"Okay, let's go." He walked back to his truck.

She followed slowly, getting in the passenger side. But she wasn't so out of it to forget her manners. Before swinging her legs inside, she turned sideways and brushed off the bottom of her feet. A few rocks and dirt fell to the ground.

HE GAPED AT HER IN HIS OLD WHITE CABELA'S SHIRT. It looked better on her than him. What in the world had happened to her? A shiver racked her body, and he reached to turn on the heat.

"I'm Jake, by the way."

She seemed to be operating in a fog. It worried him a bit. She didn't wipe the tears away or hardly move for that matter. And her voice was barely a whisper when she said, "Kya."

"Uh, where do you live?" he asked. He wasn't going to question her. Whatever it was, she most assuredly didn't want to talk about it.

"Uh, I'll point it out." She was hunched over in the seat to the point Jake didn't know how she'd point anything out. She most likely couldn't see the road.

"Is there anyone home at your house?"

"Yeah, my parents are home," Kya responded, her voice dead.

He just nodded.

When they reached her house, she climbed out of the cab of the truck, shut the door, and turned so her back was to him. She reached for the hem of the shirt, but just before she lifted it, the window rolled down.

"No. Keep it." He paused. "Unless it's going to get you in trouble."

"No, they won't notice. They will be in bed now and gone before I wake up." Her voice was a dead monotone.

"Okay, see ya." Jake noticed she hadn't moved her left hand from the strange limp position against her chest.

"Thanks for the ride… Jake." He waited until she was inside before backing up and leaving.

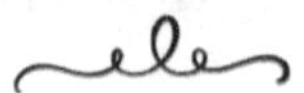

HE DISAPPEARED DOWN THE DRIVEWAY. SHE HAD never seen him before, and she pretty much knew most everyone who lived on her road. But she was too tired to fret about it. He had helped her, and she was grateful.

She made her way to the bathroom to brush her teeth, which she gave up quickly. It hurt too much to try and open her mouth. Looking up into the mirror, Kya saw she was a mess. Turning her head this way and that, pulling her hair out of the messy bun, she was grateful for one thing. The ends would have been singed off if she had left it down. A small miracle in a raft of horror.

Finally, Kya mustered up the courage to look at the burns on her hand… it was bad. Red, blistered, and charred. In some places it was black. Kya suspected it was pieces of the burned wood, stuck to her skin. And it hurt! Like the worst pain she had ever felt, and she couldn't stop the shaking. Tears began to stream her face anew. Her stomach turned with intense nausea. She had to wake her mom.

JAKE'S THOUGHTS TORMENTED HIM AS HE DROVE the rest of the way home. He worried over her. Should have made sure she got someone to help her. He prayed she was smart enough to get help.

Questions upon questions bombarded him. What happened to her shirt? Who hit her? What's his name? He planned on finding out, then kicking the shit out of the son-of-a-bitch. Whoever the fucker was would be sorry they ever touched her when he was through with them. Where were her shoes? She didn't seem crazy, but you never know. What happened to her hand?

Arriving home, he made his way to his room and slipped into a pair of shorts and crawled into bed. A thought occurred to him… *What would have happened to her if he hadn't come along?* He thanked God for staying at his sister's to watch that movie.

He lay there, and his mind wandered… all around her, Kya. The image of her in his headlights. The hem of her jeans around her hips, the curve of her waist. The bare planes of her back and shoulders. Her arms wrapped around her chest… which, even though he tried not to look, was very impressive. Her flat stomach, her face… even beaten and bruised, was beautiful. Not in the way that everyone notices, like a supermodel, it was subtle. She had shining eyes. Her dark hair knotted up on her head. The way she looked in the moonlight… the way she looked in his t-shirt… He fell asleep thinking of Kya.

KYA HIKED UP THE STAIRS, AND THE PAIN REALLY started to get to her. Her breathing hitched, and she was sobbing now. She knocked lightly on her parents' door. There was only silence in the spaces between her hiccups. She reached for the handle, and the door was yanked inward before she could grab it.

"Mom!" Kya sobbed.

"Oh, dear, what's wrong?"

"I… I." Kya stopped and took a deep breath. "I need to go to the doctor." Her last word broke with another sob.

It was dark in the hall, and her mother rubbed her eyes, not really seeing her. "Kya, it's probably just from the alcohol."

"No!" Kya stepped back and turned the light on in the bathroom across from her parents' door. She walked into the light where her mom could see her.

"Oh my…" Her mom came up to her, reaching for Kya's swollen face. She gently prodded the purple flesh around her eye. Her mom hissed between her teeth.

Kya was struggling to hold the sobs back. "Not… there… this." She lifted her hand.

"Oh my God!" She stared down at the mangled limb. "David!"

"Huh," he said sleepily from the bed.

"I'm taking Kya to the emergency room."

"What's wrong?"

"She's burned her hand. Bad. And she's beat up."

"Beat up?" He sounded more awake now.

Kya was breathing heavily through her hiccup sobs.

Her dad stepped into the hall. "What the hell! Who did this to you?"

"M… M… Mitch."

"Graaaw." Her dad growled, beyond words.

"Why? He's always been… at least with you." Her mom stopped and looked down at Kya's hand again. "Doesn't matter right now. Let me put clothes on. We're going."

THREE

Kya sat in the cramped, ill-padded, vinyl-covered, wooden-armed, worst chair ever, in the hospital waiting room. Her left knee bounced uncontrollably. They had arrived over twenty minutes ago. She held her cell phone in her good hand, tapping it from corner to corner on her leg. She held her injured hand in the air, so it wouldn't touch anything. It hurt something fierce, like someone scrubbed her skin with a wire brush. It stung and throbbed. If she attempted to move her fingers, it felt as though her skin would crack and break open, then fall to the floor in a pile of bloody scabs. She stared intently at a spot on the floor, trying to ignore the pain. The nausea had passed a while ago, but she didn't care to look at the horror that was her hand.

With a sigh, she knocked her head back against the wall, making an audible thud. Her mom jumped at the noise.

A nurse stepped out of a side door and called in a sickly sweet voice that was way too perky for the way Kya was feeling, "Kya O'Shadit."

As soon as they stepped through the door, the nurse

turned to them and spoke. "Sorry for the wait. We had a head injury come in."

"Oh, that's alright," her mother replied with a hint of skepticism in her voice as she looked down at Kya's mangled hand held awkwardly before her.

"After I take your vitals and things, we'll have a doctor in right away."

Keeping her mouth shut, as she had locked her jaw to keep from grinding her teeth, Kya only nodded.

She was led to a plain white room with pastel-colored floor tiles and pictures of human anatomy decorated with different illnesses. There was one depicting all the different types of burns. Kya shifted her eyes from the illustrations to her own hand. The only conclusion she could come up with was that the artist was being far too generous in the details. The poster was kid-friendly, where her hand appeared as though it had been put through a meat grinder, then tossed on a grill for a few seconds. Kya averted her eyes and scooted on to the lumpy old bed.

The nurse began to take her vitals, checking her blood pressure, shining a light in all the orifices on her head, and taking her temperature. She started Kya on an IV for fluids, and possibly some pain meds, because she was soon feeling much better. Then she proceeded to examine all the bruises. When she found the one on the back of her arm in the shape of Mitch's hand, an odd look crossed her face. She turned a questioning look to Kya's mom. She turned the same questioning look back to Kya.

"Mitch's hand," Kya ground out between her teeth.

"So, your boyfriend did this?" the nurse asked.

"If you mean romantic dating, then no. If you mean a friend that's a boy, then yes." Kya's snark seemed to intensify when she was in pain.

The nurse gave her a weird, angled nod and a grimace that was probably supposed to be a smile, then looked over Kya's burns. She patted her knee before exiting.

And the wait began. Kya kept her eyes off the posters and the biohazard container filled with needles hanging from the wall. Nervousness settled in her gut. What were they going to do to clean her burn? She had heard horror stories of burn victims and didn't want to even imagine what it would feel like to have it scrubbed and scraped. Bile rose in the back of her throat, and she swallowed to keep it down.

Kya's perusal of the room skated over her mom sitting in another of the uncomfortable chairs. She was staring at Kya, drowning in pity.

"What, Mom? Just spit it out."

"I'm so sorry this happened to you." She crossed the room and wrapped Kya in a gentle hug.

Tears streamed down Kya's cheeks. Sometimes there was nothing better than a mom hug.

There was a knock at the door, and it swung open. A tall, dark-haired, middle-aged woman in scrub pants and a white coat walked in. A stethoscope hung around her neck, and she held a file in her hand.

"Hi, my name is Dr. Macy." She held her hand out for her mother and Kya to shake.

She gently placed her bruised right hand into the doctor's. "Hi."

Dr. Macy looked down at the hand in hers and grimaced. "Boy, you are beat up."

The nurse returned and placed a tub, along with some tools, on the counter in the corner.

"Thanks, Tina."

The nurse sat down at the laptop with a small nod.

"Sorry for making you wait," Dr. Macy began, "but we had a head injury. So, I figured you wouldn't mind delaying having to scrape your burn since you seemed fairly okay."

Kya nodded again, feeling the blood drain from her face at Dr. Macy's words. The doctor began poking at Kya's torn lip, then to her black eye. Her touch was gentle as she prodded around Kya's purple skin.

"All of your bruises will heal in time. I'd like to take an X-ray of your eye just to make sure, but let's take a look at that hand. How did all this happen?"

Kya took a deep breath and began her tale. Dr. Macy brought over the tub and tools, placing the tub on a table next to Kya's bed. She started poking Kya's hand with some of the tools and her glove-clad fingers. Kya sucked in sharp breaths intermittently during her story when the doc poked or prodded a particularly nasty spot. It happened a lot and took way longer for Kya to spit her story out. She gently turned over Kya's hand, exposing the inside of her wrist and more burn marks going up her forearm. Kya had not realized the burn had gone that high.

As Kya mentioned the injuries she sustained, Dr. Macy

followed them across her body, like following along in a book. She peeked at the bottoms of her feet and found some abrasions to her neck, where the shirt ripped, and a few more bruises on her arms, back, and legs where she'd tripped over the log into the fire.

Kya finished her story at their arrival at the hospital. Dr. Macy nodded with a tight-lipped look as she finished examining Kya's hand.

"Well, it looks like your hand will be fine. There's no damage to anything super vital, other than your skin. You were lucky. The majority of it is second-degree, which will be painful. There are a couple of areas of third-degree, but they shouldn't leave any lasting damage.

"I cleaned a little of the dirt out and some of the dead pieces, just the big stuff that was loose. We will have a nurse take you back for hydrotherapy to thoroughly clean the burn. It's a much gentler way of cleaning burns. Then it will be gooped up with an antibiotic salve and wrapped in a nonstick bandage. I will get you a prescription for an antibiotic salve, and something for the pain. Your other injuries will heal in time. Would you like an ice pack for your eye?"

Kya nodded.

"Sit tight here and relax. I will be back in a bit. I'd like to look closer at your eye. I'll send a nurse in with ice, and she'll take you back to the hydro tanks."

Kya was wheeled back to the physical therapy wing of the small hospital with her mother following. They didn't trust her to walk that far. She entered a room that smelled of rubber. To one side, through another door, stood several stainless tubs.

The nurse wheeled her to a tank and began filling it with water.

When it was full, she parked Kya next to it and had her submerge her hand. The water was pure, unfiltered bliss. The relief was instantaneous and overwhelming. Kya groaned and wanted to cry for the sweet, soothing sensation.

She looked down at her hand. There were nasty fiery red welts that were blistering along the length of her fingers. The worst points were her fingertips, where they were pushed into the ash. The tips were welted and swollen already. Two of her nails were charred and sure to fall off in a few weeks. She tightened her jaw and swallowed. The water rushed over her hand. Slowly, she turned it over in the tub. Her palm and the underside of her fingers were a mess of bloody red sores and blisters. Her fingers would not be bending anytime soon. The skin, or what was left of it, was marbled with white and bright red. There were also some black pieces. She leaned closer and realized they were ash particles stuck to her skin. It had only taken a split second, and this had happened.

Kya looked up at the small noise her mom had made. She stood with her hand over her mouth and tears in her eyes.

KYA LAY BACK IN THE HALF-RAISED BED. SHE couldn't really pinpoint what it was, but the bed was so uncomfortable. Her butt was numb, and her low back was aching. She held her newly cleaned hand up, keeping it from touching anything. It looked like a tenderized steak, without the charring.

Apparently, she would be okay, though it didn't feel that way. It was as though she had lost the whole limb, except she could still feel it throb with pain. It would heal in time, as long as she didn't do anything super stupid.

A nurse came in with a rolling tray of packaged bandages. She smiled at Kya and began opening bandages to wrap her hand.

"My name is Keelee. So, how'd all this happen, dear?"

With a sigh, Kya told her story again. This time she wasn't as detailed as she was with the doctor.

Once her hand was completely covered in goop, and encased in gauze and wrapped, the nurse stepped back and began to clean up from her ministrations.

Dr. Macy finally reappeared. "Well, hun, you are quite beat up. Your eye has more damage than what's visible. I'm fairly certain that this thin bone here," she gently brushed her fingers over the bone along the outside of her bruised eye, at the edge of her temple, "is fractured, based on the placement of this bruise and your description of the person who did this. It's most likely a small crack, but we're going to X-ray it to be sure. It will be tender and sore for probably a month or two. Try not to bump it or get punched anymore, okay?" The doctor smiled, trying to make a joke.

Kya twitched the good side of her face and nodded.

"Would you like us to report this?" Dr. Macy asked.

Kya thought for a bit and looked to her mother for guidance.

In the silence following her question, Dr. Macy added, "It's law that we have to report burn victims that have 5 percent or more of their body burned. Which would equal about a person's whole arm. You have pretty much only your hand, so about 2 percent. That makes it up to you."

"Would law enforcement be informed?" Kya's mother asked.

"In this case, that would be up to you. Kya was assaulted. But it's up to you to press charges or not."

"Um, I don't know. I'm not entirely sure what that would mean for me or for him. I'm not sure," Kya said.

"Oh, we are pressing charges."

"Mom," Kya started.

"Do not argue, Kya. If we let this slide, he may come after you again. From what you've described, his affection for you is not healthy. And he's clearly capable of extreme violence!" Her voice rose as she continued growing more agitated. "Or he could do this to someone else. You don't want that on your conscience."

"Okay," Kya said from the bed. "I just, Mom, uh, I just want to go home."

"Absolutely. You will need to file a report with the Weston County police. There are ways to help protect yourself against further issues or altercations with the assailant, where you don't have to be involved. The police can take care of it. Be careful in the meantime. I'll have a nurse take you back for X-rays, and then we'll get you out of here and home."

Kya's head bobbed again in a slow nod. She was having a hard time making one person out of Mitch, her friend, and the Mitch from last night, who beat and attacked her.

"Thank you, Doctor." Her mom stood and gathered Kya's things to take her home.

When they got to her mom's SUV, Kya crawled in and collapsed in the seat. Exhaustion weighing on her, she leaned into the door and fell asleep.

Kya stirred awake when they turned onto the gravel road that led to their home. Her hand was throbbing, so she lifted it off her lap to hold it above her heart. The blood instantly drained from it, back into the rest of her body. She ached all over.

"How are you feeling?" her mom asked from the driver's seat.

"Like I got hit by a bus." She breathed in deeply to try and relax.

"What are you going to do now?"

"Sleep for three days."

Her mom huffed a laugh through her nose. "I meant about that SOB."

"Hmm, I don't know. I'll think about it later."

"You need to think about it now. I don't want you to see him again. Ever. Do not answer his messages either."

"It's not like I'm gonna venture into his house for a soiree."

"Okay, but first thing when you wake up, we're calling the sheriff." Her mom paused for a breath. "I think you've learned your lesson, but if he remains out and about, he could be hurting other people."

"It just doesn't make sense."

"You are a friend to him, and he hit you. What's stopping him from hitting someone else?"

"You don't understand. THIS," Kya gestured to her face with her mummy hand, "isn't the Mitch I know. My Mitch is a teddy bear who watches romantic comedies with me!" Tears tracked down her face. "I can't condemn my teddy bear for life. I… I just… how could he do this to me?" She was yelling by the end of her rant, but quickly deflated.

Her mom didn't say another word. They finished the short trip to the house in utter silence.

FOUR

THE MOST PLEASANT SCENT SUFFUSED THE AIR
when she awoke the next morning. Musky, sort of sweet
too... there were no words except delicious. She rolled over
and opened her eyes... She was still dressed? Kya peered at
the shirt and the source of the smell, and it all came back in a
tidal wave of pain. Her hand, head, face, neck and jaw, arm,
and feet hurt like she was hit by a freight train. She had hoped
it was merely a bad dream, but no, her drunk friend had hurt
her. Hit her and tripped her into a fire. And some handsome
stranger saved her, sort of, after she saved herself, sort of.

Kya ran her fingers through her hair, pulling it over her
shoulder and nearly gagged. The rancid smell of cigarettes,
campfire, and Mitch's house was soaked into her hair. She
turned her nose away and rolled out of bed. Standing up,
she cracked her neck and ran a hand through her hair again,
pushing it back over her shoulder and away from her nose,
wincing as she brushed the side of her face. It hurt to even
blink.

Shuffling her way to the bathroom, she flipped on the
light and gazed at her reflection in the mirror. She sighed at

herself. The whole left side of her face was black and blue. Damn, he had big hands. Her eye was swollen, but she could still see out of it. The split in her lip had scabbed over in a gruesome rust-colored slash that closely resembled rotten hamburger. The inside of her mouth was raw where it had been smashed into her teeth, and black and purple-blue stained the soft pink flesh of her lips. She tipped her chin up and saw the bruises that marked where Mitch's fingers had gripped her jaw. They continued down her neck, slowly fading away to a slight redness. She lifted her arm up to see it in the mirror. The imprint of a hand marred the back of it too. Kya's jaw locked, and she clenched her hand into a fist, grimacing in pain from where Mitch crushed her fingers in his.

"Well, there is no way that I'm going to be able to hide this. Even a whole bottle of concealer probably won't do the job," she told her bruised reflection. Looking down at her gauze-wrapped hand, she sighed. There were some splotches of pink and red and yellow starting to soak through the bandage.

After an awkward one-handed shower, Kya walked back to her room to get some clean clothes. She pulled the guy's t-shirt out of the pile of dirty clothes, sniffing its heavenliness one more time. She folded it up and placed it on her dresser. How was she going to get it back to him? Jake.

Kya picked up her phone on her way out of her room. There was a text. She opened it.

Last night was amazing. Need to do it again.

It was from Mitch. Kya closed the app and headed to the kitchen.

The television in the living room flared to life, blaring a theme song.

"Tucker," Kya yelled above the noise. "Turn it down!" She could hear her mother shouting the same thing from her bedroom. Her mom had called in a personal day at work.

"Okay," her little brother called back, and the noise receded.

"Kya, get up here and get some food in you. We are going to the sheriff's office," her mother called.

"Coming," she said as she entered the kitchen. Pouring a bowl of cold cereal, she sat at the table to eat.

Graduating seemed so small compared to what happened at the party. What should have been one of the best memories in her life was now scarred and tainted. Kya sighed again, bringing her elbow up on the table to rest her head against her hand, but when pain shot through her skull, she dropped her arm, huffing out a short breath of annoyance.

"Whoa! What happened to your face!?" Tucker asked from over the back of the couch "And your hand?"

With a sigh, Kya dropped her spoon in her cereal bowl. This story was going to get told a lot. "I got beat up and fell in the fire last night."

Tucker hung over the couch, stunned.

"Close your mouth, Tucker, and leave Kya be," her mother said as she stepped into the dining room. "How are you feeling this morning?" she asked Kya.

"Sore everywhere, and tired."

She nodded.

Kya finished her cereal, gathered her things, and headed to the car with her mom. Tucker opted to stay home.

They drove the half hour to the Weston County Sheriff's office in New Castle. When they arrived, Kya got to regale them with her sordid tale. The officer recorded the story and wrote down as much as he could. They then took pictures of her and said they would check in with the hospital in Sundance.

Two hours later, Kya was completely wrung out, squeezed until every drop was gone. Thank goodness her mom was with her. It was intimidating, like she was in major trouble, talking to the police like that, but her mom was solid next to her. Someone familiar, who'd always supported and encouraged her.

At the car her mom hugged her before they got in. "I'm sorry you had to do that, but I'm proud of you. You've grown into a strong and resilient woman."

"Thanks, Mom."

Once home, Kya made her way to the living room. She flopped back on the couch, feeling ready for a nap.

"Someone's here," Tucker called.

"Really?" Kya strode to the picture window.

"Who is it?" Tucker asked.

"Uh, I think I might know."

Her mom was also looking out the window from the kitchen.

Kya turned and hurried to the front door. The black Dodge parked at the end of the line of cars out front, eating all of the extra room with its bulk. Jake got out and walked to the front gate.

Watching him stride with an air of confidence down the sidewalk, Kya was able to see what the darkness hid last night. He had wavy light brown hair tucked under a worn-out old ball cap, the ends curled around the hat. He wore the same sincere turn to his mouth she saw last night. He was about ten feet from her, and Kya was ready to face him when a tidal wave of thought washed over her. *Why was he here? What would he think of her in the daylight? She probably looked like shit.* But she turned the corners of her lips up in a plastered-on pleasant façade and opened the door. The first thing she noticed were his eyes. They were a mix of green and gold.

"Hi," Kya said tentatively.

"Hey." His voice was soft as he stared at her face with a pained expression.

Kya dropped her eyes, avoiding his look of pity. "It looks worse than it is."

"Yeah? I bet it feels exactly how it looks."

A small smile found her lips, and she managed to meet his gaze. "Okay, it hurts pretty bad, but I'll survive."

SHE FINALLY MET HIS EYES. WHAT HE COULD ONLY describe as dark last night were now beautiful, gleaming, mahogany-brown eyes framed by chestnut-colored hair. The effect gave her a warm glow. Jake realized his jaw had fallen open. He snapped it shut and mentally shook himself.

"Uh… that's actually why I'm here." He brought up a small, brown jar with something yellow-ish inside. "It's ointment for your bruises. My aunt makes it. Does wonders when you get kicked by a calf."

"Thanks." Kya took the jar from him.

"I don't mean to pry, but would you mind me asking what happened?" He glanced down at her gauze-encased hand.

"No, I don't mind. Do you have anywhere you need to be?"

"Nope, I finished my work this mornin'."

"Then, would you like to come in for breakfast… or lunch, I guess?"

"Sure."

KYA LED JAKE INTO THE HOUSE WHERE HER MOM and Tucker waited to be introduced to the stranger in their home.

"Mom, this is Jake, the one who gave me a ride home last night. Jake, this is my mom, Catherine, and my little brother, Tucker."

"Hi." Jake reached out to shake her mom's hand.

"It's nice to meet you. Thank you for helping Kya last night."

He nodded. "It was my pleasure." Looking to Tucker, he asked, "How's it going?"

"Pretty good… Do you play PlayStation?"

"Yeah, all the time."

"Cool, would you like to play with me?"

Jake flashed a look to Kya and her mom, then answered, "Sure, I can play a quick game."

"Sweet, I usually play with Mitch when he's over, but he sucks so bad I could beat him blindfolded. Kya's even better than him."

"Of course I am," Kya said.

"Would you like something to drink?" Kya's mom asked.

"I offered him lunch," Kya said.

"Then I'll get right on it. Sandwiches, okay?"

"Yes, sounds great," Jake replied before Tucker practically dragged him into the living room.

They started their game, and Kya moved to watch from the couch. After a few minutes watching them racing their digitized cars and battle it out for first place, they finished.

"Yea! I win!" Jake threw his hands in the air.

"Best two out of three?" Tucker asked.

"Maybe later, okay?" Jake got up from the floor.

Kya felt Jake's eyes on her. "Would you like something to drink?"

"Sure." Jake stuffed his hands in his pockets and glanced at her mom in the kitchen.

"How about a glass of water?"

"Sounds perfect."

The way he said it made tingles run up Kya's entire body. She filled a glass with water from the door of the fridge, acutely aware of her mother behind her. Handing Jake the glass, Kya was careful not to touch his skin. He followed her back into the living room to sit on the couch.

He patiently waited for her to begin the story.

"So yesterday was graduation… and we had an afterparty…" Kya related the events of the night, and when she finished, there was a short pause.

"Mitch hit you!" Tucker yelled, jumping up from the floor, "Oh, that drunk son-of-a—"

"Hey! Watch your language," their mom scolded him.

"Dad says it all the time."

"Well, you're only twelve, and Dad is an adult, and until you leave this house, there will be no cussing." With a scowl, Tucker sat back down and continued playing his game.

Kya focused on Jake. His hands fisted in his lap, and she could see his jaw muscle work as he ground his teeth.

"Are you okay?" she asked.

"Yes, fine," he said through a locked jaw.

In an attempt to loosen Jake's fists before something got broken, Kya asked, "So what brings you to lovely Upton, Wyoming? I haven't seen you around before."

"I just moved down here about six months ago from Montana to help my aunt and uncle with their ranch. My sister lives in town too… that's where I was coming from last night."

"So, your aunt and uncle own the ranch at the end of the road?"

"Yeah."

"They're nice people. I've met them a few times."

Jake's jaw unclenched as he nodded his head, but his fists didn't. "How much does your hand hurt?"

"It stings, and is throbbing a bit." *And I kind of want to cry,* she added silently.

Jake's fists tightened impossibly more. Kya reached over with her good hand and worked his fingers open. He wound them loosely around her dainty digits. Staring at their hands, he picked hers up and turned it into the light.

"Jaysus, even your fingers are marbled with bruises." He gently lifted her arm to find the black-and-blue handprint.

Kya could hear his teeth grinding together again. He placed her hand back in her lap and stood up from the couch. He pulled his hat off and thrust both of his hands through his wavy hair. It looked so soft, and Kya found herself wanting to run her own fingers through it. Of all the things she had to think about, her mind chose that. She mentally rolled her eyes at herself.

Jake paced in front of the fireplace. His hands alternated between his pockets and his hair.

"Jake, if you don't stop, you are either going to tear the pockets out of your jeans, or you won't have any hair left," Kya's mom reprimanded him. "Sit, please."

Without a word, Jake sank into the cushions, resting his elbows on his knees. He bounced a little on his toes like he was settling in. A huff of air tore out of him, and his hands were back in his hair. He turned his head, looking at Kya beside him, and dragged his fingers down his face.

"Kya, Tucker, Jake, your lunch is ready." Kya's mom set three plates on the dining table. "Jake, I need you to take a deep breath. Believe me, we know exactly how you're feeling. We are beyond furious with him for what he did to our daughter. But we've already filed a police report and are pressing charges. You need to calm down and let the authorities handle this." With a final nod, she returned to the kitchen.

Kya placed her hand on Jake's shoulder and offered him a small smile, attempting to contain the hysterical bubble of laughter threatening to break loose. Her life had become so insane. Friends abusing her. Strangers wanting to protect her. Her mom, mothering said stranger.

"Are you sure you're okay?" he asked as they sat down to their lunch.

"I will be, once I heal." Kya smiled again, swallowing her hysterics. Her swollen eye throbbed as her cheeks drew up. The skin of her ripped lip tugged painfully and stung.

A look of shock and concern flashed across Jake's face. He stumbled and stuttered a bit. Kya shifted back, trying to figure out what had him in a tizzy. Jake leaned forward, reached over, and pulled a napkin from the stand on the table. Kya's brows dropped, confused.

Jake gingerly brought the napkin up to Kya's chin. His hand hesitated midair, unsure.

Kya shrank back.

Jake gently touched the tissue to her chin, dabbing lightly. He pulled it down, and there was a smear of bright red blood contrasted against the bright white of the flimsy paper. Jake folded it over and wiped softly at her lip. She had reopened the cut when she'd smiled.

"Thank you."

"So, how bad is the damage? The full extent, I mean."

"Are you sure you won't break something?"

"I'll try my best." Jake glanced at her mom as she walked over and handed Kya a tube of lip balm.

"Well," she paused to gently smear the lip balm on, "I have second- and third-degree burns on my hand, and first-degree up my arm. The ocular bone in my eye is fractured. I'm fighting the mental battle of understanding how my friend, and the person who did all this to me, are actually the same person. I'm bruised, like, everywhere. The backs of my legs, my arm, my other hand, my face, lips, and elbow where I hit him in the nose, and I have abrasions on my neck where my shirt tore off me. And with that thought, I will be right back." Kya stood and combed the hair back from her face with a deep sigh. Jake met her gaze with a slightly pained and sympathetic yet confused expression of his own.

She bounded through the house to her bedroom. Her bare feet slapped against the concrete of the basement floor, only to be muffled again, as she turned down the carpeted hall to her bedroom.

Kya's home was a grand log structure, but the inside was mismatched and unfinished. But it was hers, and she saw nothing wrong with it. The horrible pink carpet in her bedroom had been drowned a few times when the basement flooded. It was worn thin and wrinkled up in some areas, but it was a relic of her childhood. Same as the purple walls covered in horses and unicorns. The dollhouse her grandparents made her when she was five sat in the corner surrounded by her boxed-up dolls. For some reason, she couldn't bring herself to get rid of them. The comforter on her bed was white, and covered in neon floral designs at the bottom. When she thought about it, her room was chaotic, but it suited her perfectly. It was all bright colors and happy childhood memories. It was the one place that she didn't need to be perfect. Kya looked down at herself. Perfect, happy, and bright was not how she would describe herself in that moment.

An image of Mitch popped into her mind. She felt tainted and dirty. As she looked around her room, she was thankful it was not stained by his presence. He had never really been into her room. They always stayed in the living room, or outside, or at his house. She dragged in a deep breath of the familiar comforting scent of her space. What would Jake think of her room? Kya's cheeks heated a bit. It was childish in many ways even though she was not anymore. Still, it was perfect to her. Kya shook herself, physically and mentally. What reason would Jake ever have for seeing her room? Who was she kidding? He didn't like her, not like that. He was only here out of concern to check on her. She squashed whatever small kindling of hope there was that he might actually like her. No sense in getting excited over nothing. Entertaining ideas like that lead nowhere but to sadness and heartache. It wasn't that he was absolutely gorgeous, and she was not. Kya was aware of her beauty. It was just that feeding thoughts of her and Jake being together would probably cause her pain later when it went nowhere. She simply figured there was no reason to get her hopes up for nothing. Yet she couldn't help the giddy grin that threatened to reopen her torn lip.

Kya brought her thoughts back to the present reason she came down to her room in the first place. She spun in a circle in the center of her room and spotted Jake's t-shirt on her dresser. She reached forward, snatched it up, and made her way back to the dining room.

"You guys have a lovely home," she heard Jake say as Kya approached.

"Thank you," her mother replied.

Kya dashed in to find Jake looking out the front windows of their house at the open field and the surrounding pine trees.

He turned away from the view and looked at Kya holding his t-shirt in her hand.

"Thought you'd want this back." Kya handed him the shirt.

"Thanks," Jake said with an odd trailing at the end like he wished to say more. His eyes shifted to where her mom sat on the couch. "I better be going. I have night chores to start."

"I'll walk you out." Kya stood, and Jake followed.

At the door, Kya hesitated. "Thank you, for the bruise salve."

"You're welcome." Jake paused. "Is your mom always home?"

"No, she and my dad work the same shift at the coal mine. So, they're gone fourteen hours out of the day, rotating night shift and day shift."

"So, it's just you and Tucker?"

"Yeah," she said.

"I'll give you my phone number. If anything odd happens, he comes here, or you get scared, I don't care. Please call me."

"Okay, thank you." Kya had no intention of calling him for help. She was perfectly capable of taking care of them, as she always had been. "Can I ask you a question?"

"You just did, but what's the next one?" Jake replied.

"Why are you helping me?" Kya looked to her blue toenails. "I mean, why come check on me?"

She met his gaze for a moment. Jake looked away from her to stare out the window.

Kya sighed. "Why did you stop last night to pick me up?"

He turned to face her. "Because it was the right thing to do. Because a girl alone in the middle of the night wearing no shirt or shoes could use a little kindness." His green eyes shone with conviction as he gazed into her eyes.

Kya returned his gaze. "Thank you. A lot of people wouldn't have stopped. They'd think I was crazy, or messed up on drugs, or some other crap. Thank you for not assuming and helping me. I don't know how far I would have made it."

"I'd do it again in a heartbeat, Kya."

Kya stood on tiptoe and kissed his cheek, then waved as Jake made his way to his truck.

FIVE

Why is it that every time there are flashing lights, everyone and their dog have to flock to them like bugs to a zapper? Maybe it's a morbid sense of curiosity. But when police lights are on, and there are a lot of them, everyone knows it's going to be a bad scene. And for some reason, everyone has to look anyway. We gawk as they come screaming by on the highway and wonder where they could be heading in such a hurry. Sometimes, we laugh at the sorry sucker who got pulled over. Other times, we gape at the mangled vehicles and crane our neck to see the more gruesome views. What is it about those red-and-blue lights that always makes us look, even when we know we really don't want to see it?

Kya had no idea what made people always have to look, but the same strange pull overcame her as she entered the bathroom. She reiterated on a continuous mental loop not to look. She tried rephrasing the thought using different words and even rationalizing with logic. Don't look. Don't look. Don't look. Every time she passed a mirror, she tipped her head down, avoiding the darkening bruises covering her face. She didn't want to see her mangled and useless hand.

The unfortunate part was there were a lot of mirrors in her house. She hadn't realized how many until she couldn't stand to look at her reflection. And it wasn't only mirrors. It seemed every surface was reflective in some way. She fought the involuntary urge to peek at her reflection every time it appeared.

Ducking her head, she hurried down the long, narrow bathroom to the porcelain throne at the end. She slipped her finger into the waistband of her comfy shorts. Then the real struggle began. She pulled one side lower on her hip with her good hand, then moved to the other side, stretching her arm across her body. Back and forth with one hand, she shimmied her shorts down. When they were down, she sat and sighed. Being one-handed was going to suck donkey balls.

Finished, she pulled her bottoms up inches at a time. At the sink, she rinsed off her one hand and dried it as best she could. Her eyes swept up, and she met her gaze in the mirror. The involuntary urge had claimed her. She didn't recognize the person staring back. Where she used to have wide, bright eyes, she now had dead, sunken sockets surrounded by bruises and shadows. At least that was the eye she could see. The other was nearly swollen shut and looking blacker at the moment, as it faded slowly to purple, and then to a sickly green around the edges.

The bruise spanned the entire side of her face. One side of her nose, up around her eyebrow, and out nearly to her hairline, all the way down, curving under her jaw. Good grief, Mitch had big hands. Purple edged around her mouth and along both sides of her jaw. The purple-and-green handprint on her upper arm wrapped all the way around. Her burned hand was hidden under clean white gauze, but she knew it to be rust-colored, and looked more like decaying flesh than living. Her other hand was purple-ish green. Glancing back to her face, she knew it was far paler than it ever should be. With her naturally darker, tanner complexion, the lack of color made her look ashy, like the dried paper surface of a wasp nest. She drew in a breath through her nose, huffed it out, and turned away.

As soon as she was back in her room, her phone rang. One-handed, she dug the infernal device from the depths of her purse.

With an exasperated sigh, she said, "Hello?"

"Ah! Finally!" Rachel's perky voice shouted over the connection.

"Yeah, sorry, I left my phone in my purse."

"You really need to stop doing that, you know. People could be dying, and you would never know! This shit is important."

"Okay, so who died?" Kya asked.

"Only the hottest guy on the planet, and hopefully he doesn't die 'cuz that would suck, and I would cry."

"Alright, so who are we talking about?"

"Uh… I forget his name, but he's in that new movie, the one with the sexy aliens that glow."

"Oh, yeah, okay." There was a pause. "Why is this dude important?"

"I have his movie in my hand, and I am en route!" Rachel practically screamed.

Kya pulled the phone away from her ear, and a small panic lit up her chest. "Um…" she stopped. "Um… I…"

"Are you okay? 'Cuz you sound off, like you just woke up. And you should be super freaking excited about this. We've been geeking out for the last six months!"

"Um, yeah, right, but…"

"Oh, whatever, I'm coming over. You better be out of this funk by the time I get there." And with that, Rachel hung up on Kya.

"Yeah, this funk isn't going away for a while," Kya said to her empty room. "She is going to freak the eff out when she gets here." Kya couldn't hide. She'd been silently hoping to hide all summer till her face healed. Her reliable good girl persona was entirely broken now. One look and anyone would know she wasn't a good girl. Good girls didn't get beat up like some drug addict's girlfriend. People would talk. Would they ever trust her again? Would she ever outgrow this incident, or would she wear it like a dirty stain for the rest of her life? Would Rachel look at her differently?

Kya climbed back up the stairs. "Mom," she called. "Rachel is on her way over. She wants to watch a movie. Is it okay if we watch in my room?"

"No, I want to keep an eye on you today," Kya's mom replied. "Tucker, here in a bit you are going to have to shut that off. Rachel is bringing over a movie."

"Yeah, okay," he called over his shoulder as he shot

an alien-looking creature from a first-person shooter's perspective.

Kya walked into the kitchen, filled a glass with water, and tossed back two pain meds the doc had given her, while watching as Tucker shot more aliens.

Her mom's phone rang. "Hello?" She held a one-sided conversation, requiring her mom to only say "Mmm" and "Okay" at certain intervals.

"There's nothing we can do to get him off the streets or keep him away from Kya?"

More murmurs.

"Okay, thank you, goodbye."

"Who was that?" Kya asked.

"The sheriff. He said Mitch is claiming you had an argument and you stormed off, and when he tried to stop you, you tripped into the fire, then took off. He told them all the bruises are from the fall and him trying to catch you." She set her head in her hands with a wary sigh.

"So, now what?"

"Now, we're in a he-said she-said battle. You sure no one else witnessed the start of it?"

"The people in the front room may have seen me. But I don't know. I was trying to hide at that point because my shirt was ripped and I was sprinting."

"Okay, I need you to be careful, please."

Kya nodded. "I will."

Out the front window, motion caught her eye. A patchwork Dodge Neon crawled down the gravel drive. The girl must have driven sixty on the gravel road to get there that fast. But now, Rachel was creeping at probably five miles an hour over the large-rock road. Kya's dad, when they laid the rock, had thought it would sink into the mud more, but it didn't, leaving a gravel road of fist-size rocks. A few minutes later, the front door opened and slammed shut, causing the house and all the glass fixtures to rattle. Rachel came running with a movie in her hand, and her mouth hanging open as she pulled in a huge lungful of air.

"I'm so excited! This is going to be so, whoa." She came to a halt as she entered the kitchen and stared at Kya. "What happened? Were you in a car accident? No, 'cuz I totally would have heard about that."

"No, no car involved." Kya didn't continue.

Rachel waited. "Bulldozing? Skydiving? Cliff jumping? Did the neighbor's bull get in your place? 'Cuz yesterday you did not look like this. Please, tell me it happened when you were doing something cool, especially since we have ruled out car crash. It has to be something awesome."

Kya picked at the hem of her shirt as Rachel surveyed her. But she knew the instant Rachel saw the handprint on her arm, because her mouth fell open, and her eyes about popped out of her skull.

"Who did this to you?" she said in a quiet voice Kya had never heard her use before.

Kya took a deep breath. How to start? Rachel tended to gossip. At that thought, she knew she had to tell Rachel everything as accurately as possible so that the gossip she spread was at the very least accurate information. Kya wasn't sure the whole town of Upton needed to know it was Mitch.

"You know I did actually go to the senior party last night, right? Totally proved you wrong, by the way."

"Yeah!? I was there schooling everyone on the pool table. I never saw you. Otherwise I so would have put you on my team." Rachel paused and surveyed the damage. "Holy shit," Rachel breathed.

"Mitch tried to kiss me." She paused. "Well, I suppose he actually did, but not in the way you or I think of a kiss." Kya pointed to the bruises around her mouth, chin, and hand. "Then I slugged him in the nose to make him stop, and he hit me." She indicated her swollen eye. "And as I turned to run, he grabbed my arm." Pointing to the handprint. "Then he snagged a hold of my t-shirt and nearly ripped it from my body. Thank God it was old because it ripped easier." Rachel stared at her, mouth agape. "Then I ran out of there so fast I forgot my shoes. And Mitch caught me near the campfire. He got a hold of what was left of my shirt, and I turned to kick him in the nuts, but I tripped over a log and fell into the fire." Kya held up her gauzy left hand. "I don't know what happened after that. I sprinted into the trees. So then, I walked halfway home barefoot."

"Oh, suck a duck!" Rachel shook her head with a hand covering her mouth. "Wait, what do you mean halfway home?"

"This is where it gets interesting." Kya leveled her gaze on Rachel.

"There's more! You had one hell of a night, didn't you? Is this where the bulldozer comes into play?"

"Oh, yeah." Kya nodded. "As I was walking home, this

pickup pulls over and…" Kya paused and looked to Tucker in the living room playing his game, and Mom on the couch with a book. "A complete stranger," Kya waggled her eyebrows, "offered me a ride home."

Rachel's jaw practically hit the floor, and a crooked smile pulled up one side of her mouth.

"He even lent me his shirt."

Rachel's eyebrows raised.

Kya mouthed the words "oh yeah" with a nod of her head and an appreciative look of her own. Kya gestured to her own torso, up and down, mouthing "the whole thing" and added silently, "Cowboy."

"Damn, girl," Rachel whispered.

"And then this Good Samaritan stranger shows up here today to check on me."

"Does this stranger have a name?"

"Jake," Kya replied.

"Damn, girl." Rachel shook her head. "Are you okay?"

"Yeah, just sore and tired, but my hand hurts pretty bad."

"I bet, third-degree?"

"Just a few spots. Mom took me to the emergency room, and the doctor had to pick dirt out of it. Hurt like hell. Then they did hydrotherapy."

"Oh my gosh, that son-of-a-bitch!" She slapped a hand over her mouth. "Sorry, Mrs. O'Shadit."

"No worries, Rachel, we're all thinking it," Kya's mom called back.

All Rachel could do was shake her head.

Kya dug a bag of popcorn out of the pantry cupboard,

stuck it in the microwave, and pressed start. Rachel climbed onto a stool at the counter. The front area of the house got quiet. Kya stepped around the corner and looked into the living room as Trucker was shutting off the game console. He walked down the hall to his room, which was probably the coolest room in the house. His room had a small loft in it. It was only about four feet tall at the peak of the vaulted ceiling and slopped down to about a foot. He had his bed up there, which left the whole bottom floor to be covered in his things, literally. Kya listened as the door brushed the carpet and clicked closed. She had to admit she was slightly impressed. Usually, it took a half hour and repeatedly asking him to get off the TV before he freed it up.

The microwave beeped, and Kya poured the fluffy pieces into a wooden bowl her father made in high school. Settling at the counter on the stool next to Rachel, she placed the popcorn between them.

"I mean, I know Mitch could sometimes get angry, but holy sh—cow." She covered her curse word, looking around to Kya's mom. "I never thought he would hurt you. He always acted like a Care Bear to you, lovable, and full of sunshine. He's in love with you."

"I know. I have been aware of his feelings for a while, but I don't think of him like that. He never really pursued it either. Like, I know he liked me, but he's never tried to make an advance, thank God. But last night was the first time I have been around him when he was drinking."

"Alcohol does some weird stuff to people… Maybe he's more like one of those angry bears, the ones that look all cute and cuddly, but when you squeeze them, their mean face pops out, and they go grr."

Kya nodded and popped a piece of popcorn into her mouth. It was kind of her and Rachel's thing, popcorn, chocolate, and a movie.

"What I want to know is what the heck was Hot Guy doing on the road at that hour? And why haven't I heard of him? This town is way too small not to know, like, everyone." Rachel shoved a handful of popcorn into her mouth. Dramatic stories and food seemed to be the only things that could make Rachel be quiet.

"He said he was coming from his sister's in town and headed to the ranch at the end of the road."

"Ooh, a ranch hand cowboy."

"You should have seen his reaction when I told him what happened to me."

"Did he yell and scream like Mel Gibson in *Braveheart*?"

"No, he got really quiet and tense. I thought he was going to break his teeth." Kya paused. "He brought me a balm for my bruises."

"Aw, and he's sweet too."

Kya rolled her eyes.

"Okay, okay, do you have a photo of Sexy Caring Cowboy?" Rachel asked.

"His name is Jake and no, I don't. But we could totally Facebook stalk him." Kya pulled her phone from her pocket and opened her app. "Um, I don't know his last name. I think he told me, but I can't remember. My brain was sort of stuck on other issues… He did give me his cell number."

"Ooh, text him. Ask his last name and if he has Facebook."

Kya swapped apps and sent a quick text. She hit the send button and had her finger over the lock button, and the reply appeared. Holy cow, Jake was fast.

"He says his last name is Lancer, and no, he does not have a Facebook."

"Huh, weird, like nearly everyone has a Facebook."

"Apparently, he's one that doesn't."

"Hmm, I wonder why."

"I don't know, but he just asked why I wanted to know." Kya typed out a reply.

"What did you tell him?"

"That my best friend wants to know what he looks like." Kya's phone buzzed, and she read the text, laughing.

"What, what'd he say? Gawd, I hate being on one side of the conversation." Rachel huffed.

"He said he couldn't leave a lady waiting." Kya's phone buzzed again. This time it was a picture message of Jake in his ball cap out in a field somewhere, and he was covered in dirt like cake makeup. Kya could see smears and creases of dirt along with track marks from sweat. He looked pretty nasty. Kya turned the phone around and showed Rachel.

"Oh… wow, he's dirty." Rachel drew back from the phone with a grimace. She snatched the device from Kya's hand and peered at the screen closer. "Dayum! He is hot."

Kya bobbed her head with a smirk. "It sucks, though, this," she gestured to her face, "is how he got to meet me."

Rachel hissed through her teeth. "Yeah, that really does suck."

"Anyway, I think I need some good vegetable time on the couch with some sexy aliens. Something where I can stop thinking."

Rachel beamed, clapping her hands, and jumped off the stool. She ran into the living room, started grabbing remotes and turning things on like she lived there.

Kya followed and flopped onto the couch.

Kya and Rachel sat zoned, watching the TV, with the bowl of popcorn and a bag of M&M's between them. The actual movie began to play as Kya's fingers reached the bottom of the bowl. She frowned.

"We need ice cream," Rachel announced and bounced up from the couch.

A few minutes later, she returned with two bowls of ice cream. She handed one covered in caramel to Kya and began mixing a little ice cream into her bowl of chocolate to create soft serve.

Kya dipped her spoon into the sugary goodness and savored the rich, chilled flavor.

Rachel lifted a heaping dripping spoon of creamy chocolate, and as she brought it to her mouth, a dollop fell and landed on her exposed chest. She wiped it up with her finger and went in for another scoop. She huffed as another drop landed on the exposed swells of her chest.

"You know, I need a man to lick this off me."

Kya spluttered, barely catching herself before she spewed ice cream all over the living room. Recovering enough to swallow and take a breath, she turned to Rachel with an amused yet exasperated look. Kya raised one eyebrow and dipped her head to the side in concession. "That's some truth right there."

"You totally just got an image of Jake, didn't you," Rachel whispered to Kya, glancing over the couch to look for Kya's mom.

"No, but now I do."

"You so want him." Rachel taunted.

"What straight woman wouldn't?"

"Touché."

They turned back to the movie, and silence descended.

Moments passed. Then Rachel said, "He is really hot. If you don't stake a claim on him, I will."

"Hey now, we just met yesterday… or today, actually. You got to give a girl time to work her magic." There was another pause. "And heal." Kya didn't voice it, but she didn't think Jake was into her at all. No other guys had been. She was too much of a 'stick in the mud' as they called her. No one but Mitch ever cared to be around her. And, of course, Rachel's stubborn butt.

"Yeah," Rachel dragged the word out, "that would probably be a good thing."

THE MOVIE ENDED, AND RACHEL WENT HOME. KYA busied herself helping prepare a quick dinner by pulling all the leftovers from her graduation dinner out of the fridge, while her mom opened the containers and began reheating some of it. She began cleaning up the kitchen and clearing the mail off the table—anything to try and keep her busy.

The front door opened, and her heart dropped to her stomach. Would her father think differently of her? She wasn't his perfect princess anymore.

He topped the stairs, dropped his lunch pail, pulled Kya from her busy work, and wrapped her in a fierce hug.

Tears spilled from Kya's eyes, soaking into his dirty work shirt. He smelled like coal and dirt, earthy, yet sulphury. He hugged her tighter.

"Hey, Princ…"

"Don't, please don't call me that." Kya breathed in a rattling breath. "I'm not your perfect princess anymore."

"Oh, Kya, that is just a pet name. I have never expected you to be perfect. And this, what happened to you, is not your fault in any way." He stopped to tilt her face up to his. Then he hugged her even tighter. "I am so proud of you. You're a fighter. You got into a very scary situation, and you fought your way out of it. You made it home to us." He pulled back and gently touched his fingers to her face. "Does it hurt? Are you in pain?"

"No, I'm okay. The doctor gave me some antibiotics, and I'm taking painkillers."

"So, how did that go? The doctor visit?"

"It was painful. They had to pick debris out of my hand." Kya held out her white-wrapped left hand for him to see.

"How did you burn it?" Her father looked down at Kya's hand, then up at her face, and feathered his fingers along her swollen eye.

Kya recounted her story for what seemed like the hundredth time. As she told her tale, her father grew angrier and angrier. By the end, he was looking for murder.

"I'm gonna kill that son-of-a-bitch!" he fumed.

"Dad, no!"

"Honey, we've already filed a police report and the charge papers. Putting yourself in jail will not help us."

He paced the length of the dining room behind the couch. His fists were clenched, as well as his jaw. The action reminded Kya of Jake's reaction to her story.

"Mom?"

"What?"

"Is he going to be okay?"

"Eventually, but I'm kind of right there with him. I've been alternating all day between fits of rage and thanking God you're okay."

"I'm okay… or I will be, really." Kya said with a head tilt and a one shoulder shrug.

"You sure you're okay?" her dad asked.

"Yes, Dad, I'm fine."

He wrapped her in another hug.

"Dad, you need to eat and get to bed. Four day shifts, remember?"

"Yeah, alright."

Her phone buzzed in her pocket. She dug it out and read, *How are you?* Jake even used punctuation.

Kya responded, *I'm okay, sore and tired. My dad is pissed.*
Yeah, I bet that wasn't very pretty.
No, but no lives have been lost… yet.

LOL, only time will tell, he texted back. *Well, sweet dreams. I'm off to bed. I have an early morning tomorrow.*

Good night, thanks for all that you've done.

"Kya," her mother called as she slid the phone into her pocket. "I'm going to have to go back to work tomorrow. Will you be okay?"

"Yeah, I'll manage."

"If you need anything, call someone, anyone. Rachel, Jake even."

"Yes, Mom."

"Make Tucker help."

"Okay."

"If anything else happens, send me a text. It will take me a little over an hour to get here, but I will be here if you need me."

"Yes, Mom, okay. I love you." Kya wrapped her arms around her fretting mom. "I will be okay."

"Okay, sweetie. I love you too."

As her parents prepared for bed and work the next day, Kya started her nightly routine by brushing her teeth as best she could without tearing the scab open on her lip. Changing into her pajamas was a little more difficult, but she managed somehow. She lay in bed with her digital camera flipping through the pictures on it, stopping on one of her senior pictures her mom had taken next to the professional photographer. She looked naïve and fake, like she was a doll on a shelf, everything painted to perfection.

Now, she looked like crap. But it would all heal, eventually. The only possible scar would be on her lip and hand… and mind. She looked horrible, felt horrible, dirty even. Kya didn't know who she was anymore.

She was still responsible, reliable, honest, kind… but would everyone else see her that way? She no longer was confident of anything, not even of herself.

JAKE LAY IN BED WIDE AWAKE WHEN HE SHOULD HAVE been asleep hours ago. They had work to do tomorrow, but his mind wouldn't calm. It circled around Kya, what happened to her, and the events of the day. He barely knew her, and yet he was strongly protective of her. Kya should never have been a victim. If he ever met Mitch, he'd give him his comeuppance.

Anger fumed through Jake's blood. He knew the price of pressing charges. He knew. Reality sucked, but a person had to face up to their actions. The crew he'd been with back in Montana were pissed when he spilled his guts about their little crime ring. Those weeks he spent in prison awaiting trial were the scariest of his life. The probation he was serving now was nothing compared to what he could have gotten. But he took his punishment. He'd damn sure earned it.

Mitch needed to answer for what he did to Kya. This was going to be hard on her. Oh, sweet, lovely Kya with her dark exotic looks. The image of her taunted him. Mentally, he removed all of her injuries. He could not wait for the day he got to see her healed and healthy. She was absolutely gorgeous now. Remove the bruises and she would be a bull kick to the chest and an ice-cold drink on a hot day. Right then, Jake knew Kya would be the death of him.

SIX

IMAGES FLASHED THROUGH KYA'S MIND OF FIRE AND darkness. And all she felt was pain. So much pain. No matter which way she turned, she was either engulfed in flames or immersed in darkness. Pain, always pain… Mostly in her left hand. It hurt so badly. Kya moved, and the pain shifted slightly. As Kya slowly pulled herself from the horrid darkness into wakefulness, she became aware that her left hand was trapped under her body. She slowly rolled off it. The bandages compressed against her raw flesh. Her hand smarted. She breathed heavily as it throbbed.

"Son-of-a-bitch," Kya breathed through her teeth. Tucker was right. That really was the proper sentiment. That, and another naughty word.

She sat up and swung her feet to the floor. They didn't hurt anymore, so that was a plus. Her breathing slowed. The pain dimmed to a dull ache.

Finally, her mind pushed past the pain. She had a little over two weeks before work started. She was not looking forward to scrubbing munchkin boogers off the desks. She'd done it for the last three summers, and every summer, it sucked just as bad. This one would be worse with an incapacitated hand. Dust, toilets, and children was all it was… yuck. And the high school was as bad as the elementary. If there was one thing Kya knew, it was that she did not want to be a custodian for the rest of her life. She was headed for college in the fall. Hopefully, she could convince her parents to let her pursue a career behind her camera.

Kya wiggled her way into some shorts and a tank top; then she stiffly climbed the stairs. Out the big front windows, the grass was neon-green, and there was a deer feeding on the lawn. The birds flew and darted about the feeder in the bright sunshine under a blue, cloudless sky. It was a picturesque spring in Wyoming. Kya knew what she was going to do that day.

She poured herself some cereal and munched her way through it. She wasn't in any hurry. Today would be calm and relaxed.

After finishing breakfast, Kya snatched her camera from her room and padded to the foyer. She searched the pile of shoes for her flip-flops. They weren't there because, of course, they were at Mitch's house. Sighing, she went back to her room to get her tennis shoes. She had no desire to see him or go there to get her sandals. Even though they were her favorite flip-flops. Maybe later she'd work up the nerve to go get them… nope, she was never going back there. Goodbye favorite flops. Her hands trembled as she attempted to tie her shoes. Failing, she tucked the laces inside the shoes and stuffed her feet in after. Right now, she was going to take some pictures.

"Tucker," Kya called up the stairs.

"Yeah?"

"I'm going outside."

"Okay."

Kya spun on her heel and stepped up the few stairs to the front door. Outside, the breeze was fresh and cool, and the sun warm. It was a beautiful day. Kya breathed in deeply, let it out slowly, and walked to the tree where the bug light hung. The trunk of the pine tree was covered in two-inch-long moths that blended perfectly with the bark. Kya pulled up her camera as she'd done a thousand times… and stopped. Her gauze-wrapped hand was pretty much impossible to use in any helpful way. And she was afraid to think what it looked like under the white wrappings.

A sigh filled her lungs and rushed past her lips. Gingerly, she rested the camera on the back of her left hand. It felt okay, but it wasn't very stable. She was having a hard time keeping the camera from sliding around as she depressed the button on top. The device shook like the last dead leaf left on a bare tree in the middle of a winter blizzard. Kya's breath rushed from her, and she dropped her hands, trembling more from the frustration than anything.

It didn't hurt so much as it was uncomfortable. Every time she moved her wrist or attempted to move her fingers, the delicate skin under the bandages would pull and sting. They were tender with pressure from fluid buildup, and parts seemed as though they would burst.

How was she to take good pictures, or do anything, with only one hand? Kya's vision went blurry as her eyes filled with tears. Blinking once, the tears poured down her cheeks. She drew in a shuddering breath and looked to the crystalline sky. They streamed into her hairline. Where was her life now? Her shoulders sagged, and her stomach fell into her butt. He had taken so much from her! A first experience she would never get back. A tainted and painful memory where there should have been only fun and happiness… He had killed her friend.

There was no way she could ever look at him as she used to. His furious features as he ripped the shirt from her body. That was the face that haunted her. She couldn't even remember what he had looked like to her before. All her memories of him were stained now with that hideous face.

Kya sank to her knees and sat on her heels. Ugly, face-reddening, monster sobs tore through her, leaving her raw. She sat there and cried till her face was nearly swollen shut and she had given herself a headache. Stuttering in a deep breath, she opened her eyes to the sky. On the branch above her, silhouetted against the blue sky, sat the most brilliantly yellow bird she had ever seen. Kya blinked a few times and then brought the camera up and clicked a picture. The small bird never moved. It was as if he was puffing his chest and posing. Viewing the digital display, the photo was perfect… in complete odds with how she felt. Then inspiration struck. Kya raised the camera to the perched bird and positioned herself, so her blackened face was in the edge of the frame, she hoped. When she pulled the camera down, she could see both the beautiful bird and the angry bruises in the frame. She clicked at least twenty pictures, posing her face in different expressions and angles in conjunction with the bird. And the whole time, the bird never flew away. Scanning through a few of the strangely dark but bright photos, Kya had to admit that they were good, though painful. She looked back up, and the bird was gone.

Kya turned her attention back to her original chosen subject, the army of giant moths clinging to the tree. Zooming in close, she started clicking pictures of the disguised bugs. She tried different angles and light. Took one facing up through the branches of the tree. Gingerly poked one and it spread its wings. Poked a few more, making them open as well. They were quite beautiful, disgusting creatures. She spent a while there, making sure she'd explored the area before moving on to a new subject.

Out in the field behind her house, Kya found a patch of small purple wildflowers. They resembled miniature hibiscus flowers. There was one that was three or four shades darker than the others. She moved in close and clicked a picture. The tiny flower filled the frame.

Then an idea struck her. There was a patch of wild Shooting Star flowers on the south end from where she was. They only bloomed when it was really wet. Then they dried up and died. They would not reappear until the next year. But now, they would be in bloom.

Kya stood and started south through the tall lush green grasses of a healthy spring in Wyoming… Her socks were going to be filled with grass stickers. She walked along the roundabout trail the horses had worn in years ago, to the one tree she knew under which these incredible flowers grew, and sure enough, there they were.

The magenta petals folded back away from the yellow-and-white center that imitated a needle-like point. The stems were a foliage red and about eight inches tall. Moss grew on the ground around them from the high moisture of the area.

After capturing her fill on her camera, she heard a vehicle on the road. Kya checked the time. It was one in the afternoon. Curious, she moved out to a clearing where she could see the house. In the driveway sat a very tall, black Dodge pickup. Kya shook her head with a small smile.

JAKE KNOCKED ON THE FRONT DOOR, STEPPED BACK, and waited… And waited. He knocked again, louder. This time, Tucker's head appeared around the corner of the door. Recognition flashed across his features, and he raced to open the door.

"Hi, Jake. Back for a rematch?"

"We'll see if I have time. I'm looking for Kya. Is she here?"

Tucker stepped back and let him in. "Kya's outside taking pictures."

"Oh, okay. Will she be back soon?"

Tucker motioned for him to follow. Jake closed the door, wondering what was up. He found him staring out the front windows.

Pointing out the window to a figure moving down the road, Tucker said, "She's on her way now."

Jake's gaze found bronze-colored light reflecting off her hair. The corner of his lips tugged back.

Tucker asked, "You sure you aren't here for a rematch?"

Jake shrugged. "You're on."

Sitting on the floor, he picked up the second controller and raced his digital car for all he was worth. He was not underestimating this kid. Jake might have won the last time, but Tucker was some serious competition.

The race ended, and Jake whooped his victory, throwing his arms in the air. Yes, he made a fool of himself. But he'd barely won.

"Best two out of three?" Tucker scowled.

"What, you a sore loser?"

"Heck no!"

"Maybe next time, Tuck." Jake smiled fondly at Kya's brother as he stood. Turning around, he found Kya watching them. A small camera dangled in her hand.

He hoped she had not taken a picture of his victory dance.

"Hey," Jake said.

"Hey, nice dance," Kya said with a small smirk, and Jake's hopes were crushed.

"WHAT ARE YOU DOING HERE?" KYA ASKED.

"I had some time for lunch, and I wanted to check on

you." Jake moved into the dining room. Kya pulled out a chair and sat. Jake sat across the table from her. "How you feeling?"

"Pretty good. This morning was rough, though."

"Yeah?"

"Yeah, woke up lying on my hand." Kya lifted her burned hand for emphasis.

Jake hissed through his teeth. "Ouch."

Kya bobbed her head.

"Everything else seems to be okay?" Jake gestured to his own eye.

"Yes, I mean it sucks and is sore, but I'm dealing."

"That's good."

The most awkward silence of awkward silences descended. Kya didn't know what to do with herself. She fidgeted with a pen on the table, looking at anything except Jake because if she did, she'd probably stare like a total creeper again. She didn't know what to do. She looked like shit in more ways than one. And a thought occurred to her. The tank top she wore showed off her purple marbled flesh… every bit of it. Kya chanced a glance at Jake. His gaze was fixed on her. She expected to see anger burning in his eyes and his knuckles turning white. Well, his knuckles were turning white where he clasped them in his lap, but the fire burning behind his green eyes was not that of anger, but of something far more intimidating. She expected him to be staring at her injuries. Rather, his stare was fixed to her chest. Kya's mouth popped open slightly. His perusal of her traveled along her neck to her face, where he lingered. His eyes seemed to study her face, committing it to memory. His tongue flicked out to wet his lips, and he swallowed. Then his gaze jerked away and landed on her purple-handprinted arm. Every emotion she first expected rose to the surface. Jake's jaw clenched. Kya prepared herself to argue the "I'm fine" case and calm him down. He looked away and forcibly relaxed, but continued to grind his teeth.

Kya opened her mouth to say something—what, she didn't know—but Tucker interrupted.

"Uh, Kya?" Kya looked his way. Tucker had his face scrunched up, staring out the front windows.

Following his line of sight, dread settled in her stomach. Legitimate fear coursed through her veins. A white Subaru cruised down her driveway like he owned it.

Kya's heart drummed out a beat a professional hip-hop dancer would have problems keeping time with. Her breathing sped up, and she thought for sure she was going to pass out.

"Did you invite him here?" Tucker asked.

Kya shook her head and whispered, "No."

"Then why is he here?"

"I… I think I know why." She dragged the words out past her panic-paralyzed lungs.

"Wait, is that…?" Jake let his question hang.

Kya looked at his handsome face and nodded.

SEVEN

JAKE FLIPPED THE SWITCH TO ANGRY SO FAST KYA was sure steam would blow out of his ears any second.

"What is he doing here?" he asked through a locked jaw.

"Probably bringing me my shoes." Kya found her voice.

"Did you call him? Did he call you?"

"No, and no." Kya turned and ran for the door. Over her shoulder, she said, "Stay here, Jake, please." Her only thought was to keep him out of the house. She had to keep him away from Tucker… and Jake, even if just to prevent a fight. Jake called something to her, but she didn't hear.

Kya sprang up the short section of steps to the front door two at a time. Through the window in the door, she watched Mitch park behind Jake's black Dodge and heave himself out of his car. As he reached the front gate, Kya threw open the door and speed-walked in her bare feet to meet him. Mitch's face broke into a huge grin as he saw her come toward him.

"That eager to see me, you had to meet me at the gate?" Mitch lumbered in a big guy sort of swagger around Jake's massive truck. Her flip-flops dangled from his fingers. "I brought your shoes for you." The strange truck in the drive caught his attention. "Did your parents get a new truck?"

Kya didn't respond to his rambles. She was numb and tried to focus on his face, judging his mood. Kya knew the instant Mitch fully appreciated her bruised physique. His face soured to pity.

"Sorry, that had to happen. But you weren't listening. And I got so angry," he said and reached like he was going to brush his hand down her face.

Kya ducked and stepped out of reach, horror and revulsion burning through her. He was sorry? Was he kidding!

"Kya, you and I are perfect together. Don't you see? There's no one out there for you but me. If you weren't so stubborn and would get off your high horse, you'd see that."

The knot in Kya's throat vanished. "High horse? You've got to be kidding!" Kya was wound up now. "I never once led you to believe that I had any feelings for you, ever. As I tried to tell you at the party, I do not like you in that way. And since you decided to physically assault me, I don't like you at all. Actually, I quite hate you." She was screaming now.

"There's always differences and fights in a healthy relationship. Who's been filling your head with these ideas? Was it him?" Mitch yelled, pointing behind her.

What? Kya whirled. Jake was leaning against the doorjamb, muscled arms crossed over his chest, looking like a bouncer at a bar. Kya turned back to Mitch, who brushed her aside like a curtain. She stumbled and moved off the sidewalk as Mitch hulked toward Jake. The testosterone battle was so thick, Kya could nearly see a red haze in the air between the two.

"No!" she yelled, trying to stop him. "It wasn't him!" But it was too late. Mitch had already thrown the first punch. Her flip-flops went flying across the driveway, and Kya cringed, waiting for Mitch's fist to connect with some part of Jake… but he stepped lithely out of the line of fire. She had always thought of Mitch as huge, and he was, but Jake stood a good half a head taller than him. Mitch swung with his other fist, and Jake dodged it, stepping back again.

"I am the only man in your life, Kya!" Mitch shouted.

"Both of you STOP!" Kya ran towards them to try and break up the fight before Jake ended up looking like her.

"No! Kya, stay back!" Jake looked away for a split second, and Mitch struck him in the ribs. He grimaced in pain, and his face contorted in anger. He clutched his side and, from his bent position, brought his right fist straight up, slugging Mitch square in the jaw.

Mitch's head snapped back, and he staggered a few steps. He began to swing at Jake with a blind rage. Kya stepped into the boundaries of the fight. She placed a hand on Jake's shoulder and shoved him backwards. One of Mitch's wild shots flung out and connected with Kya's forehead. Darkness descended.

KYA'S HEAD THREW BACK AT AN ODD ANGLE AS SHE fell, crumpling to the ground in an unconscious heap. Mitch stared, dumbstruck, at Kya's limp form. Jake strode forward, knuckling a fist. In one smooth motion, bringing his coiled hand up to shoulder height, he stuck out with one quick, well-placed jab, connecting straight with Mitch's nose. The bone cracked as it broke. Mitch fell back, too stunned to react. Blood drained from his nostrils.

"Asshole," Jake said, dripping venom. He knelt down by Kya and checked her over for serious injury.

"You sorry son-of-a-bitch." Jake stood, making himself a barrier before Kya.

"She deserved that. She needs to learn respec—"

"BULLSHIT!" Jake exploded. "There is no circumstance in the world in which a woman deserves to be beaten like you did to Kya!"

"Don't ever say her name, you scum!"

"Get the fuck off of this property before I break more than just your nose!" Jake's voice was a low growl now.

Mitch shook his head as he backed away. "She's mine! Always has been. You're no better than a corpse." He turned and marched back to his car, spitting blood on the ground as he went.

The white car disappeared down the drive.

KYA GROANED, AND HER EYES FLUTTERED OPEN. Squinting in the sunlight, she moved her hand up to tentatively touch the goose egg on her head.

"What happened?"

"Mitch punched you," Jake said.

She nodded and tried to push herself off the ground, but had to squeeze her eyes against the new pain in her head. Jake's warm, strong arm wound around her back and helped her to stand.

"Thank you." The pain in her head seemed miles away, his nearness sending her heart a-flutter. A concentrated dose of his divine masculine scent washed over her. He was so close, crouched over her protectively. Coherent thought was nonexistent, acutely aware of his proximity.

"Me? I didn't do much. You're the one who took the hit." His smile was glorious and sincere.

The gravity of him drew her in like magnets.

"Dude! That was epic! I even got it on video!" Tucker burst out the door, his phone in hand. "Watch." He held the device out, and Kya and Jake watched a replay of the fight.

"Whoa, you broke his nose?" Kya asked.

"Maybe." Jake plowed his fingers through his hair.

"Thanks for exacting revenge for me," she said with a mischievous smile.

He leaned in and lightly brushed his fingers down the side of her face, gently prodding the bright red lump on Kya's forehead. His jaw locked again, and he shook his head slowly from side to side. Stepping away from her, he shoved his hand through his hair again.

Slowly, Kya brushed herself off with her one hand. "Eh, what's one more splotch of color to my already marbled flesh?" Kya looked at him with a crooked smile and shrugged.

Jake was near to a rage, but looking at her, he seemed

to lose the battle. Kya cracked his angry mask as easy as cracking an egg, and a grin split his face.

Jake huffed out a laugh. "You never cease to amaze me."

Kya gingerly touched the goose egg on her forehead. She could feel her pulse in her brain. It throbbed and seemed to worsen with every blink. Pain meds were her first priority. Wait, no, her shoes. They were in the driveway where Mitch had thrown them. Kya marched down the sidewalk and through the gate. One shoe was lying in font of Jake's truck. The other was under the truck. She crouched down to reach for it.

"Here, I'll get that." Jake was on the ground before her and halfway under the truck before she could even extend her arm.

"Thank you," Kya said, standing up and putting her one shoe on.

Jake stood with a smile, handing her the other to put on as well.

"So… do you have to get back to work, or…?" Kya let the question hang, not sure what she was even asking.

"Naw, I was wondering if you'd like to hang out?" Jake asked. He put his hands in his pockets and rocked back on his heels.

Was he nervous?

"Uh, yeah, that would be cool, but we're hanging out here. I don't want to go anywhere."

"That's perfect." Jake smiled warmly.

Kya reciprocated his warmth, and they walked back into the house.

"Did you have any plans for today other than taking pictures?"

"Well, I'll probably need to call the sheriff and report this incident."

"Oh…" Jake scrutinized her. "You don't seem sure."

"Yeah, I'm not really. But when my mom took me in the other morning, the police said I had to report any other 'altercations.'" Kya sat at the table and pulled out her phone. "I know it's the smart thing. I mean, look at the state I'm in." She gestured to herself. "But I don't know."

"Even after what just happened?"

"I… it's complicated." She took a deep breath and held it before letting it whoosh out. "His face is familiar, but his actions are not. I don't know what to do." Kya collapsed forward, resting her head in her hand, and winced at the contact with her forehead. Pushing up from the table, she marched to the kitchen for some pain meds and stayed there until she'd finished her entire glass of water. Then she strode back to the dining room.

"Well, in any case, I better do what the authorities said." Kya picked up her phone and went back to the kitchen. Her dad had written the number for the sheriff's office on a sticky note on the counter. She dialed.

"Weston County Sheriff's Office. How can I help you?"

"Hi, my name is Kya O'Shadit. I live in Upton on Barton Road. Um…" Kya trailed off, not sure what she needed to say.

"Tell her you need to report an assault," Jake said without hesitation from right beside her.

Kya jumped a bit. When did he leave the table? "Um, I guess I need to report an assault."

"Are you in any immediate danger?"

"No."

The dispatcher took down Kya's address and phone number. "All right, dear. Someone will be out shortly."

"Thank you." Kya hung up the phone and groaned inwardly. Great, she'd get to tell the story again… "You better stick around. He's gonna want to question you, too."

"I'm not going anywhere." Jake's hot, pointed gaze dug straight into her eyes.

Was that what they called a smolder? She wasn't sure, but it had her burning up from the inside out.

WHEN KYA SPOTTED THE SHERIFF'S PICKUP RATTLING down the drive, nervous energy raced over her skin from head to toe and back. What was it about cops that inevitably made you nervous no matter the circumstances? She didn't know, but she sucked in a steadying breath and let him in.

Sheriff Rodgers was a pleasant man. He had a calm round face and a rounded belly. If someone had ever tried to run from him, by the looks of him, the potential for escape on foot was high. She coughed before the laugh bubbled up.

As he approached the door, Kya opened it.

"Are you Kya O'Shadit?"

"Yes, sir."

"You do look like you have a story to tell."

Kya raised her eyebrows with a huff of air, but didn't reply. She led him to the dining room table where Jake sat.

"Jake, how are you?" Sheriff Rodgers asked.

"Not too bad, Sheriff." Jake sat, forearms resting on the edge of the table.

"Why am I not surprised to see you?"

Jake simply shrugged, with a downturn to one side of his mouth.

Kya queried at the familiarity between the two, but said nothing.

Sheriff Rodgers lowered himself into a chair. "So, Miss O'Shadit," he pulled out a note pad and pen, "what's the story?"

Kya sighed, seating herself at the head of the table. The two men faced each other on either side of her as she recounted the morning's events.

As Kya talked, the sheriff scribbled notes. When she finished, Kya sat back and released a breath.

Sheriff Rodgers continued to write for a few more minutes. The house was eerily quiet. Kya listened to nothing but the buzzing in her ears. Then the house creaked and popped like log homes did.

"Okay," Sheriff Rodgers said as he clicked his pen closed. "You've been through a lot lately."

Kya said nothing. She bobbed her head and pressed her lips together.

"Unfortunately, this is not the first story like this involving Mitch."

That surprised Kya, but she did her best to school her features neutral.

"Though this is the first report we've gotten with this much physical evidence and a credible witness. Usually, it turns into a case of 'he said, she said,' like we told you earlier, and nothing sticks. But this time is vastly… more."

The room was quiet.

"Uh, I'll need a statement from you, Jake."

"That's why I stuck around."

"And from anyone else that's willing—your brother even, Kya."

"Tucker!" Kya hollered into the house. In the back of the house, you could hear a shuffle, a grunt, then a hard thud. "Oh, jeez," Kya said, closing her eyes and shaking her head.

"What's up?" Tucker asked as he exited the hall. "Hey, Sheriff Rodgers."

"Tuck," the sheriff responded, "can I get a statement from you about Kya's ordeal? What's your side of the story?"

"Sure, I even got a video of it."

Did everyone know the sheriff except Kya?

JAKE LISTENED WITH GRITTED TEETH AND WHITE knuckles. He wanted to punch Mitch all over again, as he listened to Kya. She was the toughest girl he knew, besides his mom.

The urge to reach out and hold Kya's hand as she talked

was intense, but they weren't that familiar… yet. And the hand nearest him was her burned hand.

He discreetly studied her face as she spoke, watching for subtle emotions, anger or held-back tears, but there were none of those. In fact, there were no emotions at all, in her face, voice, body, nothing. It was as though her story killed everything in her. Jake prayed that wasn't true, and he vowed to make sure she pulled herself out of the emptiness.

The sheriff's brow was crinkled with lines as he diligently scribbled in his notebook. Jake was grateful that Sheriff Rodgers hadn't elaborated on their familiarity. That was definitely not how he wanted Kya to find out about his record. He supposed he needed to tell her before someone else did. But not now. Not before she even got to know him… probably wouldn't make much of a difference, but he had to try. She was important, special, gorgeous. Jake swallowed thickly and shifted in his seat. Kya's eyes darted toward him as he settled himself again. Their mahogany depths sparkled at him, then died again as she refocused on her story. Her voice was a monotone as she droned on as if on autopilot. When Tucker appeared, some of the life returned to her. She stood up as Tucker played the video and gave his perspective of the story.

"You guys want something to drink? Lemonade?" she asked.

Jake almost declined, then said, "Yes, I'd love some."

The sheriff gave her a simple nod.

She brought over two glasses and returned to the kitchen to drink her own glass.

As Tucker talked, Jake discovered that the kid had a knack for action sequences with a bit of embellishment on the details.

"It was so cool! Jake dodged, like, all of Mitch's punches. He just danced out of the way. Mitch was down there swinging at air! Then Kya stepped in to break it up." Tucker sounded disappointed that the fight had been interrupted. "She took a direct hit to the forehead, knocked her out cold! But Jake was right there with an uppercut! He caught Mitch right on the jaw, snapped his head back. Mitch stumbled backwards, all dazed and stuff! It was wicked!"

Jake couldn't help but puff his chest as his head swelled. The way Tucker told it made Jake sound like a pro boxer. Which he wasn't.

Tucker finished his story as Jake tipped the last of his lemonade back. The flavor surprised him. He'd been expecting a powdered mix, not homemade. He didn't know why. He drank Aunt Cass's homemade lemonade all the time. Who'd made it? Kya or her mother? He guzzled the rest of the glass, savoring the tart flavor in the back of his throat.

"What about you, Jake? What's your side of all this?" Sheriff Rodgers asked.

Jake set the glass on the table before him and began his tale. He made sure he left nothing out, especially the parts when Kya had been out of it. The details he noticed from his very first encounter with Kya. The way she stumbled and listed in his headlights. He'd first thought she was drunk and almost passed by without stopping. Then he realized how exposed and alone she was. He gave her kudos for being leery about getting into a stranger's truck. He made note of her physical state at that time. The red marks on her neck and arms. The awkward way she held her left hand. The swollen left side of her face and mouth. And the tears. He'd never forget those tears. He'd never seen someone cry like that. And he hoped he never did again. It was as if they poured from her eyes like an overfull horse tank. She never sobbed. Her voice was steady and dead, much like how it was when she'd told her story earlier. But that night, she slowly collapsed in on herself till her arms were wrapped nearly all the way around her.

He recounted the details he could see when he saw her in the daylight. Jake talked for what seemed like hours, making sure to only share facts and observations and not personal feelings as best he could. That would get awkward fast.

Kya was a statue in the kitchen throughout his testimony. Her eyes were vacant, staring out the front windows, frozen. She never moved, even as the sheriff concluded his inquiries and stood to leave.

"Ahem," the sheriff cleared his throat.

That broke the spell over Kya.

"I'll walk you out."

Jake followed behind them slowly and leaned against the wall near the door, as Kya opened it for the sheriff. They exchanged the usual pleasantries, and Sheriff Rodgers departed.

Shutting the door, Kya turned to face him. She had a half smile on her face and a spark in her eye.

"So, now what?"

"Let's go sit outside." Jake shrugged away from that wall, taking her good hand in his as he opened the door and pulled her after him. Her hand was so tiny. He was careful to be gentle. Her fingers were bruised, and her skin was so soft. He didn't want to scratch her with his calluses.

Jake led her over to an old wooden swing in the front yard. The green paint was peeling off in large flecks. He sat and pulled her down to sit next to him. The swing creaked a little under their weight. Early evening sun cast shadows across the yard, bringing some relief from the heat of the day.

Jake sat straight with his hands in his lap. He was unsure of where to begin, how to start this conversation. He and Kya were not very familiar, maybe an acquaintanceship graduating to friendship.

"Are you okay, Kya?" he finally asked.

"Yes, why?"

"I don't mean right now, I mean in general, about this situation you're in?"

"Well, what about it?"

Kya was dodging the subject.

"Kya, you've been severely assaulted, twice, in less than three days by someone who was a friend. You should be enraged, scared, hyperventilating, something! But you're not!"

"I'm fine, Jake. Stop yelling at me!"

"You are not fine!" Now he really was yelling. "I just watched you shut down. Not a single emotional inflection! Not one!" Jake paused, waiting for her rebuttal. "You should be furious, crying, shaking, feeling something! But you're like a statue, beautiful and strong, weathering the storms, but on the inside you're dead, just stone…"

Kya's head was bowed forward, slightly hunched over herself, and extremely interested in her hands. Jake was afraid he'd gone too far, pushed her too much, and she would never open up again.

"Take it from someone who knows. It's okay to feel what you feel. You need to feel it, no matter how much you don't like to or want to. If you bottle it up, try to hold it in, forget about it. It will become like a lid on a Coke and Mentos. But you'll never know when or how much it's going to explode, or who all is going to get sticky." Jake released a heavy sigh and waited.

Kya's voice was small as she finally spoke. "You've had a friend betray you and become an entirely different person?"

"No, but I've felt the rage and tried to ignore it. I've had my whole life derail and turn upside down. And I wasn't able to move past it, or move forward, or move at all. I got stuck like a statue sitting in one place, no real purpose, unable to go anywhere. And that's where I remained, until I allowed myself to feel what I needed to." Jake leaned forward and rested his elbows on his knees. He removed his ball cap and ran his hands through his hair. It was getting long. He needed a haircut. He peeked sideways at the huddled statue next to him. There were small, wet spots on her hands, and her shoulders shook as she inhaled. Jake's heart split again for this beautiful, strong woman. Silently, he gathered her in his arms and pulled her into his lap. She hiccuped, and a huge sob escaped her. Kya fell apart right there in his arms on that swing. He held her together as tight as he could.

EIGHT

Kya wandered through the kitchen opening and closing every cupboard, even the ones she knew had no food in them, as if by opening the right combination of cupboards, food would magically appear. Sure, they had canned foods and crackers, chocolate in the fridge, and all the leftovers from her graduation party, but she really wanted pizza for dinner. So she called the grocery store and ordered two large pizzas. However, now she had to go into town to pick them up, which meant she would have to go to the store… in person. Going to the store meant entering a public area full of her community peers while looking like a boxer's punching bag.

Oh, the rumors just by allowing people to see her. She would become the ultimate seed for the rumor mill. Not that the rumors weren't probably already flying. She could lay some to rest, but that still would not solve the natural evolution of a rumor. Then, if she told everyone the truth, Mitch would become a target… or she could become a target. Mitch was a well-liked person. He could be very kind and polite. He was the star of the wrestling team. Small towns thrived on high school sports.

Consternation crinkled her brow, and her whole face throbbed. With a sigh, she stuffed her thoughts to a far corner of her mind to be examined later.

After her major cry session with Jake last night, which she was way more than overly embarrassed about, she felt better. She'd soaked the front of his shirt with her tears, and they were not cute tears. They were messy and ugly, and oh so cathartic. She wasn't 100 percent, but she was better. One day at a time, that's what he'd told her. All she had to do was be slightly better than the day before. Her heart warmed at the thought of him holding her as she sobbed. He was too perfect, too good to be real.

He didn't show her sympathy or coddle her. He just let her feel and let her know that he cared and was there for her.

Kya really didn't want everyone's sympathy. Going to town was a major step. She could just keep her mouth shut and let the rumors soar. Everyone would hear the truth soon enough. Nevertheless, she would have to hedge their questions...

Oh, this would be fun.

"Tucker!" Kya hollered into the house. "I'm going to the store. Don't burn the house down!"

"Okay," Tucker called back. "No promises."

Kya rolled her eyes and trotted down the stairs. She picked up her purse and keys, stepped into her flip-flops—so nice to have those back—and exited the shelter of her home.

The gravel road lined with trees blurred past. Why was she even subjecting herself to this torture? She could have found something different for dinner... But pizza sounded delicious. That and she could give some hella fuel to the rumor mill. If she didn't go now, she'd probably end up some old hermit cat lady. She had to go.

Driving turned out to be awkward with only one hand. Good thing her car was an automatic. Carefully, she navigated the streets to the grocery store.

Kya parked in front of the entry doors, took a deep breath, and jumped out of the car before she could tuck her tail and run away like a scared puppy. It was a quick trip to the bakery, then to the checkout. Kya repeated this mantra to herself as she pulled open the store doors.

Making a beeline to the bakery, Kya stopped before the old, orange, laminate booths set up in the small alcove. There was a coffee machine and doughnuts on the other side of them. On the table sat two white boxes stacked one on top of the other. The top one had Kya's name scrawled across it in big, black Sharpie marker, followed by the word "thanks." Next to that was the total price. Kya peeked her head around the corner to look into the alcove where the ovens were located. A girl who graduated the year before was preparing pizzas. Shaylee lifted her head from her work and spotted Kya at the entrance.

"Hey, Kya, your pizzas are right there." Shaylee pointed at the table behind her. "They turned out—whoa." She turned completely from her work to fully face Kya. "What happened? Are you okay?"

"Yeah, I'm fine. Thanks for the pizzas." Kya lifted the two boxes from the table by bracing them against her hip with her good hand. She smiled as best she could, ready to flee.

"What happened?" Shaylee asked again.

Kya froze, and a large chunk of ice settled into the bottom of her stomach. "Oh, just some bad circumstances and situations at the senior party."

"Oh my gosh, it looks a lot worse than just bad circumstances!"

"Eh." Kya shrugged. "It will all heal in time." She tried to brush off the girl's inquiries.

"Does it hurt?" Shaylee stared at Kya's face.

"This hurts the worst." Kya lifted her burned hand.

Shaylee gasped and covered her mouth with her hands. Her eyes would pop out of her head if she held that expression for too long. "Oh my gosh, what happened?"

The girl was starting to sound like a damn broken record.

"Fell in the fire," Kya said nonchalantly.

"Oh my."

"Yeah, well, I better get these home before they get cold."

"Yes. You get better, too," Shaylee replied.

Kya smiled as she left the small area and wove her way back to the checkout. She placed the pizzas on the counter. The lady behind the register was an older gal. Kya knew she should know her name, but she didn't.

"Oh, honey. It's so sad what happened to you." She gave Kya a pitying look.

Kya wrangled money out of her wallet one-handed and passed it to the lady. She tried for a reassuring smile, but couldn't muster one. So, Kya pinched her lips together and did nothing as she took her change.

"Do you need help out to your car?" she asked.

Kya thought about the question. "Yes, please."

She called over the intercom system, and a young boy came out of the back and carried the pizzas for her.

"You heal up, okay?" the lady called.

Kya gave her a smile and pushed open the door for the kid.

After placing the pizzas on the passenger seat, the kid said, "Have a good evening," without once meeting Kya's gaze. Like one glance or smile would suddenly make him rude, or, possibly, the injuries would attach themselves to his body. It wasn't a disease she could pass off. She just got beat to shit! Though she had to admit it was nice that at least one person she encountered wasn't trying to stick their nose where it didn't belong. What happened to her was between her and Mitch. Well, possibly Jake, because for some reason that was beyond her, Jake had planted himself right in the middle of this whole fiasco.

Kya's stomach tightened and dropped. What if she dragged Jake down with her? She would wear a label in this town for the rest of her life. What would this do to Jake? How would it affect his life? He punched Mitch. His family could press charges against Jake. Shit, if it went to court, the court could charge him… with what, Kya had no idea. Why was Jake helping her anyway? What was his motive? Kya could think of one reason that was way too obvious. She was sure if that's what he was after, he could find it for a lot less work. So, why?

Doing the right thing was one thing, helping when you could, sure. But bringing her salve and taking on Mitch, playing video games with her brother, letting her have a sob-fest all over his shirt? Kya made a mental note to ask him the next time he was around, if all her thoughts didn't flee like they sometimes did when in his presence. She knew he would pop up somewhere soon. That's what he'd been doing for the last two days. Show up on the road to give her a ride home. Show up at her house with salve. Show up and fight Mitch. Show up… right behind her in his sexy truck while she drove home…

What the crap? Was he stalking her? How did he always seem to find her? Kya kept glancing in the rearview mirror. She could see his shit-eating grin! He was laughing, most likely at her! What the hell?

Kya forced herself to focus on the road ahead of her, though she couldn't help but glance in the mirror to check if he was still there. As she made the turn onto her driveway, Jake's truck followed. This guy was seriously going to follow her home like a lost puppy. What the crapidy crap? She parked in her usual spot and wiggled her gimped-up self out of her car, slamming the door. Words were about to be had with this dude. Just as she rounded the bumper of her car, Jake popped out from his truck and had the passenger door to her car open with the pizzas in his hands before she could even say, "Hey."

"Hey yourself," Jake said, closing the door.

"What are you doing?" Kya asked like an idiot.

"Holding pizza," Jake replied.

"No shit, smartass. I mean, what are you doing here, following me and such?"

"Helping out a friend." He said it with this "duh" tone.

Kya paused, looking down at her painted toes in her flip-flops. "Why?" she whispered. A more than slightly embarrassed feeling resurfaced from her cry-fest yesterday. What was it about him that made her drop all her defenses?

There was a stretch of silence, and Kya was sure he hadn't heard her. She looked up into Jake's face, preparing to take the pizzas and make a run for the front door so she could wallow in embarrassment in private. But as her gaze collided with his, he spoke.

"Because some wrongs take more than a simple act of kindness to appease. You need help, Kya. And besides, I like hanging out with you."

Kya was hung up on his words and having problems forming her own. She opened her mouth to tell him she did not need help, but then it hit her—that would be a lie. She wished she didn't need help, but the truth was she had no idea where she would be right now if Jake hadn't planted himself into her life… possibly dead, if Mitch had come looking for her that night. A shiver zinged up her spine.

Jake stared at her as she worked through her mental process.

"Come on, sugar, these pizzas smell amazing, and my stomach is starting to get angry that it's only in my hands and not in my mouth." Jake paused for a breath, and a wide-eyed, stricken expression crossed his face. "The pizza, I mean."

"Yeah, I got it."

Jake hurried past her to the gate. Kya's brow scrunched

as she thought about what he'd said. Her mouth formed an 'o' as she registered the words that had Jake looking as if his parents had just tried to tell him his conception story. Kya snorted and covered her mouth as she passed, holding the gate open. Shaking her head, she walked to the door, throwing it open for Jake to pass.

Kya didn't speak as she opened the boxes and began serving up the pizza.

Tucker sock-slid into the kitchen. "Pizza! Oh, hey, Jake." He beelined it to the pizza, grabbed a plate, and went right back to the TV. Jake and Kya followed behind him, taking up spots on the couch.

Jake took a bite and made a small moan of approval.

"Happier now that it's in your mouth?"

He nearly choked on Kya's brash words. Recovering, he looked at her out of the corner of his eye. "So much better," he said around a mouthful of food.

The words were mundane enough, but they had Kya blushing as a belly-rolling laugh shook her. Jake silently laughed next to her. His face turned red because he couldn't breathe around the food in his mouth. Tears streamed down both their faces.

Tucker looked at them like they were insane.

After a few minutes, the giggles persisted, and Tucker asked, "What kind of drugs are you guys on?"

Kya shook her head and waved him off, gently wiping the tears from her swollen face, which was starting to throb.

Tucker gave her a wary look and turned back to the movie on the TV.

When the credits rolled, Tucker silently got up, took his plate to the kitchen, and went to his room.

Jake stood, picking up Kya's plate. He moved to the kitchen and deposited the paper plates in the trash.

"You don't have to do that. I could have gotten it." Kya hopped up onto the counter.

"Because these dishes are so hard, you know, I thought I would help."

"Aw, a true gentleman." Kya rolled her eyes.

"You're very welcome, Miss." Jake leaned back in front of the sink. His hands gripped the edge of the counter at his sides. He looked over to where Kya sat and seemed to study her.

Kya met his gaze. She normally would have dropped her eyes, but she found she couldn't look away, trapped by the intense expression on Jake's face.

"Your bruises have already faded a lot. Other than the new one on your forehead."

"Huh, yeah, the others don't hurt a whole lot anymore, either. Just don't touch them."

"Ha, ha. Well, that's good."

"Now, I just look like a one-eyed sick alien."

"A beautiful sick alien."

"Psssh. You've never even seen me without my pretty purple-and-green coloring. How would you know if I'm beautiful?" Kya could feel the blood rushing to her cheeks, adding another color to her rainbow complexion.

Jake pushed himself off the counter and stalked toward her. "Because you're beautiful now."

"No, I'm just some barely adult, burned and bruised, high school girl."

"High school graduate girl." Jake stopped directly in front of Kya. "Beauty is more than flawless skin." He reached out with two fingers and lifted her chin. Her skin tingled. "I know you are beautiful because I've seen you be strong in a situation that would have broken another. I can hardly tell if it's affected you at all."

"I guess you missed all the waterworks the last few days."

"And that is the only reason I know it has affected you, but you still stand tall. You grit your teeth against the pain. Shit, Kya, you went to the grocery store tonight in a small town that thrives on gossip. I'm sure that was not easy."

"I just really wanted pizza."

"Exactly! You don't let people and their nosey, inquisitive behavior dictate what you do. You know what you want, and you don't let anything stop you." Jake was close now. Suddenly, he stood between Kya's legs. She couldn't remember when that had happened. "You're more beautiful now, simply because of your strength and courage. I know it's not easy to condemn someone you considered a friend, but you are doing the right thing." Jake spoke with such assured confidence. How had he gotten so wise?

"And where did you gain these words of wisdom?" she asked.

Jake's face fell. He stepped back from her and thrust his hand through his hair. "…Um, just something I picked up along the way." He turned in a circle, looking anywhere but at Kya. "I…um…I—I better be going. It's late, and I have to be up early." He looked at her then.

"Okay." Kya nodded. "See ya."

Jake gave a small wave and bounded down the stairs.

Kya had no idea what button she had pressed, but apparently, it was not okay to ask about his past. She stood in the kitchen, letting the wind settle from Jake's rapid departure. She was slightly confused. He had been saying such kind things to her. Then he closed up and ran away. But was he running from her or from her question?

Jake knew a lot about her. He had seen her in numerous states of distress. And that scared her because she had only met him three days ago. And she knew very little about Jake. He worked on a ranch and his sister lived in town… He had good taste in trucks… He was nice beyond all reason. He had stalker tendencies. And he was a hard worker, from what she could tell. One thing Kya knew for certain was that even though she didn't know much about Jake, she knew she really liked him.

NINE

JAKE MADE SURE HE DIDN'T SLAM THE DOOR TO KYA'S home as he ran from the premises. He jumped into the driver's seat of his pickup, gripped the steering wheel till his knuckles turned white, and backed out of the parking space. Kya's house grew smaller in his mirror as he sped away. Slumping in his chair, he turned on to a two-track, rutted-up back road, pulling off at the top of the ridge. He parked and dropped his forehead to the wheel, letting out a frustrated huff of air. So stupid. It was a simple question, and he let it trigger him. She was so close; he'd been near to kissing her, finally, giving reality to his fantasies. He could vividly recall Kya's soothing scent—vanilla, warm chocolate chip cookies, with a hint of nutmeg.

Sitting straight, Jake rolled the window down, attempting to collect himself. Looking out over the expanse of evergreen trees to the setting sun, the sky flamed a raging orange and pink fading to purple and midnight blue. He could see the two water towers, the new one that looked like a golf ball on a tee, and the other a plain white cylinder. In the distance was the airport ridge on the other side of Upton. Light reflected off a few ponds scattered along the edge of the timber. Cars moved down the highway in both directions.

Climbing out of his truck, he stood at the cliff's edge and took a deep breath. The air was fresh, permeated with the scent of sage, sweet grass, and pine trees. He breathed deeply again, and his whole being seemed to relax.

He had just run from Kya. She had asked a simple mundane question that was pretty much rhetorical, and he ran. He could have brushed it off and not answered, or said some generic crap and made a joke. Or, hell, he could have told her the truth. But the truth scared him. He didn't want to go back to that place. The handcuffs, the bars, the cold concrete surroundings. He was afraid if she knew, she wouldn't look at him with kind eyes as she always did. She would see him for the monster he really was. He wasn't ready to lose her yet.

There was a voice in the back of Jake's head that whispered, *You've already lost her. You've lied to her, pushed her away, kept her at a distance. Why would she ever want to be with you after all that?*

"We barely know each other," Jake consoled himself. "No one reveals all of their demons after knowing someone for, like, two days." Eventually, he would have to tell her if he had any hope of keeping her. Why did he want a perfect stranger so badly? Because she was absolutely beautiful inside and out. Even after being beaten by that douchecanoe, she wanted to believe he was a good person. After the confrontation with the shoes, Jake doubted she still felt the same way.

His fist clenched and unclenched. He'd punched Mitch

hard enough to black out his lights for a few seconds. He'd played it down to Kya, but Jake knew that, had Mitch been any smaller, he would have been out of the count after that single punch. Jake had a hard time fathoming his own strength. It was crazy how one instant, one choice, one moment, could change your life forever. And yet that horrible mistake had brought him to the place he was now. It had led him to Kya.

Jake stayed up on the ridge till the sun was fully set. Then he took the back loop around to the ranch.

He pulled his pickup up to the second house for ranch hands, reached into the back of the pickup, and hefted out the tractor part he had picked up in town. Walking to the back of the barn, he placed the part next to the tractor.

Kole, another ranch hand who was a few years older than Jake, stepped out from the barn and made his way toward him. "Hey, man, all the chores in the barn are taken care of." He removed his dirty, weathered cowboy hat, pushed his brown hair back, and replaced it.

"Okay, thanks," Jake acknowledged him.

"Took you long enough to pick up that part," Kole said and shot a stream of tobacco spit from his mouth.

"Yeah, I ran into Kya," Jake said, opening the engine compartment of the tractor.

Kole nodded. "She okay?"

"Yeah, though she doesn't look it."

"That son-of-a-bitch." Kole shook his head.

There was a short silence. Jake listened to the frogs and the crickets in the distance.

"All right, I'm gonna turn in," Kole said.

"Yeah, that's cool. I'm gonna get this part put in and then turn in. Shouldn't take too long."

Kole spun around and made his way back to the house.

Jake sighed and turned to his work. Kya would make him lose his job at the family ranch if he wasn't careful. Uncle Kal wouldn't put up with him freeloading.

KYA SAT ON THE KITCHEN COUNTER STARING blankly at the wood floor. Nothing seemed to be occupying her thoughts. Either her mind was working so fast nothing could become concrete, or she was thinking nothing at all. She just sat.

She didn't hear the dogs bark when her parents got home, or the front door open. She didn't notice them walk into the kitchen. Didn't realize her mother was speaking to her.

Kya's mom stopped directly in front of her and gripped Kya's upper arm. "Honey, are you okay?"

"Hmm." Kya blinked slowly and looked up into her mom's face.

"Where'd you go?" she asked as she gently prodded the edges of the bruise around Kya's eye.

"Um, I don't know."

"How are you feeling?"

"Fine, it's all healing. Doesn't hurt too bad. My hand is what hurts, even simply from holding it away from everything, including myself." Kya paused. "I woke up lying on it."

Her mother hissed between her teeth and gave Kya a pained look.

"Oh, baby." She looked at Kya with sympathy for a little while longer, then turned to the pizza on the counter. "So, who got pizza?"

"I did," Kya replied.

"You went to town?" she asked.

"Yes, I got lots of questions and weird looks."

Her mother paused. "Did you say who did it?"

"No." Kya sighed.

"Good. We need to keep this quiet till it all gets put through the process."

Kya nodded. "I'm gonna head down to bed."

"Okay." Her mother hugged her goodnight.

Kya hugged her dad around the shoulders where he sat at the table eating pizza. He mumbled "love you" through a mouthful.

She stepped onto the stairs and reached for the railing, but pulled her hand back, unable to touch it. The white gauze wrapped around her burned hand glared at her. Kya drew in a breath and marched resolutely down the stairs.

Once in her room, Kya shut her door and sat on her bed. She glanced around her space. A stack of brochures on her nightstand caught her eye. She spread them out on her bed. There was one to every college in the state, which was only, like, nine. Then there were the ones that wouldn't stop sending her stuff. She'd never even asked for their pamphlets.

These places were the big names off somewhere in the east. A couple were from California. They were the photography schools. Denver was the closest one. At the bottom of the stack was Black Hills State University. It was only an hour from home and had a prestigious photography program. For whatever reason that Kya could not discern herself, she did not want to go far from home… but she knew she needed to experience life on her own.

Her parents kept reiterating in state, in state, UW, in state. Kya had no desire whatsoever to go to the University of Wyoming. In state would save money because of the scholarships the state offered. So, then there was Northwest College, which had an awesome art program.

Kya sighed, looking over the colorful images before her. There were a number of smiling students on the covers, fake and plastic. She picked up the one for BHSU. This was the one that seemed to call to her. She snatched up the one for UW. This one would be cheaper. It's what her parents wanted. It would make things easier on them…

But BHSU had the program and the atmosphere she wanted.

Kya flopped back on her bed with a groan.

THE AFTERNOON SUN WARMED THE BARE FLOOR OF Jake's small room at the ranch. He picked up his cell phone, and Kya's name seemed to magically appear on his screen. He had no idea why he was calling her. He really had no reason to be calling her except for just wanting to hear her voice. But why did he want to call her? He wasn't sure what he would say. *Sorry for running from you last night like the chicken I am.* Sounded about right. Jake shoved that thought to the back of his mind for later exploration. He touched her number, and the screen switched to calling. Jake pressed the infernal device to his ear. There was a pause, then a ring, followed by another. He held his breath. Maybe she wouldn't answer.

"Hello?" Kya's sweet voice came through the speaker to his ear. She sounded as though she were smiling.

"Uh, hi," Jake responded belatedly, and he wanted to smack himself in the face.

"Who is it?" He could hear a voice in the background.

"Jake." Kya sounded as if she had pulled the phone away from her mouth.

"Jake, from State Farm?" Kya's best friend, possibly?

"Rachel!" Yep, it was her.

"What are you wearing, Jake from State Farm?" Rachel shouted to make sure Jake heard her.

Jake chuckled low through the phone and looked down at his jeans. "Khakis."

There was a pause, and then both girls burst into laughter.

Through their hysterics, Jake heard Rachel say, "She sounds hideous."

Kya responded with, "Well, she's a guy, so."

Then Jake was laughing just as hard as they were. He could hear Kya panting on the other end of the line. Or satellite, however you wanted to look at it, as she attempted to catch her breath. Jake shook his head and took a deep breath himself.

He held the phone pressed to his ear. His frantic pacing while wrestling with the idea of calling Kya had ceased the moment her voice had come through the phone. Jake chuckled again. His hand tucked into his pocket, he bent at the waist, rocking on his heels. He could hear Kya and Rachel recovering. Jake waited for Kya to speak… And the giggles resumed. A smile crawled across his face. He wished he were there to see Kya so joyous. He also had the strange urge to meet Kya's crazy friend she talked about. Just so that he could learn more about her. Why… he didn't really want to think about that too closely.

"Ah, wheewoo." Kya took a deep, steadying breath. "Sorry, Jake."

"Eh, it's okay. If I'm good for anything, at least it's a laugh."

"Yeah, Rachel's here."

"Couldn't tell," Jake muttered.

"What's up?"

"Uh, I just finished up for the day… and decided to call you." Jake ran his hand through his hair and silently cursed himself and his incredible wit. "Figured I'd be polite and avoid my stalker tendencies." Jake grimaced. Man, he sounded like a tool.

"I was actually getting used to your stalker tendencies. The politeness is throwing me off a bit."

"Oh, my bad. Teach me to break a habit."

She laughed through the phone. "Well, Rachel and I

were just hanging out here at the house. Do you want to return to the normal stalking and join us?"

There was a muffling sound, then the scratch of clothing, and the distant murmur of voices. They sounded intense. Jake guessed Kya had pressed the phone to her shirt and was talking with Rachel. Judging by the tone of the voices, he might not be entirely welcome. Through the muffling, he caught a snippet of conversation. "How are we supposed to talk about a guy if he's sitting in the same room? That is why I am here, is it not?" Rachel, most definitely Rachel.

"Come on, it'd be a chance for you to meet him." Kya was not very good at covering up a mic.

"Fine, whatever, girly. It's your party," Rachel conceded.

"Yeah," Kya spoke directly into the phone again. "You can come over if you want."

"Uh, it doesn't really sound like Rachel is cool with that."

"Eh, she'll get over it," Kya said.

"No, she won't! This was supposed to be a girls' night!" Rachel shouted from a distance. "But I'd just *love* to meet you, Jake."

Jake frowned. That sounded sinister. What did this chick have planned? "You sure about that? I feel like I need to fear for my life."

Kya laughed. "Her bark is worse than her bite. And she'll suck it up and get over it." That last part was most definitely directed at Rachel.

"I'm not willing to take those chances. I think I'll stay here where I know it's safe."

"If you want, but you're totally welcome to come over."

"Naw, I think I'll postpone this meeting and my inevitable doom. I've already interrupted your evening… and nearly every evening previously." Jake frowned at himself. He had been seeing Kya an awful lot. "You have fun with your girls' night."

"Okay." Kya's voice sounded…disappointed. "Thanks, Jake."

He smiled at hearing her say his name. "You're welcome, Kya. I'll talk to you later."

"Okay, bye," Kya said.

Jake ended the call and slid the phone into his pocket. Now, what was he going to do? He really had been spending a lot of time with Kya. She needed time away from him. He should have been keeping his distance from her to begin with.

Nothing good would come of this. But as the situation stood, Kya needed protection. Jake didn't trust this was over. He didn't know that bastard very well, and Kya hadn't said much about him. But from what Mitch said, he wasn't going to just let her go. He'd wanted her for too long, worked toward getting her all these years. There's no way he would give up that easily on the object of his obsession.

No, Kya was still in danger. Jake would stick around long enough to see that asshole in jail and Kya safe. Then he would step aside and leave Kya be.

If he could.

She was quickly becoming the source of his own obsession. The difference was he wasn't insane about it, or violent. Not that he couldn't be, he just wasn't toward people who didn't deserve it. And he never lost his head in rage.

Was Jake violent? Yes. Volatile? No.

He remembered the first time violence had been the solution. Vividly recalled the feel of bone crunching and flesh splitting beneath his knuckles. The sound of flesh connecting with flesh and the crack of broken bone. The screams of pain. All of that he expected when he chose to defend himself. What he didn't expect was the greed it created in him. He wanted the violence, the darkness, the pain, craved it, had to have it again. It was only by sheer will and his friends' reminder that he held it together. Even now, he could feel the craving rising, wanting an outlet. Jake figured Mitch would be a good target. No one would blame him. The guy had it coming.

The image of Kya lying on the ground after Mitch punched her flashed through his mind. She had looked so small and yet so fierce. She was the reason he had not taken all of Mitch's teeth out. His concern for, and the need to protect, Kya, was what stopped him then. But she wasn't here now…

The only way to satisfy the darkness was to give it somewhere to go.

Jake changed out of his boots and into gym shorts and tennis shoes, and left the hand house, and crossed the dirt lot to the barn.

There was one thing he had insisted on bringing with him when he left Montana. Aunt Cass insisted that if he had to have it, it was only going to be in the barn. She didn't want anything in the house to get damaged.

Jake walked through the center of the barn. Stalls lined both walls. They weren't used very often except when one of the horses was going to foal. His aunt and uncle agreed he could set it up in one of the unused stalls. It had taken quite a bit of finagling to set it up so it was stable, but they did it.

Jake stepped into the stall. In the center of the space hung an old, red punching bag. The leather was cracked and worn. For the most part, you couldn't really tell it was red. It was faded so much that the only way Jake knew it to be red was from peeling back the folds at the top to reveal the dark rusty color of its former glory. The bag hung a few feet off the ground and a couple inches over his head.

A couple of days before he came down to Wyoming, he'd found it in a garage sale. His mother had been furious when he came home with it. She had raged for a few minutes, demanding where they were going to put it. Yelling and calling him foolish for spending money on the old pile of junk. Jake had stood unmoving and kept his mouth shut as she yelled. She had only quit because Jake hadn't moved at all, and she wanted him to answer her. But Jake said nothing. He couldn't explain it. She wouldn't get it. And if he did explain and try to make her understand, Jake worried he would scare her. He didn't want his mother to be afraid. But he was too late because she already feared for him. Jake was just glad she wasn't afraid of him. She might have been if she knew his motives.

Jake methodically wrapped his knuckles. The motion

was soothing. He bounced on his feet and danced around the bag.

He recalled the way his mother looked when he had left for Wyoming. She stood on the porch with one arm wrapped around her waist and the other lifted in a stiff wave. Tears tracked down her face, and the wind blew her hair in every direction.

Shifting his body forward, he slammed his fist into the bag. A loud thud sounded, and the bag swayed, creaking on the chains it hung from. Music to his ears. His whole body seemed to sigh with relief.

He remembered the look on Mitch's face as he punched Kya. The image appeared crystal clear in his mind. Jake's jaw clenched, and his lips pressed into a thin line. He wiggled his fingers, readjusting his fists. He sucked in a breath. The muscles in his shoulder tensed up, coiling into ropes of steel. The tension flowed down his arm to his biceps and triceps. It rippled down his back to his lats. His whole right side was a coiled band ready to snap as he drew his arm back. His forearm and wrist flexed. And the band snapped. He twisted at the waist, throwing his whole body into the motion. His arm projected out, his fist straight with his forearm. The knuckles of his wrapped fist slammed into the worn leather. It caved around his fist, creasing and wrinkling. The weight of the bag pushed back against the force of his punch, making his muscles flex farther. A loud echo like the report of a fired gun ricocheted around the stall. The bag swung backward at the force of his blow.

As it rocked back toward him, Jake dodged to the side,

and he swung on the bag with his other fist, and the fury began.

Coupling his jabs with kicks and dodges, he ducked and strayed as if it were a real opponent. He recalled every lesson he had learned, remembered the exact motions as he had been instructed, throwing in a few wild moves he had picked up from watching others. Many of those were cheap shots and sneaky, but anything was legal when it came down to you or the other guy.

Sweat poured off his body in rivers. It trickled down his spine and over his forehead. He continued punching and kicking. Air sawed in and out of his lungs as they labored to reoxygenate his body. Still, he kept going. Soon, his muscles ached and trembled. He launched one last punch that sent the bag swinging toward the corner. He stepped out of its reverse path and began removing the wrap on his hands. He concentrated on calming his heart and regulating his breathing.

He lifted his head from his task. Kole stood in the stall's doorway, wearing shorts similar to his, and had a towel slung over his shoulder. Jake had no idea how long he had been there. Some of the guys liked to use the bag too, and he didn't mind. At least it was getting used well.

"Hey, man," Kole said.

"Hey," Jake replied as he continued with his wrapped hands.

"Whoa, dude." Kole looked down at Jake's hands with a wide-eyed, "holy shit" expression.

Jake followed Kole's stare. He had removed the strip

across his knuckles and was starting on the weave between his fingers. The tape and his knuckles were stained a deep red. It ran down his fingers and dripped onto the floor.

"Oh, huh." Jake simply finished peeling his hands free of the wrap. He wadded up the wrappings and held his hand under it to catch the blood.

Kole stared at him like he was an alien with tentacles. "That doesn't make a guy feel inadequate at all," he muttered, as Jake headed toward the trash bins out back. He dropped the wrappings in and went back inside to the tack-slash-tool area where he picked up a couple of rags, one old and one new. He secured the new one around his fist.

Reentering the boxing stall, Kole stared at the blood on the floor. He looked a little pale as he wrapped his own hands. Jake knelt and mopped up the blood with the dirty rag.

"See ya, man," Jake called as he left, dropping the dirty rag in the trash on his way back to the house.

Once inside, he went straight to the bathroom and turned on the cold water. He plunged his hands under the spray, and the white sink turned red, then slowly faded to pink. The blood ran from three cuts along the tops of his knuckles. They weren't very big, but blood pumped out of them. The cold water slowly worked to stanch the bleeding.

Jake stripped his sweat-soaked clothes off and stepped into the shower. The warm water worked at his tight muscles and washed away the grit of the day along with the lingering black clouds in the back of his mind, leaving only the bright spot that was Kya. A small smile turned up his mouth. She was everything he'd ever hoped to dream for, and more. She was real and beautiful, and kind beyond measure. Was she asleep now? Or was she a night owl? Should he try calling her again?

The split skin of his knuckles stung in the soap.

Would she be afraid of him if she saw him fight?

TEN

Kya hugged Rachel in the entryway.

"Okay, see you later, alligator," Rachel said as she turned to the door.

"In a while, crocodile," Kya replied and waved her off.

It had gotten late while Kya and Rachel talked. The movie they had put in ended up being background noise as they discussed college and boys and college boys. Kya laughed to herself. If only their talks were ever that superficial. The subject may have been superficial, but the way in which they talked about it was not. They had attempted to answer some of life's most difficult questions and tried to figure out the future. All they had succeeded in was moving in circles and creating more questions. Rachel usually tended toward the philosophical stuff, and Kya was content to just wander and enjoy the ride.

They had discussed Jake to great lengths. The only conclusions they reached were that Rachel needed to meet him, and Kya was far too into him for knowing him only a few days.

Butterflies, or maybe it was nerves, gripped Kya's stomach.

She shuffled her way back to her room, clutching her phone in a death grip. She wasn't sure why she was about to do what she was about to do. Obligation? No. Guilt? Maybe a little. Need? Not really. Want? Most definitely, but why?

Kya sat on the edge of her bed. Her left leg bounced in a staccato beat of its own volition. She stared down at the phone in her hands. Jake's name was at the top of the screen, and her thumb hovered over his number.

Today had been the first time he had called her. And Kya felt guilty for cutting it short. He had called her, and she had shut him out. She owed it to him to apologize. But it was late. What if he was in bed? Alone... well, he better be alone, or she was going to kick his ass. Kya stopped that train of thought and took a deep breath. They hadn't even declared anything yet. She had no official claim on him. For all she knew, he didn't even like her and was just being nice. The idea of Jake with someone else had her clenching her fists—well, fist, singular—and gritting her teeth. Oh, man, she had it bad. And that scared her. Her reaction to him was... intense. She barely knew the guy, but some part of her felt it had a claim on him.

Her thumb hung suspended over his number. What if he was asleep? He worked long days. She'd hate to wake him up. Absent thoughts wandered through her mind. Thoughts she shouldn't be thinking. Like, *What did his voice sound like when he was groggy from sleep? What did he wear to bed? Did he wear anything to bed? Was he a cuddler?*

Blood rushed through Kya's body, and her abdomen fluttered. She slapped herself, like actually physically slapped herself. It wasn't very hard, but with all the bruises, it stung. She pressed her thumb down, and her phone went to the call screen. She pressed it to her ear and listened to the drone of the ringer.

Kya's foot bounced double time now. It rang three, four times. Kya was about to give up.

"Hello?" Jake's voice came through the phone sounding slightly breathless and strained.

"Is this a bad time?" Kya asked, looking at the clock again for what seemed like the zillionth time.

"Uh, uff, ow, no," Jake said.

"It sounds like you're busy," Kya said, disheartened.

"No, no, I'm not. I… had to… dive and… dig my phone out of my jeans pocket."

"Oh, sorry for my bad timing."

"Actually, it was quite perfect. I literally just walked into my room after my shower."

"Ah, well, okay then." A mental picture of Jake diving for the phone in nothing but a towel brought a blush to her cheeks. "So, what are you doing?" Kya asked. "That was a dumb question. You told me you were in the shower." Word vomit bubbled out of her mouth. Kya wanted to crawl beneath her bed. What was wrong with her? She was usually clinically composed at all times.

Jake chuckled, "I just finished boxing and seriously needed a shower."

His voice was throaty and, if Kya was being honest, sexy as hell.

"You box?"

"Eh, I dabble."

"Uh-huh…" *Liar*, Kya thought. He was probably really good, judging by the jab he landed on Mitch, and his… physical attributes. "Yeah, I bet you probably go all Rocky on dudes' asses."

"Well, Rocky was a straight boxer, and I do more like a street version of kickboxing."

"Oh, sorry, my bad. Didn't realize the distinction." Kya rolled her eyes. "So, you do something more like UFC fighting?"

"Yeah, I suppose that's more comparable. Though I wouldn't pin myself to be quite as insane as some of those guys."

Kya laughed.

"Insane, sure, but I'm not quite to their level… yet."

"There's still time, right?" Kya smiled in reflection of Jake's tone. Talking with him felt good and light. It was easy. She wished it wasn't over the phone. It would be better if it was face-to-face. And that thought made her already fluttery belly jump. She literally had only known him for a few of days, and already she felt that they were longtime friends. She wanted to know all there was to know about him.

Jake's low deep, throaty chuckle had Kya biting her lip.

"How was your girls' night?"

"It… it was good. Rachel's as crazy as ever. And I think I'm more confused now than when I went into it."

"Confused? Why?"

"Rachel says she can't form an opinion till she meets you, and that she always suspected there was something wrong with Mitch, but she's never really liked him anyway, so there's no surprise there."

"Well, I guess I can't say anything to that fact. I just met the guy. But from what I've seen, I think there's more than 'something wrong' with him."

"Hmm, I've never seen that side of him before… that night. I thought it was because of the alcohol. But, then at my house…" Kya sighed. "Either he was drunk then or… he's an abuser and a bit off in the head."

There was a pause. "I don't know. I haven't known him long enough to know for sure, which is true. And he could be a great actor and hide it well."

Kya tried to think back to a time when that side of Mitch might have appeared, and she'd just brushed it off.

Jake said, "What I do know is how he's been recently. And all the signs are indicative of an asshole."

"Ha," Kya huffed. "You're telling me." She gingerly prodded the swollen flesh on her face.

"It'll heal." It was as if he knew exactly what she'd been doing. "Every day I see you, it looks better."

"Yeah, it doesn't feel all that much better."

"Sorry."

"It's just the truth. Getting punched in the face, twice, is bound to cause a person some degree of pain."

"I only saw it happen the one time, and I have this insatiable urge to inflict just as much—no, more—pain on that fucker as he has on you." Jake paused, and Kya could hear his heavy breaths. "No man has the right to hit a woman."

Kya didn't know what to say. She was flattered by his protectiveness and a little scared by the barely contained anger in his voice. Kya could practically see him clenching his jaw and fists. She hoped he didn't break his phone.

"But I forgot. He's not a man—he's just an asshole." Jake let out a forced breath. "Sorry, I know he was your friend and all, but what he did to you is not okay."

"No, no. I agree. This was so not cool. But I… guess I'm having problems making one person out of the Mitch I've known all this time, and the one who did this to me." Kya stopped and fiddled with the hem of her shirt. "He was so kind. This one time they were offering a photography class. It was super informal, just a local photographer that did all the school photo shoots. I really wanted to take the class, but I was the only one. So, Mitch went out and bought a really nice camera. And he took the class with me. He didn't like photography, but he did it because I wanted him to. When the class was over, he gave the camera to me… That's the Mitch that I know… knew. He would go out of his way to do something nice."

Silence stretched between them.

"So, what are you going to do? What do you want to do?" Jake asked.

"I want to know the truth. I want to know what's going on. I want to get to the bottom of this. I want to understand why."

KYA LAY IN HER BED OVER AN HOUR LATER. A SMALL smile was a permanent fixture on her face. After the heavy conversation, they had talked about everything… and nothing. There was no lapse in conversation between them. Much of what they had discussed was completely pointless. But neither of them had cared. They just kept talking.

Kya lifted her phone and looked at the time. It was eleven o'clock. She had been on the phone for two hours. The only other person who came close to that record was her grandma. And that was simply because the woman never stopped talking. But even then, it was only like forty-five minutes. Two hours. During that whole conversation, she had had no concept of time passing.

A giddy little girl smile split her lips. She had a very strong need to jump around and clap her hands. And maybe even let out one of those very unattractive squeals. Goodness, she was such a girl.

All he'd said was, "Goodnight, Kya." …but it was the way he said it. There was something almost, dare she say, reverent in his voice. Whatever it was, it made her chest swell and her breath catch. She probably sounded like a doofus because she didn't have enough air to speak. So, her return, "Goodnight" came out all full of air and breathy, like one of those bimbos out of a cheerleading movie. She kind of wanted to punch *herself* in the eye.

Kya had seen people get punched in the face numerous times on TV, and she decided then that those actors really didn't capture the sentiment correctly. It hurt like a son-of-a-bitch. If they would like cry, or bawl really, maybe roll around on the floor in pain, that would be more believable. Could be that she was just a wuss. Either way, getting punched on top of a black eye was not fun.

Still, Kya couldn't figure it out. Why? Mitch'd never shown that side of himself before. If he was acting, why hadn't she seen it before now? She'd spent quite a lot of time with him. You'd think she'd have noticed something at some point. But if he loved her, he would have been kind and nearly perfect to her. It was only when she refused his direct advance that he got angry. Quiet, studious Kya with her face buried behind her camera wouldn't have seen it because Mitch had what he wanted when he was with her.

A yawn stretched Kya's mouth wide. Her eyes watered. She rolled to her side and switched off the lamp. She snuggled down into her blankets, closed her eyes, and replayed Jake's goodnight to her, hoping to rid herself of the depressing thoughts about two-faced Mitch.

ELEVEN

Gazing out the bay window, the western sky was alight with colors. The sun had set below the treetops, and a yellow glow emanated through the trees, fading to orange, then pink, gradually becoming purple, and, finally, the deep blue of twilight.

It had been five days since the senior party, and she tried to breathe in the calm of the sunset's beauty, but moisture kept leaking out of her swollen eye, reminding her of the dreadful event.

"Are you crying?" Tucker interrupted.

Kya spun around to face her brother. "No, my eye keeps watering. It feels weird. It's healing and sore. It tingles and itches all at the same time, and I can't touch it because it hurts!" Kya explained in a quick burst.

"Yeah, right, you're crying, crybaby."

Kya stared at him blankly.

"What?" Tucker drew back like he was innocent. He picked up the TV remote and turned on a movie.

Kya walked to the kitchen and opened the fridge, staring at the contents, wanting something, but not seeing anything appealing. Her phone buzzed in her pocket. The text was from none other than her stalker himself.

Meet me outside.

Kya texted back. *Ok, why?*

Tucker's voice drew her attention. "Kya, Jake's here... again."

Out the south windows, his truck make its way down the road. Kya turned and went to her parents' room. She found her mom folding clothes and placing them in an open suitcase.

"Are you about all packed for your trip?" Kya asked.

Her mom looked up, "Yeah, I think so."

They were going on their anniversary trip, their twentieth, to Jackson Hole and Yellowstone, like they did on their honeymoon.

"When do you leave?" Kya asked.

"Tomorrow morning."

"Okay, um, Jake invited me to go hang out. Would that be alright?"

"Well, I wanted to spend some time with you, but I suppose it's all right. Miss Graduate."

Kya smiled. "Thanks, Mom."

"I feel terrible leaving you after what's happened." She brushed a gentle finger down Kya's bruised face.

"Mom, you've had this planned since last year. Tucker and I will be fine." She paused. "And I bet Jake won't be far away," she said, looking at her feet.

"And why should that make me feel better? An older

guy, who seems to be smitten, hanging around my very beautiful daughter."

"Mom, no, no, don't even go there. I meant that he proved himself able to protect me when Mitch dropped my shoes off, and if he's around, you shouldn't have to worry about me getting hurt again."

"Yeah, still worries me… and I probably just put that idea in your head."

"No. We're just friends."

She gazed at Kya. "For now."

Kya's mouth dropped open at the suggestion her mother made.

"What? I know how it is, and you are far too beautiful." She leaned forward and kissed her head. "Go and have fun." She shooed her out of the room.

"Love you, Mom," she called from the door.

Kya raced down the stairs and to her room, swiped her purse off her dresser and her jacket off the hook on her door, and stepped into some sandals. She leaped up the stairs and to the front door in long bounds, sweeping it open, and calmly paced down the sidewalk.

Jake sat behind the wheel of his Dodge with his left arm laid over the top of the wheel and leaned on the center console with the right. He was the picture of relaxation.

Kya popped open the door and hefted herself into the cab. They both gazed at each other for a moment.

"Hi," Kya said, breaking the silence.

A small smile crept up one corner of Jake's mouth. "Hey."

"So…what are we doing?" Kya asked.

Jake shook himself slightly, as if waking from a trance. And that crooked smile turned into a crooked grin. "We're gonna go for a drive."

Jake dropped the truck into reverse and backed out of Kya's driveway. The truck bumped down her rough gravel road, but the instant they hit the main road, Jake hit the throttle. The truck surged forward, and Kya was pressed back into the seat. Her breath caught as adrenaline raced into her bloodstream. As she gripped the door handle, a smile stretched her cheeks, and a thrilled giggle bubbled out.

JAKE GLANCED AWAY FROM THE ROAD TO THE SMILING beauty next to him, and his heart softened. It made him happy to see Kya having so much fun. Thinking back, he believed this was the first time Kya had smiled that big for him—because of him. A sense of relief and satisfaction washed over Jake. Something about this was right. With a passenger in his truck, he wasn't scared… for now.

Jake pressed his foot to the throttle again and pushed his truck as fast as it would go without losing control. They sped down the gravel road toward the ranch. Before the turn to the ranch, he took off on a side road that branched north. It was the back road that made a loop up on the ridge behind Kya's house.

Periodically, he stole a peek at Kya, trying to gauge her reaction. He slowed his speed to begin the trek across the rough, rutted-up, two-track road. Kya's smile slipped a little, and a crease formed between her brows. She looked out the windows, then at Jake, and the smile returned full force.

"I love coming up here." Kya rolled down the window. The Wyoming wind lifted her hair from her shoulders. She breathed deeply. "Mmm, sage, pine, and fresh air."

Jake rolled down his window and took a whiff of the breeze. "Man, that's one of the best scents in the world," Jake agreed.

Kya's gaze shifted farther away. She stuck her arm out the window and pointed to the east. "Looks like a storm's rolling in." She leaned out the window and breathed deeply again. "And it smells like rain."

Jake followed where she pointed and spotted the dark gray, towering plumes of cloud. The fear returned in full force, gripping his stomach, and twisting it into knots. Tightening his fist on the steering wheel, his jaw locked shut. Maybe his master plan wasn't such a smart idea. They could turn around. Jake looked to Kya. She seemed to be enjoying herself, relaxing in her seat with her head resting against the headrest. Her eyes were closed, feeling the breeze with her hand as it hung out the window.

Jake didn't want to spoil this. Ruin whatever it was he and Kya had going on. He liked her so much. He wanted to get to know her better before she ran for the hills.

There was a voice in the back of Jake's mind that whispered he was only delaying the inevitable. She wouldn't look at him the same, and she'd leave. Hell, it was probably better that she leave. She didn't need him. She had a good life, a loving family, and a beautiful, comfortable home. She was going somewhere with her life. Somewhere he didn't deserve to go.

Jake looked back at the approaching storm. It was still a ways out there. If he hurried and timed it right, he could be back before the storm ever hit.

"Hey, is everything all right?" Kya seemed to sense his mood change.

Forcing a smile, he made sure it reached his eyes. "Yeah, I'm fine. Just worried about what the rain will do to this road."

"Trash it completely," Kya said bluntly.

Jake looked over at her with a little bit of horror.

"What?" Kya startled back. "It's true. This road sucks." She turned back to the window. "We'll probably be out of here before the storm even hits. Of course, it would make for some awesome mud bogging."

Jake looked at her with a face that clearly said, "You can't be serious."

"Don't worry. We'll be out of here."

He breathed a little easier. Kya confirmed what he had hoped.

KYA KNEW THIS ROAD. SHE'D LIVED OUT HERE HER entire life. She'd ridden four-wheelers all over these roads at all times of the year. She knew this place. It was her home. Jake only recently moved here. And she had no idea what his driving skills were like in bad weather. Not to mention there was that nasty hill at the other end of this road. And it was springtime, so the road wouldn't be in that great of shape.

Glancing at Jake and looking around at the truck, Kya wondered about either one's ability to handle mud. Seeds of doubt settled in Kya's gut. She'd not be helpful at all if they did get stuck. She stole a peek at Jake again. For some reason beyond her, she trusted him. Trusted him with her life. It was herself she doubted. She was useless and weak now. But it was never an issue around Jake. He was just so competent. He took care of everything, even her fears.

Kya checked Jake out from head to toe. His profile was strong. His nose had a slight bend in it from being broken. His eyelashes were sinfully long. Why did men always get the gorgeous lashes? Kya dropped that question, not caring because his black lashes framed devastating, heart-stopping, swoon-worthy green eyes. His lips were full, but not big. They were perfectly kiss-worthy. He had a strong, square chin and jawline. And his neck was wired with muscle that framed into his strong broad shoulders and defined chest. He wore a loose-fitting t-shirt, but it did nothing to hide his toned body and arms rolled with lean muscle. Kya could see he had a very distinct tan line where the sleeve of his shirt ended. His veins stood out in his forearms and hands. Hands, goodness his hands were perfect. They were strong and large, permanently darkened by the dirt that permeated and embedded his hands daily. There were scars along his knuckles, and his nails were kept short. A working man's hands.

Kya's gaze drifted lower to his jean-clad thighs. The

denim stretched snug over Jake's muscled lower body. They fit him perfectly, defining his sculpted behind even though she couldn't see it at the moment.

The feeling of eyes on her made her shift her stare up to Jake's. His gaze narrowed slightly, and his incredible crooked smile ghosted across his lips. His brown hair curled around the edges of his dirty ball cap and swept across his forehead. Jake was the epitome of the boy next door, but he had a dangerous edge to him that kept people at a distance. But then, why was he letting her get closer? Kya had so many questions. She wanted to get to know Jake and find out why.

"What's your last name?" she asked.

Confusion shown in his sage-colored eyes. "Lancer. You asked me that when we were texting… Why?"

"Oh, that's right, I forgot. I was just thinking that I should at least know my friend's last name."

"Ah." Jake looked away down the road ahead of them, and his expression darkened slightly, then changed again to curiosity. "What's yours?"

"O'Shadit," Kya stated proudly, and observed the emotions play across his face again.

"I think I knew that, but I'm not sure where I learned it."

He had so many expressions. Kya wanted to know their source, to know what he was thinking. But previous experience told her that to ask outright would lock him up, and send him for the hills. She would have to be patient and figure him out by observation alone.

Kya decided this would be fun, whatever the outcome.

TWELVE

T HEY'D JUST MADE THE FIRST TURN AND WERE headed up the hill to the top of the ridge. So far, the road was dry. The truck rumbled its way up the hill at Jake's command. Kya bounced and jostled around in her seat. The seatbelt locked up and began to choke her. Kya reached down and unclipped it.

Jake's head swung in her direction faster than a blink. "What are you doing?" he practically yelled.

Kya looked around, confused as to the reason for his panic. "Taking off my seatbelt. It locked up on me."

Opening and closing his mouth, he stuttered and stammered as if wanting to speak, but couldn't find the words. In the end, he settled with his hand on the wheel, staring out the windshield with rapt attention.

Kya's brow crinkled, confused at his behavior. It's not like they were going fast or like there was any other traffic.

They topped the highest part of the ridge, and Jake's expression completely changed. His eyes lightened and seemed to smile, and his crooked grin turned up his right cheek. Now she was really confused. Panic, secrets, and joy all in ten seconds.

"Why are you smiling?" Kya asked.

"Because we're here," Jake said. He turned off the rough road and on to a barren knoll. The truck glided smoothly across the ground in complete opposition to the conditions of the road. He coasted to a stop and shut off the truck. Getting out, he came around and opened her door for her. Climbing down from the truck, she followed him.

Kya glanced around at their surroundings, and her brow crinkled. What was so special about here? The hill was nothing but iron rock and bentonite. Though she could see the top of Devil's Tower far off to the northwest, the new water tower to the south, the highway to Moorcroft, and the sunset in the west along miles and miles of ranch land. Kya admitted it was a great view.

"Look there." Jake pointed straight at the sunset.

"Yeah, it's a beautiful sunset."

"No, on the horizon line."

Kya stared into the orange and pink colors of the sunset. Along the horizon there were some jagged pieces like teeth, and Kya's jaw fell open.

"Do you see them? Right there on the horizon, about exactly where the sun sets." Jake pointed.

Kya smiled like a two-year-old with a lollipop.

"It's the Big Horns."

Kya nodded. "Yes, I know. I didn't realize you could see them from here."

"My uncle told me about this."

"That is so cool!"

"Yeah, you can only see them on really clear days."

"Wow, I love the mountains." Kya covered her mouth with her hand in wonder.

"Yeah, me too. I used to go on camping trips up there with my cousin."

"My family goes every chance we get." Kya stared off at the mountains. They were slowly fading away as the sun set farther and darkness crept in. Behind her, there was a flash of light followed by a loud bang. Kya jumped.

"That was close."

"Yeah, it was." Jake looked around at the sky. The dark mass in the east crawled across the darkening sky. You could see the water sheet across the tops of the trees as it slowly approached.

"Suppose we better go if we want to stay dry."

"Yeah, prolly."

Jake followed Kya around the truck. He reached around her and opened the door. Kya suddenly became very aware of Jake's closeness. Her heart rate sped up, and blood flooded her cheeks. She took a deep breath to steady herself, and Jake's scent washed through her senses. And the lightning in the sky was now in her stomach.

The world turned white, and thunder ricocheted through the hills.

Kya jumped at the incredible noise. Her back pressed flush to a solid, warm surface. Jake's hand instinctively caught her around the waist, keeping her steady.

"They don't call this Lightning Ridge for nothing."

"Yeah, no kidding."

Kya climbed into the pickup, guided by Jake's hand on her waist, and placed her hands in her lap.

Jake's hand landed on her knee. "You okay?"

"Yes, I'm fine."

With a nod, he closed the door and moved around to the driver's side. He jumped in and started the truck all in one motion, jamming it in reverse and pulling back onto the road, continuing their journey around the loop.

Kya's nerves seized. It might have been smarter to go back the way they came; at least they knew it was dry. Kya just shrugged. Either way, they would get there. Although one might be more adventurous than the other.

They bounced and crawled over the road, through ruts and drainage ditches. The road seemed to sink farther and farther into the earth as they continued. All at once, a sheet of rain lay over them, and everything was soaked.

It seemed okay for a bit. The truck was getting along just fine. Then, as Jake powered forward to climb a hill, the back end slid sideways and fishtailed. Jake handled the motion like a pro, Kya conceded. The man knew how to drive.

They fishtailed and spun out at the top of the hill, but made it over, and started down the other side as the back end of the truck began racing the front, sliding sideways the whole way down.

Kya looked out the window at the increasing mud. Chunks of it were flung off the tires to cover the side of the truck and part of Kya's window.

"I'm so sorry, Kya. This is my fault. We should have turned around at the first sight of the storm."

"It's okay. It's just a little mud."

"Yeah, but you wouldn't be here if it wasn't for me."

"True, but I chose to come with you." Kya paused. "And I never would have gotten to see the mountains if I hadn't come."

Jake nodded and locked his jaw in concentration as he navigated the sloppy trail.

Passing a Y in the road, Kya recalled the times she had gone sledding down the other track in the winter.

Down the road a way was a turn, and they would enter the trees again, and then emerge at the hill from hell.

What was a rutted-up, two-track road would turn into a waterfall in the downpour. It would wash down the ruts slowly, digging them deeper. One used to be able to drive down the road, but now, the ruts were so deep they would swallow a motorcycle. Instead, everyone created a new road on the slight rise next to the road. The problem was a cedar tree had grown over the original road. So, to get to the newly formed one, you had to turn at right angles on a downhill slope. And in the mud, they were more likely to end up in the gully wash ditches... or the swamp on the other side of the new road.

Crossing her fingers, Kya sat back to enjoy the ride.

They slowly descended toward the nasty final hill. Jake tensed up and sucked in a deep breath.

Involuntarily, a huge grin stretched Kya's cheeks. She was having a blast. The most fun since she and Rachel spun cookies in the school parking lot on a snow day. Then they ran from the cops and somehow escaped. It had been fun, but Kya had been shouting at her to stop the whole time.

Jake maneuvered into the turn around the tree. The front end of the truck fell into the drainage ditch and slowly climbed back out. The rear end followed, but seemed to be gaining speed. The ass end of the pickup slid downhill, then stopped. The whole truck stopped. Dead standstill.

"Fuck!"

Kya jumped at the loud interruption of her delight. Jake punched the top of the steering wheel.

"Hey, now, it's not the truck's fault."

"I know. It's mine." Jake bent forward and pulled the gearshift into four low.

Kya leaned forward. Through the mirror, she could see the rear tire sat cradled in the ruts. The very bottom of the tire wasn't touching the ground. It turned slowly, spinning in its slimy cradle. That wasn't good. The engine revved, and the tire spun faster, but the truck never moved. The tire cradle deepened with the increased rotation, then stopped and spun in reverse. Still nothing.

"Yeah, we're not going anywhere."

"You're not stuck till you quit moving," Jake said.

"Pretty sure we've quit moving."

He leaned forward, turning the wheel and jamming gears, attempting to get some form of motion out of the truck.

"I'm so sorry, Kya. This is all my fault. I'll fix this. I'll get us out."

Kya crinkled her brow as Jake frantically moved about

the cab, his frustration visibly growing. After pausing to look up at the grey, rain-drenched sky, he reached into the backseat and pulled out a coat. He slipped it on, leaving it open, and prepared himself before he stepped out into the onslaught.

Jake circled the truck, inspecting it from all sides. He stopped in the front. His lips moved in a quick motion, and, judging by his hand in his hair, it was not a nice word. Turning in a circle looking at the ground, he stooped over. Kya quirked an appreciative eyebrow. It was not a bad view at all. He straightened with a large chunk of iron rock and walked over to the truck, dropping it in one of the ruts, and kicked it in under the tire. Jake turned and wandered the hill for more rocks. An array of emotions passed over him in quick succession. Frustration, anger, panic, and finally, it settled on worry, or maybe concern?

He kept looking toward Kya in his endeavor. Then he walked back over to the pickup, opened the door, reached in, and pulled out a pair of gloves.

"I'm sorry, Kya," he said again, for what felt like the hundredth time.

"Dude, this is so not your fault."

"But it is." And he slammed the door.

Kya bailed out of the truck and into the mud and rain in flip-flops, shorts, and a tank top.

"Jake!" she yelled over the rain and thunder.

He just kept gathering rocks. "Get back in the truck, Kya. You're getting wet," he said in a concerned tone.

"Oh, please, I'm fine."

"You already have enough ailments; you don't need a cold."

Kya blandly stared at him.

Jake turned and got back in the truck. The engine revved, the tires turned, and it never moved.

"Damn it." Jake cursed, getting out of the truck again. He resumed his frantic rock gathering like an animal looking for grubs.

"Jake!" Kya hollered.

He ignored her and ferried himself between the truck and the small embankment of rocks.

Kya reached down and picked up a small rock, slogged over and dropped it in the rut, and spun on her toes, but her flip-flops stuck in the mud, surging her weight in one direction as the straps of the sandals tripped at her feet. Her legs tangled, and she landed on her knees in the muck.

"Kya!" Jake ran over and helped her up. "Why don't you just get back in the truck? You'll be safe there."

"Jake, I'm fine!"

"Please, Kya, just get back in the truck." Jake turned and slogged back to get more rocks. "Then I can get us unstuck and you back home safely."

"No!" Kya stood barefoot in the slippery mud holding her flip-flops.

Jake continued to work. "Why do you have to be so stubborn? I got this." He trudged through the mud, piling rocks.

Kya stomped through the gook. No one was going to tell her what to do or treat her like she was made of porcelain.

That façade was shattered. Hell, to the no! She might seem like her daddy's perfect princess, but she knew how and when to get dirty. Hard work didn't scare her. She splashed over to where Jake was gathering rocks, his back to her.

"Jake!" she shouted.

"I can physically put you back in the truck, Kya," Jake said as he turned and stood straight.

Kya made sure she positioned herself directly behind him. When he turned, they were inches apart.

Dropping her sandals, she reached up with her good hand, wrapped it around the back of Jake's neck, and pulled herself up to his height.

Jake froze.

She locked her gaze with his. Kya looked deep into Jake's sage and gold eyes, where she found nothing but worry. Worry for her. He seriously took responsibility for her, everything that happened to her, and her safety. She read it all in that one look.

Jake never looked away from her.

Kya leaned in and pressed her lips to his. That had not been her intention when she'd grabbed him. She'd just wanted his attention. But now that she'd started, she found she couldn't stop. Didn't want to stop.

The initial kiss was a soft touch of skin. Kya pressed her lips together more firmly over Jake's bottom one and delved a little deeper. Rain tracked over their faces. She pulled back a hair's breadth with a small sucking sound.

He never moved, didn't outwardly respond at all. But

Kya could feel his heart tapping out a tempo against her own chest.

"Kya," Jake breathed as he remained statuesque.

Looking up into his eyes again, the worry she saw before was still there, but now a fire burned in their depths, and Jake seemed to be fighting an internal battle.

"I…" Jake began, searching Kya's face frantically.

Kya knew what he saw. A damaged girl. Jake's jaw tightened, but his hands remained gentle, and his thumbs began rubbing circles on Kya's hips. Her belly jumped, and she froze. When had Jake grabbed her hips? She couldn't recall, but hoped he wouldn't let go.

Jake brought his hand up to brush along the less-bruised side of Kya's face. "I don't know where to touch you, where I won't cause you any more pain."

"You won't hurt me." Kya couldn't look away from his face.

"You say that now, but you just have so many bruises. And I know they are still painful." Jake read Kya's argument before she could voice it.

Kya turned her head away and moved to step back. Jake's hands at her waist prevented the motion. She glanced back up at him through her lashes. He studied her intently.

"You put yourself here. And I'm not letting you go." Jake pulled her back into his body.

Kya's hands landed on Jake's firm chest.

Gentle as a butterfly, Jake tipped Kya's chin up, leaned down, and pressed his lips to Kya's with no more weight than that of a feather. He started to pull away.

Kya threw her arms around his neck, locking herself into his embrace. Screw the bruises! She wanted to feel something other than pain. Something that burned and stung stronger than her hand. Something that ached of pleasure rather than of pain. Something that flushed her skin with a blush instead of a bruise. Kya sealed her lips to Jake's in a desperately fierce kiss. The fingers of her good hand curled into the hair at the nape of his neck.

Jake's lips pressed against hers with as much need as she offered. A low rumble came from deep in his chest.

The kiss then turned wild and hungry. Small breathy gasps of air escaped Kya. She wanted to be embarrassed, but his hands gripped her hips and plastered her to his body. She forgot everything except the feel of Jake.

He groaned into her mouth and, with a small peck, broke the kiss and rested his forehead against Kya's.

She sucked her bottom lip into her mouth, savoring Jake's incredible kiss. His thumb worked up and down the bare skin of her lower back. Kya's shirt had somehow been hiked up to her waist.

Rain fell in a torrential downpour, soaking them both. Kya's hair clung to her face and neck. Jake's shirt shaped out every defined muscle of his torso. His jeans hung low on his waist, completely drenched along with the coat he put on. Water dripped from his eyelashes. He blinked through the rain gazing into Kya's eyes.

In that heated stare, Kya read his emotions. Now, there was only caring passion and a fierce devotion, maybe even… no, not possible.

"Kya," he breathed.

She shifted her weight forward, leaning toward Jake. Faster than the rate of her racing heart, Kya lost her balance in the slippery mud. Her arms flew backwards to try and right herself. The soggy ground slipped out from beneath her feet, and her butt splashed into one of the deep gooey ruts in the road. She caught herself with her good hand, and it plunged up to her elbow in the mud. Jake's hand gripped her forearm. His startled face looked down at her. Kya looked back at his large, rough hand curled all the way around her forearm. Her gauze-wrapped hand hung out in the rain, untouched.

"Thank you," Kya said.

"What do you mean? I didn't catch you." Jake looked at her, confused. "Are you alright?"

"Yeah, I'm fine."

Jake pulled her up where he had a hold of her. Kya lifted her butt out and tugged her hand free of the rut with a nasty squishing sound.

She stood there holding her limbs away from her body.

"Come on." Jake tipped his head toward the truck.

Picking up her dropped flip-flops, she slogged after Jake, who maintained his grip on her arm, steadying her.

He walked them to the back door on the passenger side, then dug around in the back for a bit.

Kya stood stationary praying for balance. Bright flashes of light flooded the area, followed by the thunderous bang that seemed to shake the earth. The rain slowly dissipated. The clouds remained, but were slowly drifting off. Now, only the random, intermittent drop fell. Kya inspected her soggy self. She was a mess, mud up to her knees, all over her butt and arm. She was soaked to the bone. Jake turned around with a towel. Behind him in the seat lay a couple of blankets. He held the towel out to Kya and looked to the sky.

"Storm's almost over," he said.

"Yeah." Kya looked to Jake, ready to take the towel. Her hand was covered in mud. She started scraping the mud off onto her bare leg and the small scrap of cloth she called shorts. There wasn't a whole lot of material to remove the mud onto.

Jake's eye was caught by Kya's vigorous scraping motion. "Um, can I help in any way?"

"Well, I was going to dry my hair before I wiped mud all over the towel. But…" Kya dragged the word out.

"Oh, here." Jake wiped his hands on his jeans and took the towel.

Kya was slightly confused as Jake maneuvered around her, towel in hand, and stopped directly behind her. His callused fingers brushed along the bottom of her jaw and under her ears, to gather the mass of her hair at the nape of her neck.

Jake wrapped the towel around Kya's long, soft tresses, then gently squeezed the water into the towel. Dropping the mass of her hair, he placed the towel over Kya's head and patted it down. Drops of water clung to her bare shoulders. He gently dabbed them dry.

Kya giggled.

"There," Jake said when his ministrations were finished.

He quickly scrubbed the towel through his own hair and gave it over to Kya.

Wrapping the towel around her muddy hand, she stuffed it between her knees, holding on to it and pulled her hand out. She wiped the rest of the mud off on the end protruding from where she held it.

Jake watched this whole thing. "Resourceful."

"Well, I don't always have help, so I figured some stuff out." Kya proceeded to wipe the rest of the mud off. Her jean shorts were pretty much a lost cause, soaked and slimy.

Jake took back the towel Kya offered and brushed the worst of the mud off his pant legs. He wadded up the soiled towel and dropped it in the back of the truck bed.

"Get in and get warm," Jake instructed Kya.

She slogged up to the door and popped it open. Kya grimaced at the pristine grey cloth seats. She twisted her upper body around to look at her butt. Mud. Mud and pristine seats. Yeah, not going to happen.

Jake jumped in and slammed the door on the driver's side. "What's the matter? Get in here." He had taken off his coat.

"I am covered in mud."

"So… it'll wash." Jake hesitated for a second.

Right then, Kya made up her mind. She unbuttoned her shorts and shimmied out of them.

"Whoa, whoa, whoa! What are you doing?" Jake asked, surprised.

Kya wasn't sure she knew what she was doing herself. "I don't want to get your truck dirty." She bounced up into the seat with her feet hanging outside the cab and flung the mud off of her feet, shorts, and shoes as best she could. Placing them in a neat pile on the floor in the corner, she turned her body inside the cab and shut the door. Jake's jaw hung slightly open, and his eyes were hooded. He blinked once, cleared his throat, and faced forward.

"What?" Kya asked. "I had a dilemma, so I solved it."

"That you did," he said, refusing to look at her.

"It's not like I'm naked. Besides, my undies cover just about as much as my swimming suit." She was telling herself as much as Jake. What was she doing? This was not Good Girl Kya. What happened to Good Girl Kya? Nervous, giddy energy washed through her gut.

Jake looked at her then. A smile cracked his shocked expression, and he relaxed, a little.

"You seem to be healing quickly."

"Yeah, not quickly enough." Kya sighed. "Being one-handed sucks."

Jake chuckled. "I'm sure it does. Just give it a little bit."

Kya paused for a breath. "Nope, not healed."

"Smartass."

"That's right," Kya sang. A shiver racked her body. Who was she? A version of Rachel had hatched inside her and taken over.

THIRTEEN

JAKE REACHED UP AND FLICKED THE HEAT ON.

Kya's tank top clung to her every curve. Her bra was distinct through the wet material. There was probably more material in a tissue than in her tiny blue panties. Jake swallowed heavily and returned his wide eyes to the view out the windshield. Though the only thing he really seemed to see was Kya's smooth bare thighs out of his peripheral vision. He shifted in his seat, trying to get comfortable. He was overly warm. Blood rushed around his body… probably from throwing rocks. He didn't dare turn the heat down; Kya still shivered in the seat next to him. She'd be warmer if she removed her soaked shirt.

An image flashed before Jake's mind's eye. He cleared his throat again and clenched his hands in his lap. A shiver racked Kya's body. He reached behind the seat and handed her a blanket. He swallowed again as she spread the blanket out over her bare legs, hiding the expanse of creamy flesh.

He focused on the muddy road before them and found the spot where he had stood while Kya yelled at him. He could nearly feel her lips burning into his all over again.

Kya shifted in her seat, picking at the wet material of her shirt, pulling it away from her skin.

"You know, you'd be warmer, and dry faster, if you took that off." Jake held his breath. What had he just suggested? He sounded like such a complete lowlife tool. Presumptuous as all get-out, and suggestive, verging on perverted… though it was true.

Jake smashed his lips into a line and chanced a glance at Kya. One corner of her mouth was curled in a small smile as she looked at him. Her eyes sparked with intrigue and mischief.

"Survival 101," Jake said.

Kya's head tilted as she agreed with his logical explanation.

"You can wrap up in the blanket, and I won't look."

"And here I thought you'd suggest the skin-to-skin contact stated in the hypothermia survival handbook," she said.

"That is true, but it might be a little extreme for this situation."

A shiver racked Kya's body again, and she convulsed. "Alright, mountain man, look away."

Jake complied. Covering his eyes with his hand, he turned toward his window. His mind was a cruel devil. It taunted him with images of what was going on only two feet behind him. It tempted him to look. Just once, sneak a quick peek. Come on, how often was a woman as gorgeous as Kya going to strip in his truck? He had to be dreaming, or perhaps this was an alternate universe where the movies were now real life, because this stuff just didn't happen in reality. Jake bit the inside of his cheek, and it did hurt, so this was real. It was actually happening.

He dragged his hand over his face, releasing a heavy breath, and his window fogged over. As the moisture cleared from the glass, moving like globs of goo, he could see his reflection. His dark hair was stuck to his forehead with water, and his face was overly red. His green eyes were in direct contrast to his current complexion, making them stand out. It was a familiar image. One he'd seen every night since that day.

He averted his eyes from his mirrored self. A bright spot caught his attention, and he was pulled from his dark thoughts. The dome light overhead glowed off Kya's bare back. Her muscles flexed under her bronze skin as she peeled the straps of her bra off her arms. Holy shit, there was a naked girl sitting in his truck…with him. Fuck. He hadn't expected her to take off her bra, too. Kya swept the blanket around her back and wrapped it around her front and over her legs. She settled into the seat and adjusted the blanket so there were no gaps. Jake wished he had given her the small blanket. He mentally slapped himself and shook his head. It was a crude thought, but what could he say? He was a guy.

"Okay, I'm decent," Kya said behind him.

Jake slowly turned to face forward. With a tight fist, Kya secured the blanket under her chin, like they were in the Arctic, but she had stopped shivering. Small miracles.

"What?" Kya said.

"What?" Jake asked back.

"You were staring."

"Was I? Sorry." An awkward silence descended. The frogs and the crickets sang outside of the truck.

After a bit, Kya spoke. "So, what's the plan?"

"For getting out of here?"

"Yes."

"Well, we have two options. Either we wait till morning and try to get out in the daylight, or we call my cousin to come pull us out. Which, if we wait for morning, we may still have to call my cousin."

Kya scrunched her face in thought. "Any way you slice it, it's going to be highly awkward."

"How so?"

"Either your cousin shows up and finds you with a naked girl wrapped in a blanket. Awkward. Camp out on the back road, just the two of us, and your cousin shows up. Awkward. Or we get out and have the walk of shame in the morning. Awkward."

Jake nodded. "True." He paused for a stretch. "We could wait a few minutes for the rain to quit and the road to dry itself out a bit. That way, we don't risk getting two of us stuck."

Kya gave him a raised eyebrow look.

"Okay, rephrase, the *potential* for getting two of us stuck will be less." He looked at her pointedly. "Better?"

Kya nodded.

A blinding light lit up the landscape. Jake could see the whole marsh bowl before them as if it were daylight. Within the same second, a crack of thunder rattled the truck and shook the earth.

"Whoaaaly shit," Kya said beside him from her blanket cocoon.

There was a small plink that sounded from the roof of the truck.

"Aw, fuck no!" Jake said as he craned his neck to look up through the window as the sky opened, and the plinking became deafening. Pea-sized white balls of ice fell from the clouds, peppering his truck. They grew in size as the storm continued, varying from pencil eraser to the size of a ping-pong ball. Jake knew his truck was going to look like it had been in a war zone when this was over.

"The worst part is we can't even hide the truck under a tree," Kya said.

"Not sure it would help in this storm." Jake wanted to cry. His truck might not have been new, but it sure had looked like it. There wasn't a scratch or a single dent till now.

Eventually, the plinking lessened, and the icy assault stopped.

"Whoa, dude, look at this!" Kya pointed at the ground outside her window.

Jake leaned up and stretched his neck to see. "What?"

"No, come here." Kya tilted her head frantically, like whatever it was she was looking at would disappear.

Jake lifted the center console and slid across the bench seat. He braced an arm on the door panel behind Kya so he wouldn't squish her and looked over her shoulder at the ground.

It looked as though it had snowed. The ruts in the road were filled with hail, covering the ground in a sparse layer.

"Wow," Jake said.

"Do you wanna build a snowmaaaaan?" Kya conspired out of the corner of her eye.

"Um, you're naked…"

"Well, Captain Obvious, I'm actually wearing a blanket. But we totally could. We could even make snow angels!" She sounded so excited.

"You first, turbo." An image of a naked Kya lying in the ice making a snow angel popped into his head, and he shook it away. She had to be kidding. He imagined her standing up afterward with ice balls stuck to her skin, kind of like how your tongue stuck to a popsicle. Jake chuckled under his breath.

"What?"

"Nothing, but I would really like to see you try."

"Why?"

Jake didn't want to answer that one truthfully. "Do you have any idea how cold that is? I don't think you're that stupid. You just got warm."

"Wanna bet?" Kya said forcefully. "Don't tempt me."

"Nope, just sayin'."

Kya released the blanket and reached for the door handle and pulled. Jake's weight was thrown off balance where he was braced on the door, threatening to shove the door all the way open and toss him and Kya, since she was directly in front of him, to the icy mud.

He threw his weight backwards and wrapped his other

arm around Kya's waist to keep her in the truck. His one knee was on the seat, so his left shot forward and planted on the floor, catching himself and Kya. She dangled from his arm halfway out of the truck and over the muddy ice slurry. He pulled her body into his chest and yanked the door closed. He reached and smashed the lock down.

"Ohhhh, that was close," she said as she let out a breath she had apparently been holding. "I didn't mean to actually pull it. I'm sorry."

Jake's arm was still wrapped around her waist. His left leg was over her legs, and his right knee was at her hip in the seat. Her back was pressed flush with his chest. His one hand caged her in, and his other was secured around her waist. It was one hell of a position. Jake leaned back, pulling her with him. His fingers flexed at her waist. She was slim in his large hand, the curve of her hip was tantalizing, and her skin was soft and warm.

Realization tingled its way down Jake's spine. Her bare arm gripped the door. He sucked in a breath that smelled delightfully of Kya. Her naked shoulder rested inches below his mouth. The round end of her shoulder swept up in a smooth line to the curve of her neck and to the space below her ear. Her shoulder blade was exposed, and his arm only rested partially against the blanket wrapped around her. He released a breath over her skin, and Kya shivered.

Jake knew what he wanted to do. Her skin was so pristine and soft and so close to his lips. "Kya, your hand," he said to distract himself.

She pulled her burnt hand away from the door. It trembled slightly. She gingerly wiggled her fingers. "It's fine."

"You sure?" Jake didn't move from where he held her.

"Yeah." She released a breath that shuddered out of her, and her whole body trembled.

Jake slowly pulled his arm from her waist, sliding his fingers over her skin.

Kya's good hand clamped down on his wrist. "Don't."

Jake froze.

She moved his hand back to where it had been on her waist, and she tipped her head, exposing her neck below his mouth. "Don't let me go."

"Never." Jake lowered his lips to the top of her shoulder at the base of her neck and pressed a tender kiss there.

Kya hummed deeply.

Kissing up her neck to the delectable spot below her ear, he held her firmly against his chest. Grazed his left hand up her exposed arm from the elbow to her shoulder. The feel of her skin was electric. His fingers drifted over her bare back to the edge of the blanket where it had fallen. He pulled at the edges of the blanket, shifting the material in his hand up, and placing it back over her shoulder. He then wrapped it around her front.

Jake leaned back and placed Kya in the seat, so she sat straight. His legs were tangled beneath him. He shifted and sat half turned toward Kya.

Gripping the blanket with one hand, Kya held it around her. There was a question in her eyes, one Jake couldn't answer. He could claim chivalry, or concern for her injuries, or even that the setting was not right. But he knew Kya would not accept any of those explanations. She would see through the lie and demand he tell the truth. The truth was he wasn't ready. He wasn't ready to drag such a wonderful woman with a bright future into his dark, abysmal life. On the surface, it seemed perfectly fine, like quicksand, but once you stepped in it, it sucked you into its depths and suffocated you.

He couldn't, or wouldn't, enter into anything other than an honest relationship with Kya. And that wasn't going to happen. He was selfish and wanted to keep her. Honesty would only send her away. So, for now, he would remain silent. Eventually, she would find out. But before then, he would enjoy what time she gave to him.

"Jake?" Kya asked. Her hand rested on his cheek. Her eyes searched his. "What's the matter?"

He shook his head and looked to the mud he had stuck under his nails, a tiny thin line that made the end of his nail black, like a negative image of a crescent moon at its final phase before the new moon, where its light was no longer seen.

Making an instant decision, he lifted his hand to Kya's face. His skin looked grimy compared to her golden flesh. He gazed into her dark chocolate eyes, and he dove in. His mouth captured hers. The kiss was fierce and demanding. Jake put everything into that kiss. His longing, fear, desolation, passion, and love. He felt it. An emotion he thought he would never feel again. Like the missing pieces were never gone, the broken cracks sealed tight. He was whole. Kya made him feel whole.

KYA COULDN'T BREATHE AND DIDN'T WANT TO. TIME seemed frozen, and if she breathed, it would start ticking by again. Jake's kiss, oh, how Jake could kiss, but this one was different than the first. It was almost painful, desperate, like a goodbye. And that, too, stole her breath. She didn't even want to think of Jake leaving. If this was his goodbye, it would be one hell of a parting memory.

His hands held her viselike to his chest. Kya wished she could release her grip on the blanket and touch him, wrap her own arms around him. But she was sure if she did, this incredible kiss would end. So, she settled to bask in what he offered.

He was a complete gentleman. Where most guys would have seized the opportunity her clumsiness provided, he just kissed her tenderly and wrapped her back up. She knew it was just Jake being Jake, always kind and never selfish. But the look in his eyes had scared her. It was as if he had already said goodbye, not only to her, but to life, to happiness. Like he had nothing left, and she knew that to be a lie.

He may have given up, but Kya would never give up on him. He had so much vitality, so much going for him. He was so kind, always thinking of others. Fierce in every aspect of his life.

But that look in his eyes haunted her.

Jake broke the kiss and rested his forehead on hers. A rush of air blasted over Kya's chest, and she allowed herself to breathe again as well. He took her face in his hands and kissed her forehead. When he pulled back, the haunted look was gone from his eyes. It was replaced by caring and… and… and something stronger, something Kya was afraid to give voice to.

"You know I'm here for you, no matter what," Kya told him as she fell deep into his sage eyes.

Jake nodded, and his gorgeous crooked grin made an appearance. He moved back behind the steering wheel, dug his phone out of his pocket, touched the screen a few times, and then held it to his ear.

"Hey, man." Jake turned and looked at Kya as he spoke to whomever was on the phone. He reached out and threaded his fingers through hers. "Yeah, not much, but I'm stuck… Yes, like in the mud… I'm up here on the back loop, top of that nasty hill on the east end… Well, that's a story for another time, but could you come pull us out… Please… Yeah, you might want to bring the big truck… Just get up here and help." And he hung up.

"I'm guessing that was your cousin."

"Yep, he should be here shortly." Jake's thumb rubbed circles on the back of her hand.

So, now she was really confused. It was a good change, but what the hell happened to sad, moody Jake? If kissing her was all it took to make him smile, then she'd kiss him every hour of the day.

A quarter of an hour passed, and headlights appeared

at the bottom of the hill. An engine roared, and the lights swiveled every which direction as the truck spun its way up the muddy slope. It stopped near the front passenger corner of the truck.

Jake jumped out, and Kya pulled the blanket tighter around herself, making sure it covered all of her from the neck down. Being naked in a blanket around Jake was fine, but anyone else was just uncomfortable.

There was laughter outside of the cab. Kya lifted her head to try and see through the inky darkness. She thought a few shadows moved, but wasn't sure what they were exactly. Then the night got still… and utterly quiet.

Thu-wack! Two hands smacked into her window out of the darkness. Kya screamed and jumped into the center seat, losing her hold on the blanket, scrambling as the door popped open, and laughter followed.

"Aw, man, that was priceless!" Kya knew that voice. "You should have seen your fa… whoa…"

"Connor!" Kya shouted his name, and he backed up and turned away.

"What the hell did I walk in on?" Connor said as he strode to the front of the truck.

"What do you mean?" Jake asked.

"You do know that there is a naked girl in your truck, right?"

"What the hell did you do, Connor? If you touched Kya in any way…"

"Whoa, dude, calm down. I was just messing around. She jumped and lost her… blanket."

There was a pause, and Kya could practically see Jake burning holes into Connor.

"But seriously, why would you call for help if there was a naked girl in your truck?"

"Shut your mouth and hook up the rope." The tone in Jake's voice was almost scary. It rang with authority and menace, like what she imagined a prison guard would sound like. There was no doubt who was boss in this situation.

Jake opened the driver's side door and started digging under the seat.

"Why didn't you tell me your cousin was Connor Cayman?" Kya asked in a harsh whisper.

"Sorry, I figured you already knew." His voice was completely different when he spoke to her than when he was talking to Connor.

"Guess I just hadn't put the pieces together… You know we went to school together, right?"

"Yes, I was at your graduation." Jake straightened with a wrench in his hand. "I didn't know who you were when we first met. But Connor put the pieces together for me later."

"Then, do you know he was there the night that… Mit… that he… did this to me?"

"Yes, Kya, and he and I have talked about it too."

"He practically witnessed the whole thing. He's Mitch's best friend!"

"Yeah, and he told me if you took that dickwad to court, he would testify against him."

"Really?"

"Yes, Kya. Connor has known for a while how Mitch's

feelings for you were verging on psychotic, but had no way to stop it. So, he's mostly been playing buffer. There were times when he couldn't, though."

"What do you mean…?"

"Well, he couldn't be around all the time, and he'd hear stories from Mitch later bragging. Connor's been compiling a list of people he may have threatened or even got violent with, who might help strengthen your case against him."

"I… wow, thanks… it's still weird, but I'm afraid of him."

"I know, babe, but you're safe with me."

"Thank you, Jake. You're such a wonderful man." Kya scooted forward and kissed him. It was a simple planted kiss, but it was perfect. She went to pull away, but Jake followed, not breaking contact.

"Yo, we gonna get this done or not?" Connor shouted, breaking the spell.

With a growl, an actual growl, Jake reentered into the abysmal dark again. Moments later, he returned and climbed into the seat. His jaw set in determination, and he was all business.

Kya moved back into her seat. The headlights kicked on, and Kya could see a braided three-inch rope attached to the front of both trucks.

Jake rolled down the window and shouted, "Ready."

"Okay, get after her," came the distant reply.

Jake pulled the clutch out and dropped some throttle.

The truck in front moved backwards and jerked, yanking Jake's truck sideways down the road. The truck wanted to follow the ruts, and given the limited space to work in,

Connor's truck was at the wrong angle. But they kept at it. The trucks slowly advanced down the hill, Connor's backwards and Jake's sideways. Jake dropped the throttle and turned the wheel toward the downhill side, toward Connor. The front right tire bucked, and the driver's side sank as the back end of the truck swung around so they were nearly parallel with the road. The front tire was trapped in the ruts, but the passenger side was on a little bit higher ground. As long as the passenger side stayed high, they would get out. If it fell into a rut, they would end up high-centered, and no amount of pulling would get them out. Only shovels, a jack, and some ingenuity would do the trick if that happened.

Jake flipped the wheel in the opposite direction to try and pop out of the rut, but nothing happened. Connor kept pulling. They had motion, which was more than they had a few minutes ago, but it was slow. Straightening the wheel, they rode the rut out till it disappeared at the bottom, and by that point, the worst was over.

Jake and Connor jumped out and unhooked the rope. Connor dropped it on the flat bed of his truck and turned to wave at Kya.

"See you later, Kya! Sorry I scared you, but I do say that Jake is one lucky man." He smiled a shit-eating-grin, jumped in his truck, and spun a cookie, flinging mud everywhere. He peeled out and headed on down the road toward his house.

Kya felt like such an idiot for not putting it together that Jake was Connor's cousin. She had known Connor her whole life, and he had always lived in the same place. Jake had said the ranch at the end of the road… there was only one ranch at the end of the road, and it was the Cayman ranch. She felt about as sharp as a spoon. And Connor had gotten an eyeful of her goodies. The man she liked hadn't even seen them.

"Hey, you okay?" Jake asked with a hand on her knee.

"Yeah, just feel dumb for not realizing the connection between you two."

"If it makes you feel any better, Connor was beet red when he came back to the front of the tuck."

"The question is was it embarrassment or an arousal flush?"

Jake growled again; he was really turning into an animal. "It better have been embarrassment, or I'll send his testicles back into his body cavity."

Kya laughed. "You're funny when you're jealous."

"Of course I'm jealous. My younger cousin saw my girl before me. A beautiful woman like you, every male becomes a threat."

"Aw, that's so sweet… I think." Kya was flattered by Jake's protectiveness. She craved it, needed it like an addict. It was the only thing holding her together, it seemed, lately.

JAKE PARKED HIS TRUCK BEHIND HER PARENTS' SUV.

"Well, that was fun," Kya said as she picked her wet clothes off the floor.

"Yeah, sorry we got stuck."

"Don't be. It turned out pretty cool." She leaned across

the center seat. Jake just looked at her. "I went 80 percent, you go twenty."

Jake's eyes got big for a moment, and his mouth formed an O. He leaned forward and kissed her soundly on the lips.

Kya smiled, leaning away, and popped the handle on the door. "I'll see you later." She slid out to the ground and noted the clothes in her hand and the blanket she clutched over her shoulders. She hesitated.

"What's the matter?" Jake asked.

"My parents are going to have lots of curious questions if I walk inside wearing a blanket." Kya shut the truck door, turning out the dome light. A large clump of mud fell from the truck and splattered on the ground with a heavy squish. She bent forward, draping the blanket around her like a curtain from her shoulders. She stepped into her soaked and muddy shorts. She wiggled and jumped to get them pulled all the way up. Then, keeping her back to the truck, she hung the blanket over the side mirror. With her hands free, she pulled her tank top on. It stuck to her skin and was stretched in the wrong ways. She adjusted and placed it on her as best she could, making it cover the important bits, and stuffed her bra in her pocket.

Kya opened the door again and gave Jake back his blanket. "Okay, I'll see you later."

"Bye, Kya."

She shut the door and made her way to the front gate, looking to the bay window as she trekked up the sidewalk. Her mom's silhouette was stark against the lights of the house. It was past midnight, and she was about to get ripped up one side and down the other. She opened the door…

"Kya, come here, please," her mom said.

There would only be more severe punishment if she prolonged it. Kya trudged up to her.

Her mother stood at the top of the stairs with her arms crossed over her chest, waiting to speak till Kya was level with her.

"Why are you so late? You know your curfew. And why are you soaked?"

"We got stuck. The rainstorm surprised us. I got out to try and help us get unstuck," Kya said in a matter-of-fact monotone.

"Where did you go that you got stuck?" She was not relenting; the rigid posture remained.

"Jake took me for a drive on the back loop. It was fine, perfectly dry, till the storm moved in. It came in really fast, too. We got caught on the bad hill at the east end." Kya pointed in the general direction of the hill that was not too far from her house.

"Well, did you get out or walk back?"

"We got out. Conner, who happens to be Jake's cousin, pulled us out."

"Conner, as in Mitch's BFF."

"Yeah, but I'm pretty sure that no guy in the world wants to be called a BFF."

Her mother waved the comment off. "Well, as long as you're safe." She paused. "Did you have fun?"

"Yes, it was awesome. He likes a lot of the same things I do."

"That's good. Now go get in the shower and get warm, then bed."

"Yes, ma'am." Kya turned and slumped downstairs… she didn't even get grounded.

FOURTEEN

The next morning, her parents were gone. They'd left before Kya was out of bed. She hoped they had fun and came back soon. It's one thing to be home alone knowing your parents will be home that night and an entirely different thing for them to be on the other side of the state. She was okay with it, but the house always felt empty when they were gone.

Kya drove into town. She stepped out of the icy air conditioning of her car and into the thick, heavy heat of summer. Beads of sweat instantly broke out on her skin. She made her way to the door of the café and welcomed the A/C that was chilling the inside. Her swollen eye watered, and she very carefully wiped it away.

She looked through the restaurant. It was fairly crowded. There were five people out front, none of which were Jake. She turned and made her way to the back area around the corner. There were a few people, and in the far corner was Jake.

Kya smiled and sauntered through the room to seat herself across from him in the booth.

"Hey," he said.

"Hi," Kya replied.

"Sorry for the short notice. I was in town getting some stuff from the hardware store and got really hungry for a burger and a milkshake, but I didn't want to eat alone. I hope I didn't disrupt your day too much?" Jake explained.

"Not at all. I was just having a lazy day when I got your text." Kya pulled a menu toward her.

"So, what's your favorite here?"

"The chicken cordon bleu, and of course, any milkshake." Kya smiled warmly. She didn't know why she bothered with the menu. She knew all the items on it.

"I usually go for the bacon cheeseburger."

"Classic cowboy."

"Yeah, I suppose. Now that I work on the ranch, I'm a legit cowboy."

Kya grinned. She'd thought that things might have been awkward between them after last night, but everything was perfect.

Jake reached across the table and wrapped his fingers around hers.

The waitress arrived to take their orders. Kya knew her. Lacy was a sophomore.

When she left, Jake asked, "So, I need to know, for more than one reason. How old are you?"

Kya's brow scrunched. "Eighteen… why more than one reason?"

"Well." Jake seemed to brighten at her answer. "I just wanted to make sure, you know, since I'm twenty-two…

if you weren't legally an adult yet, I could get in a lot of trouble."

"Oh, yeah, my birthday was February eighteenth."

Jake gripped her hand, and Kya smiled.

When their food arrived, they ate in companionable silence. Jake wolfed down his burger.

"Did you taste it?" Kya asked him.

"Li'l bit, but my stomach is happy now." He reclined in his seat, slurping his milkshake.

Kya only ate half her sandwich, so she asked for a to-go box when their waitress returned.

As Kya was loading her food into the white Styrofoam box, Jake's phone dinged.

He dug it out of his jeans pocket. When he read the screen, panic flooded his features. "Oh, shit! I have to go right now. Sorry, Kya."

"What? Now?"

Jake tossed a wad of cash on the table and rushed from the room.

Sitting back, as the air settled after his rapid departure, Kya's mind whirled, unable to latch on to a single thought. When it stopped, all she could think was, *What the hell was that?* He evaded her questions. Ran from them even. Acted like he knew so much more than she did, but wouldn't let her inquire about his past. And now he ditched her without even a 'call you later' while on a date? There was no other way to describe the two of them having lunch together. It was a date.

Fury boiled through Kya's blood, and her heart latched

onto one solid thought. Maybe this relationship, or whatever it was they had together, wouldn't work after all.

If he wouldn't tell her about himself or open up, there was no point. Kya had been laid bare, emotions filleted open to him. But she wasn't allowed to know him at all? Communication, on both sides, was the only way a relationship worked. She'd seen it with her parents. If they ever got angry with each other, which was rare, it was usually because something hadn't been communicated properly, or they were holding too much to themselves. Emotions were like water. They needed to flow, or they would get stagnant and start to stink.

Kya gathered her things, jamming her purse strap over her head. She wadded up Jake's money in her fist, leaving enough on the table for a tip, and fumed her way to the counter with her leftovers to pay for their meal.

As Kya waited, reeling from Jake's abrupt ditch, the two women sitting at a table near the door whispered like they stood next to a jet engine.

"That's her!" one of them said, leaning forward.

"Who?" the other asked, shifting her position toward her friend.

"The one whose father beat her for sneaking out."

All the eyes of the restaurant's patrons bore into her. She glanced to either side. It was obvious the direction of their gaze, the giant bruise on the side of her face that swelled her eye, and the half-burnt pork chop she had wrapped up as an excuse for a hand. Her anger rose another degree.

"Oh, I'd heard she'd asked her friend to beat her up to get the attention of some guy."

"Humph, wouldn't surprise me."

Kya peeked over her shoulder. The two women lounged back in their seats, eyeing her with a combination of disgust and hatred.

Kya's blood pooled in her face, neck, and rushed into her ears. She clenched her jaw and made a single fist with her good hand. She could feel them glaring at her back.

Kya took a deep breath in an attempt to calm herself. It didn't help much.

Smiling sweetly to Lacy behind the counter, she paid for her food and turned with the to-go box in her hand.

"Gossip whores shouldn't speak of what they do not know," Kya said, looking from one to the other with the same amount of disgust they showed her. "And learn how to whisper," she added as she passed and pushed open the door. She looked back at Lacy behind the counter. Her mouth hung open, and her eyes nearly fell out of her head.

Kya struggled to get her car door open with tears in her eyes and a carry-out box in her hand. She finally gritted her teeth, placed her burned hand under the box, and opened the door with her good hand. She deposited the leftovers in the passenger seat, as she slid in. Angry tears leaked from her good eye. Her bad eye seemed to always leak. So, now she's a self-mutilating, boy-crazy liar.

Talk about putting a cherry on top of what was turning out to be a horrible day.

The fluffy clouds she'd been walking on earlier had evaporated, dropping her into an abysmal bottomless pit.

Who was she? She wasn't this angry person. And she'd never tell anyone off to their face. She was responsible, kind, levelheaded. She felt as though she'd been switched for a changeling. What had happened to the good girl she used to be?

It didn't matter. She couldn't deny her emotions now. She was angry, furiously angry. Angry for the struggle she had with simple tasks like opening a door. Angry for the pain she was in. Angry for looking like a human punching bag. Angry that it all made her cry. Angry at Mitch for causing the entire situation. Angry with Jake for making her feel worthless. Angry for being angry.

She looked up at the side of the restaurant, thankful there was no one to see her cry. She dried her tears with the heel of her hand, put the car in gear, and started the trek home.

As she was about to pass the turn to the post office, Kya realized that she'd forgotten to get the mail all week and maneuvered her car parallel to the curb in front of the post office. She turned off the engine, and immediately, the heat of the day radiated into the car. Although her anger was radiating hotter.

Stepping from the car into the summer sun, she looked both ways before crossing. Not sure why, the town wasn't big enough to even have traffic lights… or traffic. And if someone did hit her, she most likely would know them. She breathed deeply again to calm herself. It still didn't work.

She pushed through the doors and, halfway down the

row of grey boxes, knelt before number 478. She inserted her key, and the lock wouldn't turn. Frustrated, which quickly turned to anger, her emotions were so high, she cranked on the key. The mechanism scraped and shoved against the contents of the box, which was stuffed full, and yanked the little door open. The tiny box was jam-packed with mail. You'd think they never picked it up. She began ripping the contents out and stacking it on her legs as she crouched on the floor. The box seemed to have infinite depth. Kya imagined a precisely placed Jenga stack of mail protruding from the back of the box, the mail ladies carefully placing the next piece so as not to fell the tower. Finally releasing the last of it from the confines of the box, she locked the door and jerked her key free, gathered the mail into her arms, and stood.

Kya turned to leave, and Mitch's large frame filled the door. Her stomach dropped out. Every emotion fled her in an instant.

"Hey, Kya. How's it going?" he asked.

Kya was frozen in place, not sure what to do or how to take him. Was he sober? Was he the Mitch that used to be her friend? Or was he the possessive beater she'd seen recently?

"Uh, hi," she choked out. The bruise on her face took this moment to twinge painfully.

"How you been? Seems like I haven't seen you in forever."

"I, uh… I'm good," Kya said, trying to keep the tremble out of her voice. "How have you been?" Kya's subconscious survival mode kicked in. Keep him talking.

"Oh, not too bad. Just did an interview out at NARM."

"Yeah, how did it go?" It appeared for the moment that she was speaking to Sane Mitch.

"I don't know. They haven't called yet, but I feel pretty good about it. No reason they shouldn't hire me."

Kya could think of a few reasons why the North Antelope Rochelle Mine, the second-largest mine in the county, wouldn't hire a mentally unstable abuser. *Just sayin'.*

"Yeah, I put in for pit operations. Should be easy. Sit on your ass and drive all day."

Kya simply nodded continually as he talked, blocking the exit.

"It'll be awesome. I'll have my own place. We could even live there together." Mitch paused and took a step forward. He raised his hand.

Kya flinched, then froze. Fear gripped her.

"I can't believe what you made me do. Such a horrible thing to such a beautiful face." Mitch's fingers gingerly touched the swollen skin on her cheek.

The urge to knock his fingers away and scream at him burned through her. Possibly deploy those dirty tactics she knew. But she stood there frozen, scared that if she moved, it would set him off. The reek of cigarettes and body odor wafted to her as the door behind Mitch was pulled open by none other than the county sheriff himself.

Mitch dropped his hand and stepped away from the door to let the man in.

"I'll see you around, Kya?" Mitch said.

"Sure," Kya mumbled and bolted past the sheriff and through the door. She piled into her car with the stack of mail clutched to her chest, dumping it in the passenger seat on top of the food box. With shaking hands, she fumbled for her key, jammed it into the ignition, locked the doors, started the car, and waited.

She wanted to run, but needed to know where he was. And she was safer with the sheriff than on her own.

After watching the front of the post office for a minute to see what would happen, Mitch walked out, looking furious. Then the sheriff followed.

Mitch got in his white car and left.

The sheriff watched him leave, waiting until he was around the corner. Then he came over to where Kya waited in her car and knocked on the window.

"Hey, are you alright?"

"Yes, just a little shaken."

He nodded. "We've been monitoring his movements. What did he say to you?"

"He… he asked…" Kya swallowed. "He asked me to live with him. Said I made him do this to me." She took a deep breath to steady herself.

"Okay, at this point, I believe we need to file for a restraining order." The sheriff was watching her closely. "Can you follow me to the station here?"

Kya nodded.

"Okay, follow me." He left and got in his truck.

Kya followed him as he made a U-turn and drove a whole block to the police station. They went into the office and filled out the necessary paperwork, along with another report for this incident.

"Try your best to avoid him as well. He was mad after we spoke, and he may search you out."

"Okay." Kya left the office and got back in her car. She was freaked out, continually looking over her shoulder and all round, sure Mitch would pop out somewhere.

She threw her car in drive. The tires squeaked slightly as she stomped the throttle and sped away from the curb. She didn't stop until she was in her driveway. Taking a moment to catch her breath, she gathered the scattered mail and the food, then climbed out. She huffed it inside, locking the door behind her, even though they never locked the door. After depositing the mail on the counter, Kya took another steadying breath as she looked out the front picture windows at the road, which cut a diagonal across their land to the house.

Paranoia swam through her, making her feel twitchy. She blew the breath out and ran to lock the back door, then sprinted to lock the French door. Mitch was well informed about her home. He knew where her room was, how to climb the deck from the trampoline, and how the windows worked. Kya scrambled to the basement, locking all the ground-level windows, then booked it back upstairs to watch out the windows again.

After a while, she finally was able to control her fear and moved away from her surveillance to sort through the mail. Most of it was either hunting or clothing catalogs and bills. She piled them up. At the bottom of the stack was a large, full-size envelope. Black Hills State University was printed on the upper corner. It was addressed to her. Hastily, she ripped open the envelope, all other drama forgotten for the moment, and read the first few lines. She laid the packet of papers on the counter. Now she was nervous for a whole new reason. She had to find a way to tell her mom and dad that she didn't put in for UW, and that she'd been accepted into the photography program at BHSU. After going through the papers, she took the easy way out and left the stack on the counter next to the rest of the mail, acceptance letter on top.

Kya leaned back against the counter. A headache pounded behind her eyes from the spectrum of emotions she'd whipped through that day. Once Mitch was handled for the moment, making the house as secure as she could make it, Jake's date-dash-ditch had her livid all over again.

PERCHED ON THE EDGE OF THE COUCH, KYA SAT WITH her back rod straight so she could look out the windows. She'd double-checked the locks on every door and window in the house and moved the spare key to a new hiding spot. She contemplated getting a gun from their gun case in the corner and placing it where she could get to it fast. But that seemed a bit excessive.

Kya sighed and tried to relax. She felt like the bogeyman was behind every corner and kept wishing Jake was there. Then she'd get pissed at herself because she was still mad at him for ditching her at the café. But her heart whispered he always made her feel safe. And on the other hand, he was a huge distraction, which she could use right then, but she also needed to maintain constant vigilance. Constant vigilance.

However, she continued replaying the kisses she and Jake had shared. They plagued her mind, making her lose focus. Butterflies assaulted her belly, and her cheeks heated every time she thought of those kisses. Mmm, he was something else, with those green eyes, big hands, and luscious lips. Kya shook herself. She was getting distracted again. She was also supposed to be *mad* at him.

Kya was alone in the house. Tucker was at a friend's. Trying to keep herself busy, she'd already cleaned the kitchen and planned dinner. She glanced up to the ceiling fan hung from the vaulted eave. Strings of dust bunnies dangled from the lights. Kya's nose crinkled, and her lip drew up. Gross. She snapped her eyes back to the front windows, then over to the mounted elk and deer heads over the fireplace. Cobwebs strung between their antlers and ears… She checked the road again. Well, she could dust. Her gaze drifted to the stacked logs that made up the walls and decided she wasn't even going to open that can of worms. The house was huge, and the logs shredded any duster that touched them. Kya imagined herself swinging around the house with the extend-o-handle duster and breaking all her mom's knickknacks. It would be doubly bad, since she had an unusable hand.

She lifted her phone. The screen showed nothing but the time. She'd texted Jake hours ago, and he hadn't responded. She'd even called him three times. There was no way she was letting him get away with ditching her like that without a confrontation. Kya had no idea why he wouldn't answer.

He usually texted back before she could lock her screen. Honestly, she was worried about him. Stupid heart. She speculated about what had pulled him from their date—ranch emergency, car accident, other girlfriend. But none of it seemed good enough for him to leave her like he did. It was really odd, and with everything else going on, it had her a bit anxious.

Kya jumped up from the couch. An idea stirred in her. Jake was always coming to see her, often times without an invitation… Maybe it was her turn to surprise him. She smiled ruthlessly.

This was probably going to backfire horribly, but what the hell? She wanted answers, and sitting there watching the road was sending her into mini panic attacks.

What better way to avoid Mitch than to be where he never expected to find her? Though the ranch was Connor's home as well. Mitch's other friend. She hesitated. She was going to risk it. It was better than being where Mitch knew to find her all alone.

The inside of her car was an oven. She cranked up the air, and it turned into a blast furnace. The air conditioning finally kicked in when she reached the main road.

The red gravel on the road pinged against the fenders of the car as the tires turned and flung it behind her. Nerves shook her fingers. She'd never done anything like this. What if he didn't want to see her? What if he was angry with her? Kya shook herself and pressed down on the throttle. She was going to see him and get some answers.

She turned toward the ranch and crept along the drive.

The main house came into view. Everything looked normal. Although she hadn't been out there that much to really know. The car lurched and sat back on its wheels before the impressive front yard. She turned off the engine and slammed the door. Kya paused. Was this a good idea? Probably not, but too late now. She pushed her shoulders back and made her way through the small gate. A mini oasis of vibrant green and colorful flowers lined the porch and along the fence.

What was she doing? She'd never been in this house except for Connor's sixth birthday. She prayed Cassie, Connor's mom, wasn't angry at the intrusion. Pausing at the step, she looked back at her car. She could leave. Turning back to the house, a figure was standing in the window. There went her plan to leave.

Kya mustered her most pleasant smile and approached the classic white front door with square moldings. A fancy silver knocker hung in the middle. But rather than using it, she rapped on the door with her knuckles. A few heartbeats passed, and the door swung in to reveal Cassie. Her blonde hair was pulled back in a ponytail; a dish towel hung from her hand.

"Hi," Kya said with a smile.

"Well, hi, Kya." Cassie's voice seemed overly cheerful to Kya's mood.

"Um, I just stopped by to see Jake." Kya's smile wavered. "Is he around, or do you know where he is? He isn't answering his phone."

"Uh." Cassie glanced down at her watch. "Um, why

don't you come in? Jake should be back in a few minutes. I'll get you something to drink." Cassie opened the door all the way to allow Kya to pass.

"Thank you," she said and stepped over the threshold. As the air conditioning of the house wrapped around her, Kya's hot temper seemed to melt with it. Cassie's simple kindness was a balm on her over-energized mood.

Cassie led her into the house. They walked through an archway and to the dining room. The kitchen was to one side, and sliding glass doors opened onto a patio at the back.

Cassie went straight to the fridge and started digging. "What would you like, hun?" she asked. "I've got tea, lemonade… water?"

"Um, lemonade will be fine, thank you." Kya sat on a stool at the peninsula bar.

Cassie spun around and slid a tall, dripping glass of ice-cold lemonade across the counter.

Sipping the cold beverage, Kya had to admit it was probably the best lemonade she'd ever had. Tart with just the right amount of sweetness to tone it down, and maybe a slight hint of mint?

"So, how have you been?" Cassie asked.

"Oh, pretty—bad, actually. But I'm alive, so I can't complain," Kya replied.

"Ain't that the truth. But I'm sorry to hear that." Cassie opened her mouth to say more, then closed it. She thought for a moment and tried again, but said nothing.

Kya would usually have helped by being forthcoming, but she wasn't in the mood today. She had way too much dirty laundry to open the bag for just anyone. And if she did open up, she was sure everything would explode.

A weird pregnant silence followed, broken only by the sound of the front door opening.

Kya listened to whomever it was, sigh from the other room. She turned slightly toward the doorway.

Jake stepped through with his eyes on his shoes, a hand stuffed into his hair. His steps were slow. He dragged his hand through his hair and around to his neck. His eyes looked up and instantly locked on hers.

"Kya…what," Jake looked over his shoulder, "uh, brings you here?"

Kya stood up from her stool. "I was worried about you. You weren't answering your phone. Are you okay?" The blast she had prepared to give him had lost its fuse.

"Yeah, I'm fine. I left my phone in the truck."

"Oh, you usually answer quickly is all." Kya looked over to where Cassie stood in the kitchen listening to their every word. "Why'd you have to leave in such a rush?"

"It's not important. Come sit with me a bit." And Jake led her from the house to a porch swing out back.

Kya didn't sit. She closed the door behind her, glanced over her shoulder through the window at Cassie in the kitchen, and turned to Jake.

"I have to say I did not expect to see you here," Jake said as he sank in the chair.

"What else was I to do? You wouldn't answer you phone." Kya's voice sounded strange even to her.

"I suppose. Sorry about that." He adjusted his jeans

and shifted in his seat. "What did you need that made you come here?"

"I told you. I was worried." Kya kicked a pebble with the toe of her shoe. "Why did you ditch me?"

"I, uh, forgot I had a meeting I couldn't miss."

"With who?"

"No one important."

Kya ground her teeth. His words heated her blood to boiling again. "Why won't you give me a straight answer? Don't you trust me?"

Jake stood. "I do trust you."

"Then why won't you answer my questions? Why am I not allowed to know anything about you?"

Jake thrust his hands into his hair and turned away from her.

"Answer the question! What was so important that you ditched me today?"

He kept his back to her.

She waited, bouncing her leg. "Fine. I'm out." Kya turned and stomped around the house to the front. My gosh, when had she gotten so bold?

"Kya, wait." Jake grabbed her arm as she reached her car.

Kya flipped around, throwing his arm off her. "I have had probably the worst day of my life. Even worse than getting beaten up by my friend. Do not touch me!"

Jake looked confused and a little disgusted. "Me leaving our date early is the worst day of your life?"

"Do not patronize me," Kya shouted. "If only that was all."

"What do you mean?"

"What I mean is not only was I ditched on a date, but then I got called an attention-seeking, lying whore in front of the whole restaurant! Then I got to have a meet and greet with Mitch at the post office. He wants me to live with him, by the way. And the crème de la crème to top it all off, you won't even tell me why you ditched me like last week's trash!"

Jake's statue façade crumbled before her. "Who called you a whore? I'll kill 'em," Jake spat.

Kya shook her head. "I'm out of here." She turned to her car door.

"Where are you going?"

"Home." Where she could throw something through a wall and drown in a bucket of ice cream. Hurt soured her stomach and stung her eyes. She gritted her teeth and opened her car door. She would not let him see her cry. She couldn't believe she actually thought she had a shot with him. He was four years older… and fucking hot! She'd been naïve.

"I was with my probation officer."

"What?" Kya flipped around to face him.

Jake looked at his boots, then brought his gaze up to meet hers. He held out a hand to her. "Come with me."

"Jake, I…"

"Please?" He cut her off. "Come with me and I will explain everything."

"Really? You're going to answer all my questions?"

"As best I can."

Kya sighed. "Fine."

Jake captured her good hand and dragged her off toward the barn. At the back of the barn, in the shade, sat a four-wheeler. Jake stretched a long leg over the seat. He stood on the foot pegs and bent slightly as he gripped the handlebars. He turned the key and pressed a button, and the engine revved to life.

"Well, don't be shy. Get on," Jake said with a tip of his head.

"Where are you taking me?"

"Someplace special."

Kya warily climbed onto the back of the ATV. She wasn't so sure about this. Her front was going to be pressed flush to his back. The inside of her thighs were going to be right along the outside of his. Being that close would soften her heart toward him. She needed to stay resolute. She needed answers.

Kya scooted back as far as she could so Jake could sit down. His large frame filled the seat of the four-wheeler. A solution to her problem presented itself in the form of the cargo rack on the back. Kya reached down and gripped it with her good hand.

Jake simply sat there unmoving. He twisted at the waist to look at Kya, frowned, and turned forward. His hands folded around the back of her knees and drew her forward so that, just as she thought, they sat leg to leg. He reached back and took her forearms and latched them around his waist, having her grip the wrist of her bad hand with her good hand. Satisfied, Jake popped it into gear and took off.

Clinging to Jake, her face pressed into his back because

there really was no other place to put it given the position he'd placed her in… literally. She had no idea where they were going, and she couldn't really see either. But Jake smelled heavenly. Kya savored this moment with him. It felt like it might be the last. She sighed, rested her forehead on his back, and closed her eyes. The motor of the four-wheeler rumbled beneath her. Jake's abs flexed under her hands. His legs were taut against her thighs. The sun baked down on her back. The smell of sagebrush wafted past her nose, herbal and spicy, yet soft.

The ATV bounced and bobbed along whatever trail they were following… and they seemed to just keep going. After what seemed like an hour, Kya tightened her arms and leaned up to rest her chin on Jake's shoulder.

"Where are we going?" she shouted past his ear.

Jake tipped his head toward her. "We're almost there."

Ahead of them, the tree line loomed closer and closer, as they zipped over an old two-track road. They entered the timber, and the sun's heat left, replaced by cool refreshing shade. The smell of pine was heavy in the air. The trail continued into the trees, and Jake slowed the four-wheeler.

The road made a sharp turn and then disappeared. Jake slowed and crawled around the turn, shifted the machine down, and rolled to a stop.

An old, wooden, two-track bridge spanned before them across a twenty-foot-wide ravine. The wood was old and worn. Holes gaped in the center, and one side was nearly completely missing. It was decrepit and in need of repair. But the whole setting was rustic and beautiful. Pine and cedar trees surrounded the area. The cliff banks of the ravine were layered with different colors of sand. A small, clear stream flowed beneath. Sunlight streamed through the trees in shafts of golden light, illuminating the dense forest floor.

Jake shut off the engine. Kya could hear the faint trickle of the water. Wind breezed through the trees with a wonderful, calming noise. Kya fell in love with the place.

Jake slid forward, and Kya stepped off the machine and approached the bridge. It looked as though it had come from another time. She stared at the beauty before her.

"Do you like it?" Jake asked.

"It's beautiful!"

"It's my favorite spot."

Kya simply nodded.

She could feel Jake standing behind her. For a moment, the beauty of this place had distracted her from her pain. Reality returned, and she felt as though she stood at the edge of a precipice all alone, but instead of being swept back from the edge, she would surely plummet to the bottom.

Jake's hands wrapped around her upper arms gently as he stepped close behind her.

Kya stiffened at his touch. She shrugged her shoulders, squeezed her eyes shut, and side-stepped out of his embrace, wrapping her arms around herself, and turned to face him.

"Kya...?" Jake chewed his lip as he thought. "I'm not sure how to begin."

"Why won't you answer my questions?" Kya whispered.

"I don't want to lose you. I wanted to keep you as long

as I could. It was selfish, but I don't regret the time I got to spend with you."

Kya scoffed in the back of her throat and scuffed her foot in the dirt.

"I'm sorry I blurted it out like that, but I didn't know how to stop you from leaving. If you left, I didn't think I could get you back. No matter what you think of me now, know that I'll always care for you, deeply." Jake stared into her eyes. His face was painted with pain as though his heart had fallen to somewhere below his stomach.

"Can you please explain? Why do you see a probation officer?"

Jake hesitated again.

"I won't play these games. If you're not going to talk to me, then why are we together?"

Jake breathed, "You're right. You deserve the truth. I'm just afraid that once you know, you won't want anything to do with me."

Kya waited.

Jake took a deep breath. "I'm serving probation as an alternative to prison."

FIFTEEN

Jake said the words gently, looking at Kya dead on.

Kya's mouth fell open. She was not expecting that. "I don't know if I believe you." Kya looked at him skeptically. "If you are telling the truth… for what crime?"

"It's the truth! Kya, have I ever lied to you before? Or gave you a reason not to trust me?"

"No! But you certainly weren't being forthcoming. Why are you on probation?"

"I was released from a prison sentence about six months ago."

Kya's jaw hung slack. "Wha… What? Why were you in prison?"

"I wasn't exactly *in* prison," Jake said with a stretched mouth. "I had been booked, but not charged. So, I did a short stay awaiting trial."

"Okay, what did you do?"

Jake paused, fidgeting with his fingers.

"Three cases of vehicular manslaughter." Jake's voice was

robotic, as if he'd practiced it or repeated it on a loop. "At least that is what started the whole mess."

"Manslaughter…? Like in you killed someone? I—well—yeah—that's what manslaughter means… three… vehicular?"

Jake stood silently as she worked it out.

"A car accident?" Kya looked up into his eyes, asking the silent question.

"A really bad one that was all my fault." Jake stared at his hands, fiddling with his fingers.

Kya released a breath and turned to look over the creek. How was she to react? She felt sorry for Jake, horrified at the tragedy, slightly betrayed, and wary of Jake's past.

"I was fifteen." Jake's voice startled Kya and she turned to face him. He sat on a fallen tree near the ravine. There were ghosts in his eyes. He didn't see her. No, he was watching a haunting from a memory where death lived. "It was in late February, when I lived in Billings. My mom had gone to bed early. She'd been working a lot.

"I heard about a party that was going on outside of the city. So, I called my friends, stole my mom's keys, and a bottle of wine." Jake paused. "I thought I was so cool and above any repercussions for my actions." His elbows rested on his knees. His hands were clasped before him; his knuckles were bleached of color.

Kya was cold and overly warm at the same time. Her stomach hollowed.

"The roads were fine in the city… but outside of town, on the back roads, they were snow-packed. I remember it being warm that day, but it was super cold that night. The melt from the day was frozen.

"And the party, it turned out to be a total bust. No one was there. Those who were there were hiding in cars because it was so cold. One of my friends that was with me had a bottle of… I don't even know what, something strong. She'd stolen that from her dad.

"We started drinking, every one of us. Then we got bored, and so we thought we'd be cool and go cruising on the back roads… Sheri was in the front with me. Miles and Tanya were in the back.

"There was a bridge… it spanned a shallow ravine. And I…" Jake's voice caught. "Sheri had a little sister. She was too young to even remember Sheri now. Miles was an all-star football player. He would have had a full ride scholarship to the school of his choice. Tanya was top of the class with a 4.0 GPA. She was planning to go to Harvard when she graduated. Not even sure why she was hanging out with us. I… I can still hear the noise Sheri made when we started sliding and went through that guardrail. She never screamed. She just sucked in a sharp breath." Jake paused. His Adam's apple worked as he swallowed thickly.

Kya waited patiently for him to continue.

"Tanya and Miles had passed out in the back seat. Tanya was lying in Miles's lap when we wrecked. She was thrown forward onto the floor. She was pinned under the front seats. The mounting bracket for the driver's seat dented in her skull, and the center console broke all but four of her ribs… Miles… he was tossed forward so hard that the residual whiplash broke his neck… Sheri… sh… she was completely ejected from the car through the windshield. Her body was ripped open from one end to the other from going through the glass." Jake stopped… it didn't seem he would continue. He was going into so much detail, like he forced himself to remember every gruesome image, like he was punishing himself.

"And…" Kya hesitated, afraid of interrupting whatever moment he was having or reliving. "What happened to you?"

"Broken leg, broken arm, and a busted cheekbone… I was never even knocked out. Stunned, yes, but conscious. I found a phone and called 911. I thought Miles might have been alive, but it turned out when the paramedics arrived, it was Sheri who was still alive. There I was, trying to save a dead guy when Sheri was bleeding out on the snow. No one would have thought her alive… There was so much blood." Jake stopped.

Kya couldn't breathe. Her body shook, and her stomach turned. Three people in one accident, one car, one survivor. And all Kya could think was, *Thank God it was Jake who survived.* And that thought sickened her, too. Kya couldn't speak or move.

"Every one of them would have gone on to do incredible things in the world." Jake pushed himself up and thrust his hands into his hair. "And none of them even got to live." He stood abruptly and paced in a harsh line and turned on his heel. "But no, NO! The guy with no future. The deadbeat delinquent, he—he gets to live! His dumbass idea ended their beautiful lives, and he is the one that survives? Now, where is the justice in that!?"

Kya gawked open-mouthed, stunned into silence. Jake stomped across the ground. He was fuming.

"And they did nothing to me! I got off free and clear. I had to do a bit of community service, but that was it. Three people dead and I get nothing!" He continued to storm over the ground.

"Jake?" Kya took a small step toward him. But he kept marching. "Jake." Kya raised her voice. "Jake!"

Jake stopped mid-stride, frozen.

Kya walked up to him. Her earlier consternation was now replaced by much softer emotions. She placed her hands on either side of his face, forcing him to look at her. "You made a mistake. It's in the past and you can't change it."

"I know. That's what's ..."

"Shh." Kya cut him off with a finger to his soft lips. "You've paid the price for that mistake… probably every day, and probably will continue to for the rest of your life. Your own mind and heart are the worst punishment anyone ever faces. What happened was tragic… But if it hadn't happened, where would your life be now?" Kya paused and looked directly into Jake's eyes. "And I really like the man you've become. I'm sorry for getting so angry. I had a rough day."

Kya kissed Jake's cheek.

"Yeah… so, you're okay with dating an ex-con?"

"I like bad boys."

"I wasn't just bad… I aided and abetted. Killed three people. Three of my friends."

"Everything happens for a reason. We may not know what the reason was now, or ever, but it's all in God's plan."

Jake simply nodded.

There was a stretch of silence as they both processed everything.

Kya's brow crinkled. "Wait, before you said the accident is what started it—started what?"

Jake rubbed his palms on his jeans. "After the accident, I was in a dark place. They made me see a therapist. That's where I picked up the kickboxing. My therapist thought it might help with my anger. Turned out I really liked it, and then I met some people who set up matches and promised me winning money. I took it. But once I was in, I was stuck. I made some very bad choices, and, turns out, I was in with the wrong crowd. But it felt good to have some sort of purpose. Then they started asking me to do more than fight and place bets.

"At first, it was driving people places. Then acting as the muscle, you know. Then it was 'take this gun and to pick up some packages.' I didn't know what most of the packages were. But then they asked me to join a group of them going to sell drugs. And I went, but right when we arrived at the location… I don't know. I couldn't do it. I left and went home for the first time since my eighteenth birthday.

"My mom was so mad, made me explain where I'd been. Then she was scared for me." Jake looked at his boots. "I was arrested later that week because the crew I was with had been caught, and they had mentioned my name. They gave me a plea bargain, and I spilled my guts to the police. I was only booked for a little while awaiting trial, but when I was in... I... actually fit in, like I belonged. I had a lot in common with the other inmates, and that scared me more than anything.

"Once I was out, my mom got my probation sentence moved here. She's a lawyer, which probably had more to do with my light sentence than I will ever know. I think she thought they would try and come after me. Which they may have. So, yeah, here I am."

Kya swallowed thickly, processing everything he had said. She turned her gaze down to her feet. He'd been on a dark path indeed. He had been in it bad, criminal activity, a criminal. And it all led him there, to Kya. "What would have happened to me if you weren't here?" Kya whispered.

Jake stiffened before her. He brought his hand up from his side and tucked a finger under her chin. He gently lifted, so she was looking up into his eyes.

"I'll always be here for you." Jake leaned in and touched his supple lips to Kya's in a soft kiss. It wasn't hungry or desperate. It was sweet. When he pulled away, Kya wrapped her arms around his waist and pressed her face into his chest and held on.

Jake tucked his head into her neck and hugged her as tightly as she clung to him. When Jake's breathing was back to normal and he'd relaxed, she released him. He stepped back and looked over the ravine.

"It's kind of ironic that I like coming here," Jake said.

"Yeah, why is that?" Kya asked.

"Because it looks very similar to the place of the accident… Except for the trees. There weren't any trees on the other road. Maybe that's why I like it. It's so similar, but this place is beautiful and warm rather than cold and desolate."

Kya smiled up at him in a sad knowing smile.

They sat on a log near the edge of the ravine. The soft sounds of the remote outdoors returned as they settled in and digested these revelations and their new realities.

After they'd sat and listened to the sounds of non-human life for a spell, Kya stirred.

"I ran into Mitch today."

"…and?" Jake asked. He pulled her tighter into his side.

"…and it was hard and weird. He acted like how it used to be, except, now, I'm not who I used to be." Kya let out a deep sigh. The pure truth of the words she'd spoken collapsed her chest, leaving a dull ache and hitch in her lungs as she tried to reinflate her ribs. "I… I was just so scared." Kya continued, "I didn't know what to expect. I was like a deer caught in the headlights. I didn't know which direction to run, so I froze… Thank God the sheriff walked in. Mitch stepped out of my way, and I pretty much ran to my car."

"I'm glad nothing happened. Are you okay?"

"Yeah, I'm okay. Just frazzled. Can you believe he suggested I live with him? What do you do in that situation?"

"I don't know. That's a tough one. You're in a confined space with not many exits. And your assailant is blocking the main one." Jake thought for a moment.

"I suppose I could have darted into the counter area and around through the other door. Using my smaller size and agility?"

"Yeah, that could work, but it's Saturday. The doors to the counter are locked."

"Oh, damn, that's true."

"Your best bet would have been to keep talking and slowly migrate, so you were by the door, giving possible suggestions like, 'Let's move out of the way to talk.' Or possibly some self-defense to allow you to escape. But that one is a long shot, given the size difference between you two."

"Hmm, yeah, I didn't think to migrate. I wasn't thinking much at all."

"The hard part is keeping your head when the fear sets in."

"Yeah. The first time I witnessed Mitch's wrath, we were in sixth grade. I was being bullied by some eighth graders for my skin tone. They were calling me an injun, as in Indian, or really Native American. I'd explained till my tongue was numb that I wasn't Native American. But they wouldn't drop it. The teachers told me to ignore them, and it would stop. We had all even been called into the office for it. But it *still* didn't stop. They just did it when there weren't teachers around.

"One day, it escalated. They started pushing me, and I fell down on the sidewalk. Peeled my knees and my palms open. When I stood up to face them, Mitch appeared next to me. He was the huge, silent new kid that everyone was too scared to talk to. I'd tried to include him before, but he'd only stared at me.

"Anyway, the eighth graders came at him as one, deeming him the bigger threat. One kicked at his shins, and the other punched his face. Both attacks made direct connection, but Mitch didn't even twitch. They went for the second round, and he put them both on the ground so fast I didn't see what had happened. The eighth graders were suddenly laid out, holding their faces.

"I'd planned on fighting dirty but never got a chance. Mitch offered me a shot at them after they were down, but I couldn't do it. Seemed wrong." Kya took a deep breath. "In the end, it worked. Those kids never bothered me again, and Mitch and I were friends from then on."

Kya stopped, and silence stretched between them. "Hey, you mentioned that you do some fighting stuff, right?"

"Yes?" Jake turned, so they were facing each other on the makeshift bench.

"Would you teach me some, like, self-defense?"

"I don't know. I'm more of a fighter. What I'd teach you could help with self-defense, but it could also endanger you even more."

Kya sagged. "It would be cool to know how to defend myself, something more than my dirty tactics," she said with a sardonic huff. She'd always wanted to learn to fight… not that she ever planned to use it, and hoped she never needed to, but it would be fun.

"Fighting dirty works nearly every time… But I'll see

what I can come up with. I'll do some research and we can go from there."

Kya brightened with a huge smile. She pulled Jake forward into a hot, excited kiss.

They stayed out there for the rest of the afternoon and talked about everything and nothing. Jake continually caressed circles into Kya's arms. She relaxed into his chest and absorbed his warmth. She shivered in the cool air, and he wrapped her up tighter. Overhead, the stars glowed, luminous. Their light was beautiful and comforting to her.

"Ahhh," she gasped, and jumped out of Jake's lap.

"What's the matter?" he asked, following her motion to stand right behind her.

"The stars!"

"What about the stars?"

"They're out and in full force! There's no light on the horizon!" Kya turned in a circle, then stopped facing Jake. "It's got to be past ten." Her eyes got big, and she pulled her hands tightly over her neck. "My parents are gonna kill me! They have probably been calling for the past three hours!"

"Oh…crap, well, I guess we better get going."

"Yeah."

The four-wheeler ride back to the house was long and cold. Kya clung to Jake like a spider monkey. It was rough and bumpy, since Jake was going way faster than he did on the way out. He skidded to a stop at the back of the barn. Kya sprung from the ATV using Jake's arm as a handhold. He followed right behind her. When she reached her car door, Jake grabbed her arm, stopping her from making a Cinderella getaway.

Jake gripped the tops of her arms, his thumbs caressing circles on her skin. Kya was going to feel those circles for the rest of forever. He leaned in and kissed her soundly on the lips. Kya melted in his embrace. When he pulled back, he kissed her once more and bade her goodnight.

Kya stumbled, and pretty much fell into her car, and made her way home in a fog.

SIXTEEN

It was late, and the night was dark. A long sigh escaped Jake. He was tired. It seemed like he never got a break anymore. Since he met Kya, he'd been going nonstop. He smiled to himself. It was a good kind of tired. She had just left him minutes ago, and he already missed her. He hated when he had to leave her, kept telling himself that she was safe. He had to believe she was safe, or he'd go insane.

Jake stepped away from the empty parking spot where Kya had been. He looked up to the billions of stars that shone on the dark moonless night as he made his way to the main house to get a glass of lemonade before he collapsed in bed. He knew that the only thing in the hand house was tap water.

Jake quietly opened the door and snuck into the house in the dark. The light of the fridge was blinding in the darkness. He pulled the pitcher out, poured the sweet, tart liquid into a glass, and replaced it. He tipped the glass to his lips and guzzled it down.

"How'd she take it?"

The voice came out of the darkness, causing Jake to skid

to a stop at the counter. A light blinked on in the living room. Aunt Cass stood in the sphere of light from the lamp on the end table.

"Holy crap, Aunt Cass, you scared me!" Jake held the glass in his hand like it had almost become a projectile.

"Sorry, I heard you come in and wanted to know how Kya handled it," she said in a low voice. She took a seat on the bar stools across the counter from Jake. "You did tell her, right?"

"Yeah." Jake ran his fingers through his hair. "Well, she was really mad at me."

She nodded.

"It took me a while to figure out why." He paused. "When she finally told me what was up, I felt like such a jackass."

"So, how'd she take it when you told her the truth?" Aunt Cass asked.

"She was sad, understanding, relieved, sympathetic." Jake pressed his palms into the edge of the counter and leaned against them. "Why does she still want to be with me? She's so sweet, pure, and good. She should hate me. I'm more of a monster than that douchebag who blackened her face. He never killed anyone. And I've got three murders under my belt!"

"Because she's a smart girl and a good judge of character. And because she loves you."

"I don't know. Her judgment might be skewed. It was her *friend* who beat her bloody."

"Maybe so, but that boy is not clear up here." She tapped her head. "You've watched crime shows, right?"

Jake nodded.

"What's the one thing everyone always says when they discover who the serial killer is?"

Jake thought for a moment. "They never would have suspected them."

Aunt Cass nodded. "So, can you see how Kya was fooled?"

"Yeah. I never really blamed her. She's just too kind. Ready to see the best in people."

"And how do you think she felt when her kindness was betrayed by someone she was so close to?"

Jake sighed, and his shoulders slumped, defeated. "I hadn't thought of it from that perspective. I never figured she was ever at fault. I was having a hard time understanding how she never saw it."

"Kindness can do that, but maybe if more people were kind like Kya, Mitch wouldn't be the way he is... then again, he could just be entirely psycho."

"But still, she's trading one monster for another."

"I don't think she sees it that way."

"What do you mean?"

"How long have you been here, Jake, at the ranch?"

"Um, six months," Jake said, confused.

"And how many times have you smiled since the accident? And that's exactly what it was, an accident."

Jake stood straight, impersonating a fish out of water.

"There's a reason why your mother sent you here. Why she worked so hard and pulled so many strings to get your probation transferred here."

Jake shrugged. "I assumed it was a form of witness protection." Nothing more.

"The day you arrived, I saw death incarnate. There was no life in you. Your skin was pale, your eyes empty, your motions mechanical. The work helped, almost too much. You were doing so much, we weren't sure what to do with Kole. It was like we had a zombie working for us." She paused, studying her hands clasped on the counter before her and continued, "The day you rescued Kya, I got to see a glimpse of the little nephew I used to know who'd beg me to go ride horses. But he wasn't a boy anymore. He was a man.

"I called your mother that night and told her, for the first time in seven years, her son smiled. You know what she told me? She said, 'Whatever it is that brought him back to life, don't let it get away.'" Aunt Cass leaned back and took a breath.

A drop of moisture made a track down Jake's cheek. He scrubbed a hand down his face and brushed it off as he crossed his arms. He'd had no idea that was what his family saw in him.

"That beautiful girl down the road, she saved your life, Jacob, not the other way around."

Jake walked around the end of the counter and wrapped his arms around the tiny shoulders of his aunt. He tucked his face into her neck. "I'm sorry, Aunt Cass."

She hugged him back around the waist. "Just promise me no matter what happens, you'll stay with the living?"

He chuckled. "I promise."

"Okay." She patted his back and Jake released her. "I'm going to head to bed. I love you, Jacob."

"Love you too, Aunt Cass."

She walked to the hall.

"Aunt Cass?"

She turned.

"Why did my mom send me here?"

"She was scared. She didn't know what else to do."

"Scared of me." It was a statement.

"You do have a violent way of venting, but no. She was afraid of being the next parent to grieve over the loss of a child."

"From fighting or the trouble I was in?"

"From yourself, Jake… from yourself."

Jake couldn't speak.

Aunt Cass turned toward her bedroom.

Jake ghosted to the door, turning off the lamp as he went. Outside under the dark sky, bright with stars, he sank down on the porch steps. He rested his forearms on his knees and looked to the heavens.

It really was a beautiful night, and he really wished he could share it with Kya. She'd love it. The air was cool and smelled of grass and sage with summer on the way.

Bowing his head, he sent up a prayer. He didn't know where he'd be if his mom hadn't sent him to live with Aunt Cass. Thinking back to the time after the accident and before he found Kya, he'd been sad, extremely sad. He didn't deserve to live, didn't deserve to be happy, didn't deserve to breathe. He should have been the one to die, not them. His life was going nowhere. And yet he was the one to live. Fate was a bitch with a cruel sense of humor. He truly thought he shouldn't be alive, but he'd never considered suicide as an option. He simply couldn't do that to his mom and Mia, his family. That would be the most selfish thing he could do. He couldn't be the coward, the weak one unable to deal with a little, well, a heap of pain. But to know now that was what everyone else had thought, that's what they saw in him. It made Jake want to throw up. Then let Kole land a punch to his gut.

All the stress he must have caused his mom, from the fights and the criminal crowd he was hanging out with. He hadn't been on a good path. But something had stopped him that night. Divine intervention? Had to be. He had been committed to helping that crew get the money for the drugs. In the end, he made the decision to go the other way when they left the car. The crew had been pissed, but they let him go so they could finish the job.

His mom had been really scared after that, thinking they were going to come after him. When the police came and picked him up, she had been relieved, thinking he'd be safer with them, and furious for him getting in trouble in the first place.

He hadn't spoken to his mom since he arrived on the ranch. Didn't think she wanted anything to do with him. He thought she hated him, that she was scared of him. And this whole time, she was doing everything in her power to help him. To try and save his life.

Reaching into his jean's pocket, Jake dug his phone out.

He had to search for her in his contacts list. He found her in the *M*'s. Mom. He pressed the number and put the phone to his ear. It was late; she probably wouldn't answer. It rang three times and went to voicemail. He waited for the beep. "Hey, Mom… I, uh… I just wanted to say I love you. Call me when you get a chance. Bye." And he ended the call.

SEVENTEEN

KYA SCRUNCHED HER FACE UP AT THE TEXT MESSAGE on her phone.

Wanna go to a party?

She flicked her eyes to the name at the top, then back to the message, then to the name again. Confusion wrinkled her expression. It was from Jake, but the content of the message didn't seem consistent with the sender of said message.

Kya texted back, *Um… that depends… my last party experience was not the greatest.*

She wasn't really sure she was ready to attend another party. Suppose it depended on the kind of party.

Her phone buzzed. *Haha That's the truth. It's just a family ranch BBQ.*

Ah! Kya nodded to herself slowly and texted back, *Oh, yeah, sure, sounds fun.*

Sweet, can you be here around 6?

Sure… wait, I'm meeting your family?

Yeah.

I look like Rocky Balboa's punching bag!

You're definitely not a bag, and they understand the situation.

Well, isn't that gonna be a great first impression.
You'll be fine.
Says you. You already know all those people.
Well, you know Connor.
True…
You've already met Aunt Cass.
Yes.
If you want, you can bring Rachel. The more the merrier.
Hmm, ok, having a wing girl makes it better.
Awesome, Tucker's welcome too.
Well, ok then, be there at 6.
Ok.

Oh boy, what did she get herself into? Anxiety flooded through her. Kya furiously swiped at her phone, found Rachel's name, and pressed the phone to her ear.

"What's new, chicky-poo?" Rachel answered.

"Holy cow, did the phone even ring?"

"Technically, no, because I was playing a game and you interrupted it."

"Sorry, but this is gonna be way more fun than phone games."

"Oooh, I'm intrigued."

"We've been invited to a barbecue party at the ranch."

"That does sound fun." Kya heard a door shut. "I'm on my way." And the call ended.

Kya turned from the kitchen and shouted, "Hey, Tucker, wanna go to a barbecue?"

"Uh, whose barbecue?"

"Jake's family is having one at the ranch."

Tucker stepped out of the door in the hall. "Uh, not really."

"Well, okay then." Kya turned away and texted her mother about her plans.

She skipped down to her bedroom in the basement. The light smell of vanilla greeted her. She walked to her closet and stared blankly in… What did one wear to a ranch party? A summer barbecue made her want to wear a light sundress. The cattle ranch part made her want old jeans and boots. But she obviously wouldn't be doing any work, so that would be stupid. Her hands hovered over a strappy white sundress that she looked amazing in, but hardly ever wore. White and dresses weren't exactly functional in Wyoming. Kya lost track of time searching for the perfect outfit. What would Jake like her in best?

"Hey."

Kya screamed and jumped backwards into her closet. "Holy cow, Rachel, you scared the crap out of me!" Kya panted with her hand pressed to her chest.

Rachel stood bent over, rocking with laughter. "Sorry, that was the best reaction ever!" She laughed some more and sucked in air. "I thought you would have heard me come in."

"Goodness."

Rachel reached out and helped Kya out of the bottom of her closet. "Next time someone attacks, I'll be sure to remember your tactics. I'm sure I'll be able to escape from inside my closet."

"Ever heard of a place called Narnia?"

"Touché. So, what's the sitch?"

"I was just trying to decide what to wear." Kya pulled the white sundress out.

"Oh, wow, you should totally wear that."

"You think?"

"Jake is going to lose it when he sees you in that."

Kya smiled and pulled the garment from the hanger.

"Oh, and I'm gonna borrow some of your clothes."

"Yeah, it's fine, as long as you wear a dress with me." Kya laid the dress out on her bed, stripped to her skivvies, and gently slipped the dress over her body. A full-length mirror hung on the wall behind the door. Kya slowly approached it. The dress emphasized her bronze skin. Her chestnut hair hung in straight tresses down to her waist. Her gaze moved from her bare, painted toes, up her long legs to the white hem that hung a few inches above her knees, and along the floaty material up to her waist. The dress clung to her chest, shaping and outlining her figure.

It looked incredible, or at least it would if her skin didn't resemble tarnished copper. Her upper body was stained with splotches of green bruising. And her hand was an eyesore of puffy gauze. Her eye was a deep purple and red.

Kya's face soured. You know that look people got just before they're going to throw up? She was a walking ad for domestic abuse. Her body tarnished by the brutality of a man's hand. His physical marks displayed upon her skin.

"Maybe I shouldn't wear this." Kya's lips pinched.

"Why, because of your bruises?" Rachel demanded.

Kya grimaced in shame.

"Are you kidding me? You look amazing, and it's not

like Jake hasn't seen all of your bruises. And he's the only one you need to worry about."

"I'm meeting his family for the first time."

"So what? None of that is your fault." Rachel gestured to Kya's injuries. "Dress up, look nice when you meet them, and own it." Rachel paused to adjust the bodice of the deep blue dress she'd chosen. "The whole damn town knows you look like Fix-it Felix Jr., except you don't have a magic hammer to fix your face."

Kya snorted, "Gee, thanks. I feel so much better now."

Rachel simply gave her a dead look.

Kya sighed. "I know, I know, you're right. I guess this is as good as it's gonna get." Kya pulled herself out of her personal pool of self-pity. She couldn't change what happened, but she could change her attitude.

"Why do I have to wear a dress?" Rachel asked.

"Because you love me and won't let me be the only one wearing a dress."

"Okay, but know there will be consequences," Rachel said with one eyebrow raised and a finger pointed at her.

Returning the favor, Kya flipped her off.

Rachel just rolled her eyes.

Kya stepped into her cowboy boots and picked up her purse.

As they exited her room, she held open the door, and Rachel walked ahead of her. She wore Kya's cobalt-blue dress like a model, and she rocked the neon-green converse she wore. Her ash-blonde hair hung loose to her waist. The subdued freckles that covered her face and arms just made her look that much cuter. She was like punk meets Shirley Temple.

Kya marveled at Rachel's hair. It was blonde, like white-blonde, with some grey tones and pieces that were nearly black. It was crazy and completely natural. A slight twinge of inadequacy dropped through her. Rachel was beautiful and dynamic. So different. And Kya was just brown all over. Well, brown and purple-green. She loved the way she looked, but couldn't help noticing how different they were, like exact opposites. Rachel didn't give a shit what anyone thought, and Kya cared too much.

Whatever their differences were, Kya loved Rachel. She was her slap in the face when she needed it. She was her un-biological sister.

"We'll take your car, so we don't get shot pulling up there. But I'll drive," Rachel said, pointing at her again.

Kya shrugged, tossed her keys to Rach, and dropped into the passenger seat. "You just don't want to take your car out there."

"You caught me. Is it a crime to want to keep my car nice?"

"No, I was simply letting you know I caught your ploy… I'm on to you…"

"Should I be afraid?"

"Very afraid," Kya said, staring out the windshield. A few butterflies fluttered in her stomach, and her hands twitched. She sucked in a deep breath through her nose and slowly released it. It helped a little, but she was still apprehensive. She didn't want to meet Jake's family looking like a rock 'em sock 'em robot. She pulled the skin on the inside of her lip between her teeth, then released it, and repeat.

Rachel drove with her lips pursed and was nodding along to a song on the radio.

Kya sighed, wishing she could be that relaxed.

"Dude, you got to calm down. You're starting to make me nervous."

"Whatever. You're chiller than the Kool-Aid Man."

"That's because I have nothing riding on this event. To me, it's just a free meal."

Kya clenched her good hand in her lap.

"You really like him, don't you?"

Kya nodded slowly, not looking at Rachel.

JAKE RAN HIS HAND THROUGH HIS HAIR, THEN replaced his ball cap. He pulled his phone out of his pocket and checked the screen, then put it back. Taking his cap off, he readjusted it on his head. There were foot imprints in the old, worn-out carpet as he paced back and forth in his room, gnawing his nonexistent thumbnail because it gave his hands something to do. He turned on his heel and paced back the other way.

Stopping at the mirror, he looked as average and ordinary as he did every day. The t-shirt he wore, he'd selected specifically because it was slightly newer and had fewer holes than the others. He'd put on a nicer, cleaner pair of dark wash jeans. He'd even worn his nice cowboy boots, opting out of his shitkickers.

Spinning around, he paced to the bathroom, pulled his toothbrush out of the cup by the sink, and smeared a small amount of paste on the bristles. Scrubbing away at his teeth with one hand, he pulled his phone out of his pocket with the other. The main screen was blank. He opened it to his messages. The last one was from Kya. She was on her way.

Jake rubbed his hand through his hair, removing and replacing his hat in one fluid motion. He spat, rinsed off his toothbrush, and tossed it back in the cup, hand shaking as he drew it away.

Why was he so nervous? He was acting like a middle schooler on his first date. He was supposed to be cool. The cool guy. He'd got dis. He took a breath that shuddered through his chest. He *so* don't got dis. He could handle the clink, but not a barbecue with the girl of his dreams?

It was just Kya. He knew her. And she was the entire reason he was so nervous. No matter how laid-back the evening was supposed to be, he couldn't shake the feeling that this night would be important, and that nothing would be the same after this.

Adopting a calm façade, he walked to the main house. Aunt Cass was in the kitchen, running around like the floor was made of hot coals. Jake laughed to himself at the image of her high-steppin' it across the kitchen.

Out the French doors that were just off from the kitchen, the barbecue grill broiled smoke out of its lid. Uncle Kal stood before it with a set of large tongs in his hands. He talked with Rich, Jake's brother-in-law. Mia, his sister, reclined in one of the camp chairs, rubbing her swollen belly. Kole, the other ranch hand, lay in the grass on his back with two young boys piled atop him. The twins Adam and Daniel were the youngest of the party. They were Matt and Kara's boys. Matt was Connor's older brother. Kara flitted about a table they set up outside. Caleb, Connor's younger brother, was standing in the grass near Kole and the boys, holding a football. A grin stretched his face as he watched the dogpile before him. It was quite the gathering. There was only one person missing.

"What are you lazy sons o' bitches doing?" Grandpa Earl walked out from the side of the house. His grey hair was set in a deep V on his head. "Ah, what is this? A barbecue. What'chya cookin'? Got any burgers? I could go for a good burger," Grandpa Earl shouted. He pretty much shouted all the time. His hearing was bad.

Jake smiled and shook his head at the old fart. Earl's words, not his. Jake leaned against the open doorjamb to the concrete patio at the back of the house. The grill sat to one side with the table that Kara was hovering over. There was a wooden bench swing on the other side, along with some camp chairs.

Stepping through the door, he slid into the other reclining camp chair next to Mia. He pushed his chair back, and his feet came off the ground.

Mia had her chair laid nearly flat. Given her current state of being heavily pregnant, how was she going to get out of the chair?

The sun pressed down a balmy heat. It'd rained so much back in May that it was humid, which didn't happen often in this region. The rain was good, though. It meant they would have lots of grazing ground and possibly two cuttings of hay. It was strange. Everything was so healthy. The grass was nearly neon-green. But the days had been getting progressively hotter.

Wyoming was a very dry place, and though it looked like this now, the real telling factor would be if it lasted into July. It was around then that the place would burn to a crisp, unless it was a truly wet year.

Jake decided he wouldn't care if it got really hot and dry. Because then Kya's clothing was bound to shrink in size. He imagined her at the lake, jumping off the cliffs in a bikini. He sat forward, the chair sitting up with him, bracing his elbows on the arms, and hunched over.

"What's the matter, Jake?" Mia asked.

"What…? Nothin', nothin'." He swung his head in her direction. She looked at him with squinted eyes and a crease on her forehead.

"Naw, I haven't seen you this wound tight since the trial."

Jake grimaced and swallowed. The bubbles in his stomach expanded.

"Sorry." She had the grace to look pained. "Does she know?"

Jake nodded, staring at the concrete. He sucked in a shallow breath. An ant scurried around between his feet.

"So, I'm guessing she took it alright if she's coming tonight?"

"She did," he said, his voice low, not wanting everyone to hear. "She took it better than anyone so far… and I have no idea why. She has no reason to trust me."

"But she does."

Jake flipped his head in Mia's direction, confused.

"You have helped her and protected her on more than one occasion. Why wouldn't she trust you?"

"It's not exactly a simple thing finding out someone's been in prison."

"So? You weren't there long, anyway." Mia still lay lounged back in the chair, completely relaxed. It was as if she only talked about the weather.

"I'm on probation and have a felony charge on my record." Jake ground his teeth and looked away. He pulled his hat off and ran his fingers through his hair.

Mia simply shrugged.

Jake had taken his punishment with relish. It had been a lenient ruling, and he was thankful, but he believed he deserved much more. Not just for his criminal involvement, but the accident as well. Why should he get to live a full life with no consequences when they didn't? They didn't get a life at all.

"I don't see why you're nervous, anyway. She's totally into you."

"How would you know? You've never met her."

"'Cuz any girl would be crazy not to be… And it's written all over your face. And believe me," Mia leaned over the side of her chair toward Jake, "you are more than worthy of her affections."

Jake leaned toward her, so his face was inches from hers. He pursed his lips and squinted into a glare. "You need to stop reading romance novels," he said seriously.

Mia rolled her eyes and relaxed back in her chair. "You just wait, Jake. Here in a few minutes, you're going to be starring in one."

Jake gave her a small smile. He wasn't sure he believed her, but he wanted to.

There was silence in the backyard, like "listen to the crickets and frogs" kind of silence. A small conversation picked up at the grill, and the twins began taunting Kole and Caleb. It was as if everyone had taken a breath at the same time.

The screen door to the house ground noisily in its track as it slid open. What came through stunned Jake to stone. The beauty before him was ethereal, belonging to an angel. Her boots had entered his vision first. They were simple round-toe, brown leather cowboy boots. His gaze traveled up bare, bronze-toned legs to the bottom of a simple white dress. It hung loose around her thighs but clung to her hips, and was snug around the waist up over the chest, and hung on her slight frame with white straps a little wider than a pencil. Her long, dark hair swung behind her shoulders and down her back. Her lips were stained pink, making her exotic features even more potent. Her brown eyes sparkled, and a shy smile curled her lush lips.

"Hi," she said with a tiny wave of her hand at her waist.

Jake did nothing but stare.

Glancing around at everyone else gathered there, Kya smiled again.

With a burst of energy, Jake jumped from his chair in one motion, nearly knocking it over. He stood before her, sucked in a breath, and held it for a count. "You look… so beautiful." The breath whispered past his lips. He reached out and grasped her delicate hand in his and gazed down into her eyes. She smiled at him, bit her lip, and averted her eyes to the ground.

"Dude, you're blocking the door," an irritated voice said behind Kya. She hadn't even made it out of the house.

Jake pulled Kya to his side, out of the way of the door. A slight, blonde girl stepped through, followed by Aunt Cass.

"Jake, you didn't tell me you invited Kya and Rachel."

"You were a little busy in the kitchen."

"Ah, well, no matter. The more the merrier, and heaven knows we have enough food." Aunt Cass turned to Kya and Rachel. "You girls are always welcome."

"Thank you," Kya said with a smile.

"Yeah, what she said," Rachel quipped, oh so eloquent.

Aunt Cass smiled and started carrying dishes of food from the house.

There was a strange silence. "Uhhhh." Kya's voice broke it. "Jake, this is Rachel, Rachel, this is Jake."

"Nice to meet you." Jake shook Rachel's hand. It was a simple, polite gesture, but it was super awkward. "Um, that's Aunt Cassie, obviously…" Jake proceeded to introduce the family to Kya and Rachel.

Once the formalities were taken care of, Uncle Kal started

cracking jokes—well, more like flatteries—at Kya's expense. Her cheeks turned pink, and it was the most adorable thing he'd ever seen.

Kya mingled and spoke with everyone, even Kole and the twins. She fit in with his family so well. The only thing that would make this better would be if his mom could have been there. He really wanted her to meet Kya.

Connor came over and stood silently beside him. He had his arms crossed over his chest. Jake stuffed his hands into his pockets.

"Meeting the family… that's kinda big," Connor said.

"Very," was Jake's reply.

"You sure about this man? It's not just because Mitch is an insane asshole?"

"No, it's not just because of that. The fact I get to kick his ass is merely a perk."

"If you're sure, man." Connor turned to face Jake's side. "Kya's pretty great." And he walked away.

Connor approached Rachel. She stood at the edge of the concrete pad, watching the boys play football. She looked as if she wanted to join them and was silently cursing her dress. Connor stopped next to her, and Rachel leaned to her side away from him, her arms crossed, mirroring his posture, and looking highly offended. Jake had no idea what all that was about.

"Hey." Kya bounced over to him.

Jake smiled and turned to face her.

"Thanks for inviting me. This is a lot of fun." She reached out and captured his hand.

"You are very welcome. To be honest, I think everyone is happy to have someone new to talk to."

"It beats the hell out of talking to yourself." Grandpa Earl clapped Jake on the back. He stumbled forward half a step. For as old as Grandpa Earl was, he was still as strong as an ox.

"Now, what I can't figure out is how a pretty lady such as yourself is with this troublemaking fool?"

Kya smiled at the old man. "Well, who was I to refuse the knight in shining armor who rescued this damsel in destress?"

Jake smiled down at her. There was sympathy in her eyes as she looked back at him.

"Well, ain't she quick as a whip. Can't argue with that logic." Grandpa Earl chuckled and sauntered off.

"Food's ready," Uncle Kal called.

Everyone swarmed like bugs to a zapper.

Jake stayed where he was, looking at Kya as if he could subsist on her beauty alone.

"Come on, Jelly man." She pulled on his hand. "It's all going to be gone before we get there." Her grin was dazzling, and he let her drag him to the buffet line.

EIGHTEEN

Kya had no idea what was up. Jake was being… gooey. Like caramel-filled chocolates kind of gooey. He never released her hand the whole time they ate, using his left hand to feed himself, which was comical on its own. The man was most definitely a righty. At one point, Kya had had to peel her hand from his so she could eat her burger like a normal person and not the Queen of England. There was no way she was eating a burger with a fork. This was Wyoming, for goodness' sake.

Sure, his actions were extremely endearing, but a girl needed to use her hands… that was dirty… Great, now her mind was in the gutter… with his whole family around. Kya could feel her cheeks heat.

Jake leaned over. "Why are you blushing?" he whispered to her.

She shook her head and took another huge bite of her burger.

"Oh, man, whatever it is, it must be good."

Curse him. He could read her too well.

"I will find out what it is one way or another," Jake whispered again, and Kya shivered.

When they had finished eating, Kya turned around on the picnic bench and leaned back against the table. She placed a hand over her satisfyingly full belly and sighed. These people could freaking cook.

"So, what do you think?" Jake asked.

"It was de-licious," Kya replied.

They sat looking out over the green lawn toward the west, and the pasture dotted with cows in the distance. The sun was beginning to set, and the sky burned orange and pink.

Kal and Matt set about starting a fire. By the looks of their kindling, it was going to be a bonfire.

Kya sat back, leaning against Jake's side, taking in the atmosphere. She was content and warm in Jake's embrace, his arm around her shoulders. It was good relaxing and listening to everyone talk and tell stories. They had some good ones. Her favorites were of Jake and Connor. Those two were hilarious as kids.

"Or that time they about burned the house down," Cassie said.

Kya jerked to look at Cassie. She'd said it so casually it startled Kya. She turned to look at Jake accusingly. He just looked quizzical, with his brow smashed down over his eyes.

"Um, but we weren't kids then," Jake said.

"Yeah, that happened like a few months ago," Connor supplied.

"You're not making yourself look any better," Kara said.

"Yeah, you're just proving you're still delinquent children." Cassie sat back with a smirk.

"How'd they almost burn the house down?" Kya asked.

"Well…" Caleb dragged the word out. "These two geniuses thought they'd be awesome and cook steaks for lunch."

"They were delicious steaks, mind you," Jake said.

"They were the only ones here," Caleb continued, "I was at work at the time… couldn't save me any… the grill at the hand house was broken. The legs had fallen off it. It was one of those small, black, round charcoal grills. Well, they thought, 'We'll just set it on its bottom.' They were on the back porch, which is made of wood. They finished cooking and eating and were going to let the briquettes burn down and go out.

"I got home that afternoon, and I went to find them, see what was up. Chores and all that. I walk in the house, and it smells like a campfire, something burning. So, I asked about it. Jake said, 'Oh, we just cooked steaks.' And he went back to playing video games. So, I's like, yeah, okay. I walk toward the kitchen, and looked out the back-porch door, and this grill is like tipped sideways and halfway through the porch floor."

Kya's eyes bulged.

"Yep. So, I grabbed a bowl of dirty dish water out of the sink, ran it to the porch, and dumped it on it. I kept going back for more water, trying to get it to stop sizzling. The dang deck was soaked. So, I moved the grill and looked through the hole in the porch at the stacks of wood underneath for the fireplace. They were smoldering. So, I dash out the freaking door and hunt down the garden hose. I get the water turned on and start spraying down the house. And here comes Jake." Caleb adopted his best idiot voice. "'What'cha doin'?'" Caleb gave Jake a dead one eyebrow raised. "I'm like, 'Puttin' the house out!'"

Kya chuckled and shook her head, looking over her shoulder at Jake. He merely pulled her tighter to his side.

"Hey, we fixed the deck! We even matched the peeling paint," Jake defended himself.

"It was a beautiful patch job. No one would have ever known, but someone had to go and tell Mom," Connor said with a pointed look at Caleb.

"It was an epic story. It had to be shared," Caleb said.

Everyone chuckled and shook their heads. There were even a few eye rolls.

Then, Kara came out of the house carrying a speaker box. She set it on the table behind Jake and Kya. She pulled her phone out, and "Down on the Farm" blared from the speaker.

"Ouh, ouh!" Mia catcalled and hefted her pregnant butt out of the camp chair, hips first. She braced her hands on her lower back and started doing a small shimmy to the beat, which really was more of a pregnant truffle shuffle.

Rich stood and grabbed his wife. He pressed her swollen belly to his and started a fast two-step.

They looked so funny together. He was a six-foot-five beanpole, and she was a five-five curvaceous, very pregnant woman.

Matt and Kara spun around in a country swing. Those two were good. They did everything from hip sits and dips and spins to high kicks.

Kal grabbed Cassie and started propelling her through a… uh, two…stomp? Kya had never seen anything like it.

It was fascinating watching the couples. Every dance was different, yet they all danced in time to the same song. She herself wasn't really much of a dancer. She loved music, but dancing was not her thing.

Kya sucked in a sharp breath and jumped from the bench, and Jake's arms. She sprinted around the side of the house and to her car.

She could hear Jake calling after her.

In the backseat of her car was her camera. She grabbed the whole case and sprinted back to the party.

Jake stood at the edge of the congregation, staring off toward where she had disappeared. As she reappeared, his stance relaxed, and he smiled.

Kya set the case down, removing the camera, and began walking around the dancers, snapping pictures. She lay down in the grass and took some. She was able to get some closeups of faces without invading anyone's space too much. Kya smiled. They looked dreamy. They were all only wearing street clothes, but they were angelic.

That night, she discovered something. For the first time, she photographed people. She captured emotion and had frozen it in a single stage forever.

Kya looked up from her camera and saw Jake watching her. She bit her lip and brought her camera up.

Her finger depressed the button, and it clicked.

A smirk graced his full lips, and he shook his head.

Kya turned back to the dancers and took more pictures.

Arms wrapped around her waist from behind, and she was drawn back into a warm, solid wall of muscle.

"Dance with me," Jake whispered in her ear. His warm breath tickled. He took her hand and led her out to join the others.

Kya deposited her camera on the picnic table and followed Jake where he led her.

He wrapped his arm around her waist and pulled her snug against his body. He drew her hand up in his, turning it to press their palms together.

Kya's left arm curved around the crown of Jake's shoulder. She couldn't even begin to see over him. Their clasped hands were tucked close to their sides, bodies pressed together. Kya stood with one of Jake's feet between hers. Her nose was inches from the soft t-shirt he wore, and he smelled so good, like the deepest evergreen forest. Kya was pretty sure it wasn't cologne either. She pulled the inside of her lip between her teeth.

Jake lowered his head and rested his cheek against her temple, her hair catching in his scruff. His fingers flexed on her back, and he pressed forward slightly with his large, callused hand that held hers. He propelled her backwards and stepped forward, his leg moving between hers. Kya backed up, following his lead, and then they were dancing.

Their first dance. Kya thought she should probably try to remember what song was playing, but she couldn't concentrate long enough to figure out what it was. There was nothing in her mind except the feel of Jake against her.

They swayed and moved to the music. Jake guided her effortlessly through the grass. She'd been to prom and danced there, but that was nothing compared to this. There were no awkward jerking movements as you tried to figure out your partner. She and Jake were like water. They just flowed together. Her mother once told her seamless movement between two people came from ultimate trust, and from that trust, they relaxed into each other, forming one body of one mind. Kya had thought it a bit farfetched at the time. How could two people be one? But dancing with Jake, she understood exactly what her mother had been talking about. They didn't need to figure each other out because they knew each other like they knew themselves.

Jake's cheek shifted against Kya's. His nose brushed her temple, and his warm breath feathered over her neck and shoulder. He removed his hand from her back, and Kya quivered at the loss of his warm touch. Bringing it up, his rough fingers wrapped around the back of her neck. His palm was against her jaw and his thumb on her cheek. Jake gently tilted her head back, never breaking their rhythm.

Kya looked up into his green eyes, and he gazed right back at her, and Kya felt it all in that one look. Jake lowered his face to hers. He set his nose directly alongside Kya's. Her eyes closed, and she could do nothing but feel. His lower lip touched her upper lip in the softest of caresses. He hovered there, not moving.

Kya couldn't take the torture any longer. She gripped his

neck using her wrist, leaving her mummified hand dangling in the air, and tipped herself up onto her toes, bringing their lips into full contact, breaking their rhythm. It was as soft and sweet as his caress, not frantic, but it was still incredibly fierce.

Jake's lips moved gently against Kya's, and she marveled at the velvet texture of his kiss. Everything she had seen in his eyes was reflected in that kiss. He sucked her upper lip, and her teeth grazed his lower. They pressed their lips together again and savored one more kiss before breaking to rest with their foreheads pressed together. From all around them, catcalls erupted. Jake's entire family cheered as he laid claim to her.

Kya smiled against his mouth, and his chest rumbled as he laughed. She turned her face to the side, rolling her forehead along Jake's, resting her cheek on his. Her cheeks heated as she smiled at their audience.

"Well, there's no going back now," Jake said, looking down at Kya with his heart in his eyes.

"Most definitely not," Kya replied, smiling uncontrollably. She probably looked like a goober, but didn't care as long as Jake kept looking at her like that.

Just as the cheers were dying out, a heavy beat started pumping from the speaker on the table.

Rachel jumped in the air with her fist held high. "Oh yeah, this is my jam!" she shouted, shaking what her momma gave her.

Kya smiled at her friend. "Gotta love her 'cuz she's crazy."

"Yep. She's also really good at taking the attention off of us."

Kya nodded as Rachel spazzed around the yard. Rachel looked over her shoulder and glared, like "set you on fire and drop you in the Yellowstone super volcano" kind of glare. She spun around, turning her back to the area she'd just turned to ash. An expression flashed across her features that had Kya's stomach clenching and her heart aching for her friend. The emotion was brief, but it contained so much pain and hurt. Kya wanted to go hug her, but stopped herself before she could broadcast Rachel's pain to everyone when she was working so hard to look happy.

Kya followed the direction that Rachel had cast that glare. On the bench at the picnic table, Connor sat with his elbows on the table and his head in his hands. There was no one around him, so it had to be him Rachel was torching. *What the hell?* Kya understood the glare. Rachel despised Connor… but the hurt? That's what had Kya confused.

"I'm gonna go get a drink," Kya said to Jake's chest since he still clutched her to him and walked to the food table. She had her glass of Arnold Palmer to her lips, chugging it down.

"Hey, Kya," Mia said, directly behind her. Kya startled, catching the liquid before it went everywhere. Kya pressed her fingers to her lips and forced the liquid down.

"Hey." Kya turned to where Mia stood at her shoulder.

Mia's hands absently rubbed her bulging belly. She smiled sweetly, but there was suspicion or wariness in her eyes. Kya didn't know which it was.

"So, that was fun," she said abruptly and looked out towards the makeshift dance floor.

"Yeah, I'm not usually much of a dancer, but Jake is good enough for the both of us." Kya smiled.

Mia nodded once with a small smile, looking out over the gathering.

Kya bit her lip and looked at her shoes. An awkward silence descended between them. She wanted to leave or maybe crawl under the table, but instinct told her this conversation wasn't over and she didn't want to be rude.

"You're right about one thing."

Kya jerked her head up to Mia. "What?"

"He is good enough. He's the best." Mia was completely serious. She even topped it off with a sneer. "He's been through a whole lot of crap, and he's finally getting his life back and living again." Mia turned and faced her full on, her arms crossed over the belly, resting atop it. "If anything happens to him because of you and your messed-up crap, I will find you and hold you personally accountable. He's a good person and doesn't deserve to be trapped in all this bullshit!" She paused.

"Mia, I know how good he is. He's literally saved my life at least twice now. And I tried to keep my distance and keep him out of this. I warned him of the danger. And it was because of that danger that he kept coming back. And if he hadn't, I might not be here now… I owe him my life." Kya focused on Jake, where he stood talking to his cousins.

"Even with all this messed-up shit going on," Mia's voice softened, "I haven't seen him smile like that since before the accident. And that's your doing. As much as I want to protect him because he's my little brother, I understand that he's become his own man. He chose this. He chose you. Even with all the baggage and danger you now carry with you till that asshole's dealt with, you've done something that I could never do. You've given him something I never could… You can't see it because he's so much better when you're around." She turned to look at him. "But you took away his ghosts. He still feels guilty, and that may never go away, but since you came into his life, he laughs again."

Kya smiled at Mia. A lump formed in her throat.

Mia's smile dropped. "But if you break his heart, I'll break your neck." Her smile returned. "It was nice finally meeting you, Kya," she finished sweetly and waddled over to Kara.

Kya swallowed her laugh. It was hard to take a threat seriously when she walked off like that. She raised her cup to her lips and sipped the tea and lemonade. Jake broke away from the men and strode toward her.

"My sister didn't bite you too hard, did she?" Jake clasped her hand in his, threading their fingers together.

"Naw, she's just playing Momma Bear." Kya smiled up at him and breathed in his scent, calming herself. "She's worried that I'm dragging you back to the dark side."

Jake stepped closer, toe to toe with Kya. He brought their joined hands up and kissed the back of Kya's. His other hand gripped her waist. "Never. You are the light drawing me away from the dark side."

"Good, because I don't think I would be able to take it if you were Darth Vader."

"Why's that?" Jake chuckled as he pressed her against him.

"'Cuz it would mean you have really bad asthma and a son named Luke."

"Oh, didn't I tell you? I carry an inhaler and I have a secret love child back in Montana."

Kya shook her head and grimaced slightly.

"Yeah, that was… uh, yeah."

"Funny, but not funny."

"Something like that." Jake leaned down and claimed Kya's mouth with his. It scorched the tender flesh of her lips and burned through her body. The kiss burned her from the inside out. She sucked in a breath and wrapped her fingers into the material that covered his rock-like abs. His tongue brushed the inside rim of her lips and withdrew. He sucked her lower lip, and Kya flicked her tongue over his upper lip. A groan rumbled in his chest, and he released her mouth, only to press his over hers again.

A throat cleared behind them.

Jake pressed one more kiss to Kya's lips, and pulled away a few inches, gazing into her eyes.

Kya broke the trance and turned to whoever interrupted them. Rachel stood behind Kya, fiddling with the stack of plates on the table. She looked more uncomfortable than… if she had walked in on her parents.

"Um, Kya, it's getting late, and Dad gave me a curfew."

"Oh." Kya dug her phone out of her boot and checked the time. It was 10:30. "Oh, man, it is late." She looked back up into Jake's eyes. "We'd better head out."

"I'll meet you at the car," Rachel said and walked away.

Kya wrapped her arms around Jake's waist, hugging him to her. "I don't want to leave you."

"It's just for the night. I'll see you tomorrow," Jake said.

Kya nodded and stepped up onto her tiptoes and kissed him once, twice, three times. She dropped back on her heels, stepped back, and turned to grab her camera. Cassie was sitting at the table.

"Hey, Cassie, thanks for having us over. It was a lot of fun."

"Oh, any time, hun. You're always welcome."

"Okay, thanks. I'll see you later."

"Bye." Cassie smiled and gave a small wave.

Kya strolled around the end of the house toward her car, where Rachel sat behind the wheel with the motor already running. She approached the passenger door.

"Kya!" Jake yelled from behind her. He ran across the driveway and stopped directly in front of her. "I don't want to leave you either," he said, and both his hands swept up to press against her face. His palms on her jaw, his fingers wrapping around the back of her neck, and his thumbs were at her cheeks. In the same instant, his lips descended on hers in an achingly fierce kiss. He kissed her like it was the last time. He was a starving man seeking his only source of sustenance.

It wasn't like before. This kiss was almost painful. She could feel his fear, his excitement, and his surrender. Kya drank him in. She absorbed everything he poured into her and returned it in full.

He pulled away, putting a breath of space between them. "Then don't," Kya breathed the words against his lips.

NINETEEN

Back home, Kya drifted through her nightly routine. She wasn't fully aware of anything she was doing or anything that was happening around her. Jake's words replayed on a continuous loop in her head. The giddy grin she seemed to be perpetually sporting had her looking half demented and the other half was crazed.

His words hadn't been the traditional three little words, but they might as well have been. In fact, Kya thought them better than the traditionally overused phrase that she was not allowing herself to say. Their words were special, and theirs.

Kya pulled the inside of her lip between her teeth. Toothpaste ran down her chin. She snapped back to the task at hand and finished quickly, then, in a daze, walked to her room. She slipped out of her dress and into a skimpy pair of shorts and a tank top.

She thought back to the dreaded task of physically leaving Jake. He'd stood in the red glow of the taillights as she and Rachel drove away. Kya had left her heart there. It was the oddest feeling. She was so happy, beyond euphoria, yet she ached. She was so blissed out she slipped into the car on a cloud.

Kya had looked at Rachel, wanting to share this incredible feeling, but her face was set in grim, angry lines. She asked her what was the matter. "Nothing" was all the answer she got. But, out of the corner of her eye, she caught Rachel smearing her palm under her eye. They had driven the rest of the way to Kya's house in silence and said a stilted goodbye. Rachel climbed into her own car and left.

Kya pulled the blankets back on her bed, crawled in, curling her hand into the pillow, and closed her eyes. One deep breath and she relaxed. Two deep breaths and she floated on the edge of sleep. Three deep breaths and she plunged into the darkness.

KYA TWIRLED IN CIRCLES, ENDLESS CIRCLES. JAKE clasped her hand in his, smiling brightly at her as she twirled. Then his fingers were lightly brushing across her forehead and down her cheek to her lips. She was lying down. His caress flowed down her arm to her fingertips. The bed dipped to one side beneath her. His gentle fingers were at her temple again.

"Kya," he whispered.

She could only murmur in response.

"Kya, babe," he said again, slightly louder.

"Mmm, shh." She nuzzled into his touch. "Just come to bed," she said.

He became very still.

"Over here." Kya threw her arm to the pillow closest to the wall.

The bed dipped, and his lips pressed a gentle kiss to her forehead. She sighed and breathed in his scent. The bed shifted, and his weight settled more evenly beside her. Scooting closer, she curled into his warm, solid body. His arm wrapped around her and settled at her waist. Kya relaxed completely and drifted on blissful clouds of dreams.

THE MORNING LIGHT WAS MUTED THROUGH THE blinds across the west-facing window. Jake gazed around the room. The walls were completely covered in stuff. Not only posters, but a whole bunch of other junk: CDs, scarves, keychains, bows, you name it. It was like the most unique page of an *I Spy* book. The walls themselves were… purple? He thought he could see pieces of it peeking through the jungle of wall accessories. It was beautiful and unique. Kind of how he imagined the inside of Kya's mind might look. And it smelled divine. Like cookies in a spring rain. It was made even more heavenly because the source was lying half on top of him. Kya's silken hair spilled over his shoulder and arm. Her head nestled in the soft flesh where his arm connected to his chest, and her hand rested on his stomach. Her front, from chest to hip, was pressed to his side. One of her knees curled over his hips.

Jake lay there soaking it all in. It was perfect. She was

perfect. He couldn't even bring himself to feel guilty about being in her parent's house.

He listened to the quiet murmurs of the sleeping house. There was a snap and creak somewhere deep within the house, possibly upstairs. Jake tensed and held his breath. He listened for footsteps, anything to indicate life within the house. He prayed if someone was up, or that if her parents were miraculously home, they didn't come into Kya's room. He wasn't sure how he would explain the situation to them… *"No sir, my intentions were completely platonic."* Yeah, right, he wouldn't be able to hide it no matter what he did. Jake shifted, adjusting slightly beneath the beauty sprawled across him.

Kya stirred and wiggled with a small stretch. Jake stiffened. She sighed and settled. Her fingers flexed and rubbed across his stomach. That torturous hand drifted up over his chest, and then down to his waist, and across the band of his pants. He groaned and snagged her dangerous fingers, stopping their exploration. Kya shifted the leg she had thrown across him. Jake's groan caught in his throat as his breath hitched. He released her hand and gripped her leg around the back of the knee to stop her from moving it. She resisted slightly and huffed a breath. Kya pressed her hand into his chest and lifted her head. She blinked sleepily and frowned at him, confused.

"Hmm." Kya looked around a little. "What…? Jake?"

Jake brought his free hand up and cupped her cheek. "Hey. Good morning."

"Wha… what are you doing here?" she asked.

"Well, I was sleeping, but then I woke up and was admiring the view." He looked directly into her eyes as he spoke.

"Whe… last night." Realization dawned on her. "You came last night… I thought I was dreaming… a really good dream!"

Jake smiled. "I thought maybe I'd tried to wake you. I didn't want you to be scared. I mean, by waking up with someone when you went to bed alone. But you spoke to me… sort of. You told me to go to bed right here." He patted the bed.

Kya was waking up more. "Wait, so you were being literal when you said you didn't want to leave me."

"Yes, and metaphorical, too. So, I rode my dirt bike over. Figured it would have been really awkward to ride home with you and Rachel."

Kya's brow scrunched. "Yeah, good call."

There was a loud bang from upstairs. Kya whipped her head toward the door.

"My paren… nts are not here." She dragged through the word as her panic settled. "They would so kill me if they ever found you here."

"Probably. But I figure I'd get it much worse than you. They love you, and I'm just some dude in bed with their precious daughter. Being cautious, though, I parked the bike on the other side of your car. They wouldn't see it even if they were here."

"Unless my dad decided to go to the barn for something." Kya looked at Jake, then relaxed into him. She rested her head back against his shoulder with a small sigh. "I'm glad you're here."

Kya stretched against him, and he gripped her leg again, holding it in place. Her hand stretched out and covered Jake's on her knee.

Jake looked her in the eye and shook his head. His grip tightened.

Kya pulled her lip between her teeth, eyes blazing.

A low rumble worked its way up Jake's throat. Kya shifted, sliding her body up his entire side. Tingles spread over him from hip to nose. The large gulp of air he sucked down was a really bad idea. His senses were overwhelmed by her scent, and the expansion of his lungs pressed her chest flush with his.

Kya crawled up the length of his body and planted an elbow on the bed next to his head. She wavered over him, her hair forming a curtain, her luscious lips mere breaths from his.

Jake held himself immobile, curious what she would do.

The fingers of her hand scorched over his skin as she brushed them over his forehead, and through his hair. He shivered under her light touch as her fingers moved over his face and down the side of his neck. She grazed the bottom of his jaw, and her thumb brushed across his lower lip.

Jake's breath stalled in his lungs, though his body was running at full throttle. If she didn't release her hold over him so he could breathe again, he was likely to overheat. Kya's touch, her scent, the way she was looking at him, it all lit him on fire. He was sure to self-combust. Her nose swept along the side of his. Her bottom lip was a feather touch on his. Her upper lip joined the bottom one. She sucked very slightly, and Jake couldn't hold himself immobile any longer. His lips captured hers. A small gasp escaped her, and Jake silenced it with his mouth. He drank from her as if she were an oasis in a desert. Her tongue slipped along the seam of his mouth, and he opened for her.

They devoured each other. Kya's hand fisted in Jake's hair. Jake's hand on her knee slid up her thigh; his other hand trailed down her spine and drifted under her shirt, so they were skin to skin. The feel of her soft skin on his set him ablaze.

Jake shifted and rolled Kya on to her back. She made a sexy, surprised noise. Jake groaned again and shifted over her.

Gathering his shirt in her fist, she clung to the material, pulling Jake's weight down to her. She broke the kiss and expelled a frustrated breath. She pulled his shirt up his torso. It gathered around his flexed shoulders. Jake pulled his arms free, and Kya yanked the infuriating garment over his head.

Kya's hand seared a path down his chest and abs. Jake rumbled deep in his chest and clenched his jaw. His cheek rested against Kya's, and he breathed in the sweet scent of her hair. He wrapped his fingers around the back of Kya's neck and guided her mouth back to his.

Jake was lost, and yet he had found something he had no idea was missing. He was lost in everything that was Kya, her deep, warm eyes, her scent that surrounded him, her warm body pressed into his, her hands on his skin. He was lost to the point where Kya was the only thing that existed…

in losing himself, he'd reawakened who he truly was. His body burned with more sensations than he'd ever thought to feel or would allow himself to feel. His heart was swollen in his chest to the point of breaking through his ribs. His head was clearer than ever, and he knew exactly what he wanted. He wasn't drifting anymore. He was ready. Ready to forgive himself. Ready to remember the friends he lost. Ready to live a full life. Ready to savor every moment with Kya, ready to make her his, forever. It was a conviction that settled in his heart and in his soul.

She was soft and delicate beneath him. Her lips were tender, but her kiss was fierce. Her good hand was all over his skin. And Jake burned.

He retreated a few inches, their heavy breaths mingling in the space he'd created.

"Hmm." Kya's sweet sound was almost a purr. Her eyes were closed, and her hand was frozen on his chest.

"You are so gorgeous, Kya."

Her eyes flicked open, and Jake stared into their chocolatey depths.

"I," Jake paused, "Kya, I want this. I want you. So much…"

"I want you, too," she whispered, but made no movement.

Jake rested his hand on her cheek, careful of her bruises. "We need to stop now, before I can't."

"I didn't think you could be any more wonderful. Then you go and surprise me."

"We have every opportunity, but I want to do things

right… responsibly… for once," he said with a dead chuckle. His brow crinkled as he looked away.

Kya placed her injured hand on his face and drew him back. "Thank you, Jake. And I agree." She stopped and looked down like she was ashamed, and her cheeks pinked. "I, uh." She swallowed hard. "I've never done anything like this, like anything ever." Her eyes were back on his.

Jake rested more of his weight on his knees, lifting himself off her. No need to scare her with the obvious things she was doing to him. He held her gaze as he braced himself over her. "Kya, you have nothing to be ashamed of. I figured as much given who your friends are… or were. But that is not a source of shame. You should be proud of that. That takes courage, strength, discipline…"

"Lack of opportunity," Kya said.

Jake smiled at her. "Naw, I don't buy that. Though it may be true. I think you're a girl with a plan and morals."

She said nothing.

"Am I wrong?"

"No…" She fiddled with the sheets on the bed. She sat up quickly, and Jake retreated. She settled herself with her legs folded beneath her. "The way I see it, sex has become so commonplace, especially for teens…" Kya's face took on a slightly disgusted look. "And I've always been the kind of person that, if there is something that everyone is doing, I want to do the exact opposite. That's why the senior party was my first party. I've just never followed the crowd. And as archaic as it is, I made a deal with myself that I would wait till, well, marriage."

He smiled. "Kya O'Shadit, you are the most amazing woman I have ever met. Don't ever change."

TWENTY

Jake lay on the ground with his shoulder, and hip pressed into the dirt and grass. He'd left Kya and her amazingly comfortable bed earlier that morning to attend to his duties on the ranch. He dug through the toolbox next to him, searching for a wrench. After beating his knuckles seven times on the points of the hammer that lay in the bottom, Jake gripped a handful of wrench handles and dragged them from the bottom of the metal box. The back of his hand came out black with grease from whatever was spilled in the bottom of the box. Jake ignored the stain and started sorting through the wrenches in his hand. He pulled out each wrench individually and checked the number size etched on the side.

"Yes," he laid one next to him, "no, no." Those two went back in the box on the opposite end from where the rest were. "Aha, yes. Finally, jeez." He dumped the remaining wrenches in the box and rolled back under the truck he was working on with the wrenches in hand. A sharp rock stabbed him in the spine as he rolled and slid across the ground. What he wouldn't give to have a concrete floor. Oh well, such was ranch life. He pulled the oil pan under the truck and placed it where it should hopefully need to be. Jake slid to the side and out of the way of the oil spout. He tried one wrench, but it was too small. He switched to the other wrench, and it fit perfectly. He slid out of the way farther and used the wrench to twist the nut on the bottom of the oil pan. Dark-colored oil spewed from the opening. It got the side of his wrist before he could snatch it out of the way.

"Damn it. Every freaking time I get covered in oil. Uncle Kal comes out and barely gets his pinkie wet." Jake sighed and reached for a rag.

His phone in his front pants pocket rang and buzzed against his leg. Jake scooted out, scratching rocks down the length of his back. He wiped his hands quickly with the rag and dug his phone from his pocket. The name on the screen read, "Mom." He pressed the button and put it to his ear.

"Hello," he answered.

"Hey, Jake, how are you? Sorry I haven't called sooner. I did get your message."

"Hey, Mom. I'm good. How are you?"

"Oh, you know, busy with work, court and a few big clients…"

"Yeah, same here, mostly just work."

Both ends of the call were quiet. A loaded, awkward silence hung between them. Jake scuffed his boot in the gravel, stirring up dirt. It had been so very long since he'd talked with his mom. Longer than the six months he'd been at the ranch. Since before the accident that ultimately landed him in jail. He hadn't *really* talked with her since… he couldn't remember when. Maybe when his dad left.

Jake took a deep breath and started in, "So there's something I wanted to talk to you about."

"Yeah, what's up?"

"Is there any chance in the near future you would be able to come visit?"

"Well, I recently started a case with a really big client, so I'll be tied up for about three weeks or so." She paused.

Jake's stomach began to sink.

"I could probably take some time off afterwards, though."

"Really!?"

"Yeah, actually, I could really use a vacation, and I'd love to see my sister for a bit."

"Awesome! Great! That's really great, because there's someone I want you to meet."

"Oh, yeah? Someone like who?"

"Her name's Kya." Just saying her name made him smile.

"Ah, I see. A girl, huh?"

"Not just any girl, Mom. It's still early. I really have only known her for…" He counted in his head. Had it really only been that long? "Uh, about two weeks. But I feel like she's not just *a* girl, but *the* girl…"

"Oh, really?" she said, with a skeptical ring.

"Yeah. She's amazing, Mom."

"Oh, man." Jake could hear the catch in her voice and the moisture gathering. "My little boy's in love."

"Yeah, I think I am."

"My goodness, you've grown up so much. Make sure that

you tell this girl. Tell her before something stupid happens. Make sure she knows how you feel about her."

"I will, Mom." Jake shuffled his feet again. He couldn't believe how this conversation was going. He was delighted in every fiber of his body. All the pieces were falling into place. But… "There's more, Mom," he said. Even he could hear his voice fall.

"What is it?"

"Well, she's in a bit of trouble."

"Oh, no! Jake, you cannot be getting messed up in trouble. If this girl is going to drag you down the wrong road again, when you finally are starting to tread on the right one, I will not have it!" The mom voice was out full force.

"No, Mom, it's not what you think. She's not the trouble—she's practically a saint. She got into a situation that put her *in* trouble." Jake waited for what he'd said to sink in.

"…Well, are you going to tell me what happened?" she asked.

Jake recounted Kya's tale to his mother. He practically gushed to her. He hadn't talked so much in all his life, but when he was finished, his throat was raw, and his shoulders were removed of a burden. He took a deep breath, filling his body to capacity, and let it out, feeling light, like he did when Kya was around. But she wasn't here now. Still, he felt as he did when she was, and that was an amazing feeling. It was as though, now without the weight on him of his broken relationship with his mom, he'd be able to truly give Kya what she deserved in a man, someone who could give their whole selves to her. He had needed her not just for her, more like a drug that numbed and distracted from the pain. But now all was pure want for Kya. It was euphoric, no conditions attached.

One thing was for certain: he was definitely not without scars. He imagined his soul looked about like Kya's face and hand. But Kya's soul was pure and unblemished. Aside from her recent encounter with the dark side of humanity, she was pure as the rain that washed the earth clean. Just as she was doing for him, making him clean, scrubbing the dirt from his scars. Sometimes it hurt, but it was worth the small pain knowing it would all heal cleaner and better than before.

When Jake finally ended the call with his mom, he was sure they had talked for hours. The call length read forty-five minutes. Smiling to himself, a true genuine smile of his own creation, he sat heavily on the ground, his arms draped over his bent knees, the oily rag in his hands. He smiled again, and tears washed clean tracks through the dirt on his face.

KYA SAT STRAIGHT UP IN BED. HER HEART POUNDED, and her breaths were heavy. She'd been in a deep sleep, and something had startled her awake. The ringer on her phone rang again, making her jump. She picked it up. Jake's name was on the screen.

"You scared the crap out of me," she said when she answered.

"Oh, I'm sorry." His tone said that he was anything but.

"I was sleeping." They'd stayed up late that night talking about anything and everything and nothing. It was wonderful. She'd learned so much about him. About his family, his mom. She was fascinated and infatuated with him.

"Well, you're awake now."

Kya didn't respond, and she couldn't help but smile.

"You're smiling. I know it."

She smiled even wider.

"You should come to the ranch today."

"Why?" she asked.

"Because I have a surprise."

She sat for a moment. "Fine."

"Cool, see you soon. Oh, make sure you wear jeans and boots." And he hung up.

Kya threw her covers off and sprang out of bed. She dressed in jeans and a tank top, and her cowboy boots and a ball cap, too. She grabbed her keys and phone and ran out the door.

A few minutes later, she was pulling into the driveway at the ranch. She parked her car, and her phone dinged.

The message read, *Meet me in the barn.*

Kya smiled and made her way across the yard. Inside the barn, the light was dim. It took a moment for her eyes to adjust to the muted light, blinking a few times.

"Jake?" she called.

"Over here."

She followed the sound of his voice around a corner and down a wide hall lined with stalls. At the end stood Jake, flanked by one horse on each side, in full riding tack and ready to go.

Kya grinned and strode toward Jake and the horses.

Jake smiled. It was sweet and excited, with a touch of shyness.

"Hey," he said as she approached.

"Hey," she responded.

"Have you ever ridden before?"

"Yeah, not very much, but yes, I've ridden before."

"Good, you can have Cream Puff here." Jake passed her the reins to a short black horse. There was nothing special about the horse. He was black, short, and slightly overweight.

"Is his name really Cream Puff?"

"Yes, yes, it is."

Kya quirked a brow at that.

The horse that stood next to Jake was a tall, sleek buckskin. He was tan all over, with a black mane and tail. He stood a good foot taller than the black Cream Puff.

"What's your horse's name?"

"Nasty Nork," he said.

"…Like, from the old video game with the dragon?"

"Yep!"

"Ooookay then."

They led the horses out of the barn and into the sunlight. Jake flopped his split rein over his shoulder and walked toward Kya. His horse followed obediently.

"Do you need a boost up?" he asked.

"Um, well, let's give her a shot." Kya looped her

tied-together split reins over her horse's head. She reached up to grip the saddle horn in her left hand and stopped. She wasn't sure it would support her weight up to the saddle. She grabbed the back of the saddle in her right hand and prepared to fall on her ass.

"Just catch me if I fall, please," she asked.

Jake looked at her as he nodded, and the expression on his face told Kya that nod meant way more than just in that moment.

Kya gave Jake a small smile and tucked her chin to hide her grin. She breathed deep the smell of horse, leather, and summer, then reached up and hooked her wrist around the saddle horn rather than her burned hand. She lifted her left foot and curled it up to her belly to reach the stirrup. She placed her weight on her foot in the stirrup and heaved herself into the saddle. Jake's hands were on her waist, helping her up. It wasn't graceful or the proper mounting practice, but she was up, sort of. She lay on her belly across the seat of the saddle like a beached whale. Kya pulled her right leg up and shimmy-wiggled her way into an upright seated position. She reached down and placed her right foot in the stirrup, picked up the reins, and took another deep breath.

Jake smiled, shook his head, and walked to Nasty Nork. He swung into the saddle, graceful and professional. He sat tall, proud, and in control. He looked comfortable, like he belonged there.

Kya had to admit there was nothing sexier than a man on a horse. Everything he did seemed to be perfect, kind, and gentle. Her heart melted a little more for the man who had rescued her.

They nudged their horses into a leisurely walk and turned their path toward the pasture to the north. They crossed behind the house and had to open a wire gate in the fence to get through. And all they did was cut a slow path north. Riding and relaxing. Kya was so at peace. It was blissfully amazing.

She had no idea what their destination was, or if they even had one, and she didn't care. She enjoyed the silent sounds all around her. The birds, the wind, their horses' hooves in the grass and on the ground, the bugs... probably could do without the bugs, actually. But she was loving this ride with Jake more than any other thing she had done before.

After a while, they entered a grove of trees, and it got 400 times better. The light was muted, but the sunshine glowed in shafts between the tree branches. It was amazing. There were small ponds of water collected in the shale beds between the trees. There were flowers Kya had never seen before. She kicked herself now for not bringing her camera. She was definitely coming back here one day.

Jake stopped his horse and motioned for her to ride up next to him.

"What?" she asked.

Jake clicked his tongue and tapped one foot on Nasty Nork's side. The horse shimmied to the side, stepping closer to Kya's horse.

"Neat trick."

Jake stopped when both horses were smashing their feet between them. He leaned over and beckoned her closer. So, she leaned over too. He wrapped his hand behind her neck and kissed her.

He seemed to know exactly how to pull the perfect emotions out of Kya. He treated her like a princess, even though she looked more like Quasimodo.

Jake pulled back from the kiss, and they resumed riding.

Kya was dazed for a moment, then fell back in line with Jake.

"You know, I think there's some irony or sarcasm, if you will, to these horses' names."

Jake barked out a laugh, but said nothing more.

They continued on their sunny ride, and eventually, they turned and made a wide loop back to the barn.

Upon their return, Kya stopped her horse next to Jake's. He stepped down lithely from the saddle. The muscles in his arms bulged, and his jeans stretched tight around his backside. A sly grin turned up one side of Kya's face. Jake came around to her horse. He took the reins from her and looped them around a post. As he made his way back, he ran his hand down the length of the horse's sleek black neck, stopping at the saddle and gripping Kya's leg. He looked up into her eyes with the same sly grin she was wearing. Jake gripped her waist and lifted her from the saddle like it was no effort at all. He set her on her feet and gripped her neck, tipping her head back and to the side. He leaned in for a kiss with his head tipped so the bill of their hats would miss. Jake's other hand gripped her waist snugly, pulling her body into his.

Kay gasped lightly between lip-locks. Her head swam, her lips tingled, and her body pulsed, all from Jake's kiss.

He leaned back as their lips parted, tucking a wisp of hair back behind Kya's ear. "So, you know, you look sexy as hell in boots and jeans sitting on a horse."

Kya chuckled softly. "Funny, I could say the same to you."

Jake grinned, like a full-watt grin. His teeth even showed, and his eyes sparkled. It was the biggest smile she'd ever seen from him.

"So, was this the whole reason you scared me out of a dead sleep this morning?"

"Yep, it's best to ride in the mornings when it's cooler."

Kya shook her head and rolled her eyes. She helped Jake unsaddle the horses and brush them down. They worked in companionable silence while flinging mushy smiles back and forth. They would touch each other any chance they got, simply walking past one another. A gentle finger brush on the arm or a small shoulder bump, anything to create physical contact. Kya was beginning to doubt her resolve where her relationship values were concerned. The whole "waiting till you're married" was all good in theory, but no one ever took into account the raw attraction two people could create. Kya couldn't get enough of Jake. She wanted to spend all her time with him and never stop touching him… or kissing him. Now *she* was starting to sound a little obsessed.

TWENTY-ONE

Time moved weird. Sluggish and slow, yet there never seemed to be enough hours in a day. Jake had been busy on the ranch and thus wasn't hovering around as much. Kya was running out of things to do.

She had a checkup appointment for her injuries three days ago. It had gone quite well, actually. All they did was remove the bandages and look at the burn, trim a few dead skin pieces back, and do more hydrotherapy. Then they poked a bit at her eye, happy to see the swelling had gone down. In all, it was an easy visit.

Her parents had returned late the day after her doctor visit. Her mom had done a closeup inspection of her injuries again. Then Kya had to fill them in on all the happenings since they had left… with one exception. She left out the part where Jake stayed the night. No need to ruffle feathers unnecessarily since nothing happened. The talk her mom and her had was exactly what she needed.

Her mom had sat beside her, looking tired and sad, but trying to be happy. "I feel like I haven't seen you in forever." Was that pity in her eyes?

"Well…" Kya stared down at her hands, one smooth and the other red and puckered. "I've been hanging out with Jake a lot."

"Jake?"

"Yeah…"

"And!?" her mom implored.

"He's pretty awesome," Kya said with a small, guilty smile. A knot released in her gut, and the floodgate opened. "He's amazing, Mom. He invited us to a family barbecue. He's so kind and gentle and honest, and…" she paused, "and I think I love him." Kya peered up to her mom, waiting for the wrath.

"That's amazing, sweetie. Just make sure you don't rush it. Take it slow. You've got time," she said, and reached over to grip Kya's good hand.

Kya's mouth hung open. "You don't think I'm a lovestruck teenager? I've only really known him for a couple weeks!" she asked, baffled.

"Kya, you have never been a teenager. You were more like a, uh, a young adult. And the look in your eye, and the way you talk about him… it's not puppy love. I can see you really care for him."

"I…" Kya paused. "Thanks, Mom." She leaned over and hugged her.

"Oh, I love you, Kya."

"I love you too, Mom." Kya leaned back, "Do you think Dad will be mad?"

"Well, I'm not sure… guess we'll find out next time Jake's around."

"I'll be sure to warn him."

"Probably a good idea."

"Yep."

There was a short silence. "So, how is Rachel?"

"She's good. Being a little weird, though, moody and sad. She won't talk about it either."

"Hmm." Her mom sat for a bit. "And Mitch?"

Kya swallowed hard and clenched her jaw. "He's… He's… um… I don't know who he is, Mom." Kya's vision swam as tears filled her eyes. She blinked, and they spilled down her cheeks.

"Oh, sweetie." Her mom slid closer and wrapped Kya up in her arms.

"He was my friend! How could he hurt me like he did? He was never like that before. He tried to take out Jake!" Kya sucked in a sob and let it out again. "What he did to me is… it's permanent! I have to live with this for the rest of my life!" she sobbed again.

All the while Kya sobbed, her momma held her in her arms.

"He was supposed to be my friend. You don't maim your friends!" Kya pulled in a ragged breath.

Her mother pulled back. "You were not raised to be a victim. You're strong and resilient. I know you will conquer this. One messed-up hand doesn't make you ugly or useless." She wrapped Kya up again in a hug. "I'm sorry this happened to you, Kya. I wish I could have prevented it entirely. Maybe if I hadn't let you go to that party…"

"Mom, stop, this would have happened no matter

what. Mitch is volatile. He would have flipped the switch eventually. His infatuation with me goes way deeper than a crush. It's quite scary, actually." Kya pulled in a huge gulp of air. "He's always been prone to violence. And a lot of it was because of his feelings for me. I'm a fixation for him. How did I not see it?"

"Because you have a heart of gold, sweetie. You have never looked at him as more than just a friend. You've never led him on."

"I stayed his friend even after I knew how he felt."

"It would have only made all of this happen sooner. His family has never been the most kosher. Lord knows his father is at the bar nearly every day, and his mom always seems to have a new bruise… But you were the one to have the courage to give Mitch the benefit of the doubt and not judge him by his parents or his past. I'm just sorry that he couldn't be what you chose to see in him."

Kya stopped. Her tears had dried up, and she sucked in a steadying breath. A question came to her. "Do you think a person is always what their past makes them to be?"

Her mom thought before answering. "Yes… Yes, I do. Our pasts are what make us who we are. The experiences we've had shape us and take us down certain paths. What makes the difference is our choices and decisions that we make after. Our reactions to our past are truly what we become."

Kya sat back a space and studied her mom's face. It shone with love, honesty, and truth. "Jake's on probation in lieu of prison," Kya blurted and waited for her mom's reaction. Her brow creased quizzically as she thought.

"He's not much older than you, is he?"

"Four years.

"So, he's twenty-two."

"Yeah…"

"That's awful. What happened?"

Kya's heart swelled for her mom. She didn't judge him or accuse him of something. There was only sympathy and a want for understanding.

Kya held her mother's gaze and told her Jake's story.

"Oh my, that's so terrible. I'm glad he was able to get off with probation." She waited.

Kya didn't know what to say in the silence that followed.

"And how did Jake react?"

"He picked up boxing or more UFC."

Her mom's brows raised impressed. "Does he compete?"

"No, it's mostly an outlet for his anger."

"Has he ever shown aggression to another person?"

"Only Mitch that I've seen. When he showed up here with my shoes…"

"Hmm."

Kya stared straight ahead. "Mom, Mitch is the one who needs to be behind bars, or heavily medicated." Kya turned to her mom and gripped her hand. "Mom, we have to stop this. I don't want to be scared anymore… I have to lock him away. Many people knew what he was and how he was, and they did nothing. Maybe if someone would have spoken up sooner, I wouldn't look like this." Kya's jaw clenched.

"Okay. You are absolutely right. If you want to do this, you will need help. Start a list of people who would back your story or have an account of their own."

Kya nodded. "Okay, that sounds like a good idea."

"Have your friends help." She kissed her forehead. "I love you."

"I love you, too."

It had been the best talk they'd ever shared. Cathartic and comforting. She felt stronger now with her mom fully on her side and backing her.

AFTER A FEW PHONE CALLS, KYA SAT AT THE DINING table waiting for Jake, Connor, and Rachel to arrive and help her make a list. Papers were scattered all over it. Pens were littered across the papers. She propped her head on the back of her burned hand and tapped the page in front of her with the pen in her other hand. For the life of her, she couldn't remember the name of the kid she stopped Mitch from pummeling at the party.

"Ugh, what was his name?"

"Whoa, now, thought I was more memorable than that." Jake stood with his hands up in mock surrender.

"Hey!" Kya beamed. "I didn't hear you come in." She stood to greet him.

"Really? I even knocked." Jake's smile stretched his face, making creases form around his mouth. His cheeks lifted, making small lines at the corners of his eyes.

Kya walked to him, and he welcomed her into his arms, wrapping her up. She pressed her face into his chest, and he tucked her head under his chin.

"Mmm," she sighed. "I missed you."

"I know! It's been three whole days we've gone without seeing each other." He kissed her forehead. "But I know what you mean." He touched two fingers to Kya's chin, lifting her face to his. He leaned down as Kya pushed up on her tiptoes. His lips met hers. It was a reverent kiss, slow and languid, and full of love.

The front door opened, but Kya couldn't bring herself to care that she and Jake were about to get caught kissing each other senseless.

"Ahem!" Connor cleared his throat loudly.

Jake continued to kiss her as he held her in his arms. He lifted one hand, flying the bird to Connor.

"Come on, dude," Connor started as he made his way over. "You sound worse than the bottom of a Slurpee."

"Don't hate 'cuz you ain't got a girl," Jake said, a breath away from Kya's lips.

Kya stepped back and clasped Jake's hand. "Hey, Connor."

"'Sup." He stepped to the side, and there behind him was Rachel. Kya looked to Jake to answer the question written all over her face.

"He went and picked her up," he whispered out of the corner of his mouth with a shrug.

Kya nodded, and now she had even more questions.

"Hey, Rach." Kya gave her a quick but tight hug that Rachel returned.

The pregnant silence that followed was extremely awkward.

"So…" Connor broke in. "Why are we here?"

"Oh, right." Kya turned to the table of paper. "I'm making a list of instances and people who can give accounts against Mitch. That's why I asked all y'all to be here. I figured since you guys are more social than me, you would know more than me. I feel like I was the only one in the dark about that douchebag's obsession." All three of them nodded in unison to that. "See, so yeah, I need your help… please."

"Okay, let's do this," Connor said.

"Really?" Kya asked. "It's just that he's your best friend."

"Was. And 'best friend' is a strong phrase. It was more like I was a hockey referee." He shrugged. "We aren't in high school anymore. And maybe if I'd spoken up sooner, this wouldn't have happened to you," Connor said sadly, echoing Kya's own thoughts. "I wanted to apologize earlier, but, yeah, I didn't want to spoil the barbecue for you. I shouldn't have let you go in his room alone. I figured he's always behaved around you, so you'd be safe… but I should have done more. He was saying some weird stuff before the party. That's why I was watching you and giving you weird looks." Connor looked askance.

"You couldn't have known that would happen. I've watched movies in his room hundreds of times before with no incident," Kya said.

"That's not what I mean." Connor's comment hung in the air. "Mitch gave me a look like he'd murder me if I didn't leave you alone. And my thoughts were only for my own devilishly handsome face."

Rachel backhanded him in the arm with a loud smack.

"Ouch!" He glared down at Rach. "What I mean to say is I'm sorry."

"Yeah, I owe you as much too." Rachel looked at the floor. "I never liked him, and he'd made comments to me that were extremely creepy-possessive-obsessive. I should have warned you, Kya."

"Thanks, guys, but I didn't bring you here to place blame. I need your help." Kya thought for a moment. "And honestly, if you had said something, I probably wouldn't have listened. I'm *still* trying to reconcile the psycho possessive Mitch with the Mitch who was my friend. He made the shift that night because he thought he was out of time."

Connor nodded slowly with a wide-eyed expression. He reached into his back pocket and retrieved a folded piece of lined paper. "Jake and I—well, mostly me—already started a list." He opened the folded page at the table and took a seat. Picking up a pen and grabbing a piece of paper, he began writing. "I think we should give each person their own paper. Then we can add a list of instances under their name. A lot of these people had more than one run-in with Mitch, and there are some instances that I don't know about." Connor's gaze slid to Rachel for a brief moment.

"I like that plan," Kya said, as she, Rachel, and Jake followed him to the table.

As Jake pulled out a chair, he asked, "So, why am I here?

The only encounter I've had with him was when he brought your shoes and I broke his nose."

"Uh, moral support?" Kya offered.

"Okay?"

"Actually, he'll work great as an outside third party. He's an unbiased observer. He'll question stuff we overlook," Rachel said.

"What is this? CSI? And I'm totally biased. If you haven't noticed I kind of have a thing for one of the victims in question," Jake fired back.

"True, but this is bigger than just Kya. You won't know 90 percent of the people we put on this list," Rachel said. "And he was violent with you upon your first encounter."

Kya looked to her with a raised brow. "Since when are you all up on criminal law?"

"Since my dad leaves crime shows on the TV all the time." Rachel spoke to the tabletop, scribbling names as they came to her.

Jake reached under the table and placed his hand on Kya's knee.

"Well, okay then, who do you have on your lists?" Kya asked. Her list contained four names and a question mark. Rachel had nineteen names, and Connor had thirty-three.

"That many with actual physical contact? Violent attacks?" Kya asked.

"Well, no, some were just threats," Connor said. "Hadn't realized how many there were, and I just let them slide."

The room sat stagnant.

"Okay, we need to compare lists and make one list without duplicate names," Kya instructed.

"Then start each one their own page, and see what the number of encounters are for each, because some of these people were favorite targets," Rachel added.

"Well, that would be hearsay because it's not a personal recount, and I'm betting some of these are gossip," Jake chimed in. "And I doubt even if it happened multiple times, that the person has an exact number."

"True," Rachel said.

"Why don't we put a star by the ones who were 'favorites?'" Connor said, using air quotes. "Then it's the police's job to conduct interviews and collect official statements."

"Yeah, and the biggest thing, though, is getting people to talk. Why has no one said anything till now?" Jake asked.

"Fear," Kya said. The rest of them turned to her. "Everyone is afraid to speak. It's their word against his, and they don't want a target on them."

"We need numbers. The more people we can get to talk, the less fear or chance that Mitch will get off," Jake said.

"Alright, well, we have our list. Now what?"

"We take it to the police tomorrow."

TWENTY-TWO

Kya leaned back in her seat. Her left hand was draped lazily over the steering wheel. The beat of a rocking summer country song played on the radio. Her head bobbed in time to the music. A soft smile was stuck on her face. She straightened and flexed her cheek muscles, physically removing the smile. It came right back. She couldn't help it. She was just so happy. Looking in her rearview mirror, there was a tiny pang in her chest. She didn't want to leave, but she knew she had to. It was only for the night. Kya was sure she would see him the next day.

When Jake and she had taken the list of Mitch's victims to the police that morning, they hadn't been surprised. They started contacting the people on the list right away. And it turned out that many of them were more willing to talk now that there were other people to back their stories.

Kya now felt more secure than she had since graduation, and confident that Mitch was going away for a long time. She'd spent the rest of the day hanging out and watching a movie with Jake.

Her phone buzzed in the cupholder next to her. She

knew it was Jake. And her small smile transformed into a grin that split her face with euphoria. She didn't pick her phone up and kept driving down the gravel road. She was already distracted as it was. No need to add a cell phone to the mix.

The drive wasn't long.

She should have just taken the four-wheeler. That would have been fun. But she still couldn't really drive it. Without the bandages coving her burn, she could see the red healing flesh on her hand. Some places were fiery red. The whole thing was extremely tender too, like her nerves were exposed. She supposed that was probably exactly what it was.

She made the turn onto her driveway and bumped over the cattle guard. Powering up the dirt hill following the fence line, she took a left over her family's yellow cattle guard and on to their land. The large-sized rocks on the road rattled her little old car, and she swore it was about to rattle all the bolts from their holes and fall apart in a heap.

Gazing to the west, to distract her from the imminent doom of her car, she admired the setting sun lighting the sky on fire. To the east, thunderheads rose, towering into the sky. Kya pulled into her spot and parked. She was home, though her heart remained elsewhere. She smiled, and sighed, completely happy, utterly happy. She loved her life. She loved where she lived. It was gorgeous with green grass, fiery sunsets every night, and the smell of rain on the breeze. At last, she had a wonderful man in her life. Studying her burned hand, she smiled. If that hadn't happened, she would never have met Jake. Everything happened for a reason, even if we might not see it at the time.

Her phone buzzed again. She reached for it, smiling like an idiot all over again. The message flashed on the screen. She slid her thumb across it to open it. Her blood froze.

I'm coming to see you.

The message itself was completely mundane and might have even excited her had it been from someone else. Mitch's name in dark bold letters was at the top of the conversation thread. Kya scanned the conversation in a panic. It was really more like a monologue, one-sided, because Kya turned off notifications on his texts. It went back a number of days. Each message increased in urgency and pleading. The most recent ones were verging on volatile, containing threats, and then followed by professions of love. Kya was now truly convinced he was insane. A psychopath. And he was coming.

He wasn't going to stop. He was crazed and obsessed. And she was the object of said obsession. Her heart pounded, and blood rushed in her ears. Everything turned distant and sounded hollow. Spots danced in her vision. He was coming for her. The oxygen fled her, and she couldn't breathe. She had a death grip on her phone as she fumbled for the door handle. It clicked open, and she bailed out, nearly eating dirt in the process. She slammed the door and stumbled through the gate. He was coming. She looked up, and her heart seized. A white sedan car was halfway down the driveway.

Why now? Had he somehow found out about the list of victims? What changed? What should she do? Run? Hide? Fight?

Kya's mind raced. She could go inside and lock the doors. But she couldn't guarantee he wouldn't break a window… And Tucker was inside. She pulled up her phone and called the house phone. As it rang, the car crept down the rough driveway. He was here for her, and she had to do everything she could to keep Tucker safe, even if it meant willingly entering the snake pit. Her parents were on their day shifts. They would be home that evening around eight.

Tucker's voice came through the phone. "Hullo?"

"Tucker!" Kya took a calming breath to remove the panic. "I need you to lock the doors."

"Uh, okay?"

"Just do it. Start with the front door." The car drew closer. "Then the back door and then the French doors." Kya paused to look at the house. There wasn't any movement she could see, and the other end of the line was quiet. "Tucker, now!" Kya heard her brother jump a little. A few seconds later, he appeared in the window on the front door. He held the phone to his ear.

Kya nodded. "Lock it."

Tucker shook his head no.

"Do it, Tucker!"

He jumped again, and Kya could see fear in his eyes.

"He can't see you. He can't know you are here."

Tucker nodded slowly and backed away from the window.

"When you get the doors locked, lock yourself in your bedroom and stay in the loft."

"What if I have to pee?"

The white car crawled by the fence. "Be quiet like when Mom and Dad are sleeping."

"Okay…"

"I love you, Tucker."

"Love you too, Kya."

Mitch parked next to her car and climbed out, lumbering through the gate and down the sidewalk, to where she stood frozen halfway to the front door.

Kya sent one more message. *Mitch is here.* And he was upon her.

"Well, I see your thumbs aren't broken."

"Nope, just half mangled." Fear coursed through her, and apparently, it turned her sarcasm on full blast, channeling her inner Rachel.

"Not my fault you fell in the fire."

"But it is." *Shut up, mouth. Shut up. Shut up.* She was asking for him to hit her again.

His eyes narrowed. "No, that was all you, clumsy Kya." He teased her with her most hated nickname.

She really wasn't that clumsy. She tripped once with her lunch tray in school. And to this day, it seemed, she was thought to be clumsy.

Mitch stepped closer. "Why haven't you answered any of my texts? I thought maybe your phone was broken. But that's obviously not the case. And now I hear you're gathering an army of witnesses against me?"

The smell of sour, rotten piss washed over her as he drew closer with slow, sinister steps. He was drunk. A fresh wave of fear crashed into her chest.

"What is it, Kya? What's the reason?"

She really wished she was a better liar because right now that would be really useful.

He ripped the phone from her fingers. "Was it that douchebag who was here when I brought you your shoes?" He pulled up the lock screen on her phone. "Can you believe that fucker tried to fight me?" Mitch entered a code on her phone, and the screen lit up.

He knew her passcode… How did he know her passcode?

Mitch opened her messages. "That's him, isn't it? Jake? And you just texted him. He's the reason. He's been keeping you from me, hasn't he?"

"No, are you kidding me? Jake has nothing to do with me not texting you."

"Don't ever say his name! I can't believe you'd let some loser guy dictate who your friends are," Mitch huffed, and his shoulders bunched. "What the hell, Kya? You just throw yourself at the first guy who flashed his dick in your direction?"

Kya opened her mouth to argue, but he cut her off.

"And I know he's the first. I've made sure of that. No one would ever touch you, 'cuz I'd beat the shit out of them if they even looked at you in a way I didn't like." Standing mere inches away, he loomed over her, and whispered, "You are mine."

It was him. Mitch was the reason no one ever talked to her. He was why she always ended up without a date to prom. Then she was left with no option but to go with him. He's the reason Rachel was her only friend. Because she's too stubborn to let someone else tell her what to do. Had he ever threatened her? He was the reason. He was the reason for her social solitude. He's why she was never invited to a party before.

Kya's fear instantly converted into white-hot rage. "I am not yours!" She shouted the words in his face. "I belong to no one! You had no right to tamper in my life like that, to warn people off me. I am no one's object to claim!"

A shocked look had Mitch leaning back. Kya pressed forward. And he stepped back in response. This was a side of her *he'd* never seen before.

Kya leaned forward, locking her arms at her sides, lest she ignite his black rage, although she might be too late.

"And my relationship with Jake is none of your business! He had nothing to do with how insanely psycho you have become!"

Mitch's hand swung back. Kya saw it coming. She pushed herself in the opposite direction. Too slow. The back of his fingers stung her lower jaw. It would have been much worse had the blow landed squarely. Mitch slammed her phone straight down onto the rough sidewalk. It bounced and landed in the grass. His hand drew back again.

"I told you to never say his name. You. Are. Mine." And he swung.

This time Kya let the blow land, but she tossed her head, lessening the impact significantly. Her feet were planted firmly beneath her, but she buckled her knees and landed in the grass. She stumbled on her hands and knees. She crawled forward and clenched her fingers. She let out a small cry and rolled onto her shoulder, her arm tucked beneath her, her back to Mitch. Cool plastic pressed into her palm, and she slipped it into the front waistband of her jean shorts. She grunted and pushed to her hands and knees.

"Clumsy Kya." Mitch reached down and gripped her upper arm and yanked her to her feet. His fingers bit into her skin. "You've got to stop falling like that."

Kya glared poison into his veins as she brushed the grass from her hands and the pebbles from her knees.

"Come on, let's go do something. I'm bored." Mitch dragged her by the arm to his car.

"Actually, I can't. I have errands to run for my mom." Kya tried to jerk her arm free.

"Silly Kya. It's nearly eight o'clock. Nothing is open."

"Then where are we gonna go?"

"I was thinking Centennial for some night fishing."

"Mitch, I really don't want to go." She pulled on her arm again and swore she could feel her arm bruising.

"Oh, come on, it will be *fun*." Mitch gripped her tighter, pinching her skin and grinding her muscles into her bone. He dragged her by the arm to the gate, ripped it open, and shoved her through.

His meat hook of a fist gripped the passenger door handle. Kya decided his car was the nastiest color of white she had ever seen. The door made a wretched screech as it opened. Mitch shoved her down into the worn-out, crumb-and-dirt-filled seat. Kya righted herself. Her bare legs pressed into the grimy cushion. He reached across her and buckled her in. The rotten stench of him wafted to her, and she gagged. Oh, how her perception had changed. She'd ridden in his car before and never seemed to notice the dirt and smell. But now it was all she could do to keep her stomach contents down.

The seatbelt clicked into place.

"Safety first," he said, and slammed the door. He lumbered to the other side. The car dipped severely to his side as he stepped in and backed out of the space, speeding down the road.

Kya contained her scream of panic. He'd never driven this fast before. They entered the main road, and his speed only increased. Kya glance at the speedometer. It read slightly over eighty. Her breath caught, and she gripped the door handle.

Mitch hit the skids as they were about to his driveway and drifted around the turn into his place. The rear end swung out and nearly fell into the ditch. Kya ground her teeth and was glad that she was unable to breathe. Then she couldn't scream, and things would probably get much worse if she screamed.

Mitch locked up the brakes in the parking area, creating long, pale skid marks in the dirt.

"I'll be back," Mitch said in a bad accent and barked a laugh.

Kya watched him, watched his every move. He ambled away from the car and toward the fire pit in front of the door. They always seemed to have a fire going. It's a miracle they had any trees left on their land. Mitch stopped at the red cooler and pulled out a six-pack of bottled beer. He paused to speak to someone by the fire.

Kya slowly and carefully, without making any sudden moves, pulled her phone from where she'd discreetly stashed it in her shorts. The screen was shattered. Her plastic case hadn't helped much this time. She pressed the button, and the screen turned on and a picture of a flower she'd taken appeared. She slid her finger across it, and nothing happened. She tried again with the same result. Panic ebbed its way into her, and she furiously scraped her finger over the screen. She scribbled over the screen in every direction, trying to make it do something. A line slid under her finger, and the camera appeared. It was set to video. What kind of luck was that? She looked up as Mitch grabbed a fishing pole from the bed of an old truck and started back toward the car. She pressed the red record button, praying that it worked. The screen flashed and the timer showed up at the top and started counting. Kya carefully tucked the phone back into her shorts. She made sure the screen stayed on and away from her skin.

Mitch was at the car now. She covered the action by adjusting her clothing. Kya wished her shirt wasn't so lowcut and that she had on pants and a jacket. The night was growing chilly. And the wind was picking up.

Mitch tossed his items into the back seat and stuffed himself behind the wheel.

"Since we are going to Centennial, could we go back so I can get some warmer clothes?"

Mitch grunted, reached behind the seat, and dropped a grubby hoody from the floor in her lap.

Kya went to shove the infernal thing off her, but stopped.

Her stalling plan failed, but this disgusting hoody might help. First, it would cover her and keep her warm. She had no idea how long she'd be gone. Second, it would hide the phone in her shorts better. Kya bit down on the inside of her lip, and donned the nasty jacket in the name of survival.

Mitch peeled away from the house and down the drive. His speed increased along with Kya's fear, and the thought entered her mind that she might not make it out of this. Fear bubbled in her stomach. She wasn't ready to end this life. There was so much she still wanted to do and experience, so much that she would leave behind. It would be such a loss for so many, for something so simple.

TWENTY-THREE

JAKE WALKED DOWN THE HALL TO HIS ROOM WITH a bounce in his step. His phone chirped, and a small thrill raced through him. Kya's name appeared, and he flicked it open with the slide of his thumb. The text read, *Mitch is here.* Three simple words, but Jake's heart stopped and fell into his gut. He stumbled and caught himself with a heavy hand on the wall. Panic ruled him, and he didn't know what to do or where to turn. He took a deep breath that shuddered through his lungs. He snagged his truck keys and ran for the door.

His feet pounded the ground, and his legs vibrated with each impact. Jake sprinted to his truck parked over by the barn. Why had he parked so far away? He reached the door and ripped on the handle. It didn't give.

"What the fuck! Why is it locked?" Jake shouted into the wind. He stuffed the key in the door and twisted, wishing he had one of those button key fobs. The lock popped up, and he had the door open before he got the key out of it. Jake bounced into the seat, shoved the key in the ignition, and stopped.

He froze in his frantic procedures. Blackness was

beginning to fog the edges of his vision, and his breathing was shallow and short. The feeling was familiar. He took two deep breaths. His hands trembled as he held them out. He wasn't going to be able to help Kya. The thought scared the hell out of him. He had to help her. He wasn't able to save them, but he had the capability to try and save Kya. But he wouldn't succeed or even come close to attempting to if he freaked out. Jake took another long breath and gripped the wheel like a vise. He keyed the ignition and shoved it into gear.

The passenger door popped open.

Jake's foot hovered over the throttle.

Connor jumped into the seat, slammed the door, and buckled his seatbelt.

Jake stared at him.

Connor turned his head to look at him. "What?" he startled back. "Like I'd let you face that son-of-a-bitch alone."

"How'd you…"

"Know? Yeah, your extremely loud cursing and excessive running speed, along with the 'thirst for blood' look in your eye, sort of gave it away." Connor looked back out the windshield. "This was bound to happen… But I believe the explosion we're about to face is my fault. I lit the bomb."

"What do you mean?"

"I told Mitch off. He wouldn't leave me alone, constantly asking me to hang out or if he could come over." The words spilled from Connor like an overturned trashcan. "I told him to leave me the fuck alone. He's going to prison anyway, 'cuz Kya's got an army backing her now."

The crease between Jake's brows deepened as his anger shifted to Connor. "Why would you… You couldn't… for just a bit longer! You put Kya in…"

"I know!" Connor shouted. "You can rip into me later. We're wasting time. Kya needs help."

Jake snapped out of it and peeled out of the drive. He was furious with Connor, but what's done was done. He would deal with him later. Connor was right. Kya needed them.

It was unfathomable. Kya was just there minutes ago. She had left to fix dinner for her parents. It had literally been only twenty minutes. Yet now his bliss-filled afternoon with Kya seemed miles away.

He'd kill the motherfucker. He'd been to prison. He'd go back willingly if it meant Kya would be safe. That was if he got there in time. Jake wrenched his mind way from that thought. He had to keep his head.

Jake fished his phone out and dialed 911. He glanced at Connor out of the corner of his eye. Connor stared straight ahead, his features hard… this was his best friend they were going after.

"911, what is your emergency?" the operator intoned mechanically.

Jake paused. How did one describe this situation? *My girlfriend's psycho friend is at her house, most likely beating her to a pulp…* that didn't seem to quite cover it.

"Hello, is someone there?" the operator asked.

"Yes, um, my girlfriend is in trouble."

"What kind of trouble, and what is your location?"

"It'd be 26 West Barton Road, Upton, Wyoming. There's a guy at her house who is going to beat her up."

"Okay, we are aware of the situation, and someone is on the way."

"Thank you." Jake hung up the phone. He needed to concentrate on driving and possibly running the asshole off the road. But it wasn't just him he had to worry about now. Connor was in the truck with him. And Kya could be with Mitch.

He turned up Kya's driveway, throwing dirt behind him. The house came into view. Everything looked normal. No fugly old car. Jake parked his truck and bailed out, racing for the house, shouting Kya's name as he ran. He came to the door, twisted the handle, and smashed his body into the hard, green, metal door. His knee connected hard, and his cheek left a grease mark on the window. Locked.

"Kya!" Jake slammed his fist against the door. Through the window, Tucker's head peeked around the corner at the bottom of the stairs.

Jake looked over his shoulder as Connor walked up behind him.

"Tucker, open the door, please!"

Tucker stepped out from the corner with a .22 rifle held across his chest. His right hand gripped the stock next to the trigger. His index finger rested outside the trigger guard. The boy's left hand held the end of the wood stock, supporting the barrel. The kid definitely knew how to handle a gun.

Tucker approached the door, unlocked it, and stepped back.

Jake pushed the door open. "Tucker, are you okay? Where's Kya?"

"I'm fine, but Mitch took Kya!" His hands shook slightly, and his cheeks were flaming red.

"Tucker, is someone with you?" a voice spoke from what sounded like Tucker's butt.

"It's Kya's boyfriend, Jake."

Seemed everyone called it like they saw it. And yet he and Kya hadn't said it to each other. Why hadn't he told Kya?

"Okay, please stay on the line till our officers arrive," the voice said.

Jake heard an engine and turned toward the noise. A grey Chevy pickup bobbed down the road. On the side was a star with the word "Sheriff" written across it.

"The sheriff is here now," Tucker said to the phone hooked to his back pocket. He leaned the .22 in the corner of the wall by the door.

Jake and Tucker stepped out of the house, joining Connor on the sidewalk. They all went to the gate at the end of the sidewalk to meet the sheriff.

"Tucker, you the one who called?" Sheriff Rodgers asked.

"Yeah," Tucker replied.

"Okay, Tucker, you are in safe hands." And the line went dead.

Tucker pulled the phone out and turned it off.

"Mitch left with Kya."

"Where did he take her?" Jake asked. The sheriff scowled at him.

"I don't know. He just smacked her twice, dragged her to the car, and shoved her in."

Jake ground his teeth, wanting to tear off all of Mitch's protruding body parts… starting with the smallest. Jake took a step back, digging his fingers into his hair. He spun away from the others and threw his hands to his sides. They formed fists as he turned back around.

"Did she have her cellphone on her?" the sheriff asked.

"Yeah, but Mitch chucked it to the ground over here." Tucker walked away a few feet. He scanned the ground looking for the device… but it wasn't there.

"She might have picked it up again," Jake suggested.

Tucker and the sheriff were quiet. Both wore worried expressions. Jake guessed his face looked about like theirs, but darker.

Jake reached into his pocket and pulled out his phone. His mind whirled. Jake pulled up Kya's contact. His finger hovered over the number.

"Do not call her!" Sheriff Rodgers shouted.

Jake looked up at him.

"If Mitch tossed her phone, he probably doesn't know she has it. Calling her could get her in big trouble."

Okay, that was logical. But what was the use of a cell phone if you couldn't use it in a desperate situation?

"Tucker, do you and Kya have family sharing?" Jake asked.

"What?" Tucker's brow crinkled.

"On your phone and iPod, do you guys have family sharing?"

"Yeah, we share music." He looked confused.

"Give me your phone."

Tucker pulled a black case with two skulls and tribal patterns on the back out of his pocket.

Jake snatched the phone as soon as Tucker unlocked it. He tapped into the settings app and searched the word "find."

There was a list of devices. Tucker's phone was at the top. He scrolled through, and at the bottom of the list was Kya's. He tapped it. A map appeared with a dot in the center. And the dot was moving.

Jake released a breath with relief, and his muscles wound tight in anticipation. He moved the map to pan out. She was out south of town. Why was he taking her there?

"What are you doing, man? This is not the time to update your Facebook status," Connor growled at him.

"I don't even have Facebook. And… I found her." Jake turned the screen toward them.

"Son-of-a-bitch, you tracked her phone," Tucker said.

"Damn, that's some real spy shit right there," Connor said.

"Don't cuss and get in the truck." Jake pointed at Tucker, then turned toward the parking area and started forward.

"No, we'll all ride in my truck. You can direct me," the sheriff said. He had been chatting on his radio about the current situation.

Jake conceded with a nod and jogged to the sheriff's truck. He immediately slid into the back seat, knowing it was not very acceptable for a civilian to ride in the front of a patrol vehicle. Tucker filed in after him.

"Uh, guys, how are you all going to get back?" Connor asked from outside the door. "By my count, if I stay, you'll have five people, and one's a criminal."

"Follow us in my truck," Jake called out to him.

"Okay," Connor turned away. "Only way I'll ever get to drive his truck," he muttered.

The trip into town seemed to take twice as long as normal… and the sheriff was speeding. Jake glanced over his shoulder to the black Dodge following them. It made him nervous to have someone else driving his truck. But this was for Kya, and he'd suffer anything to have her safe.

"They're heading south out of town on the highway," Jake said. His stomach dropped at the familiarity of being in the back of a police car. Though the situation was a lot different, it was reminiscent of the same feeling. The memory of the last time drifted before his mind's eye. Jake shook himself to get rid of the dark thoughts and focused on Kya. He had to find her. He had to stop Mitch.

DARK CLOUDS SHROUDED THE SKY, GREY, OMINOUS, and heavy. The horizon to the east was obscured by grey sheets of rain moving in their direction. Lightning flashed in the south, followed by a low rumble that reverberated in her chest. The wind whipped Kya's hair like a flag tied to a pole. The ends made a snapping sound as the wind tore through the strands.

She wrapped her arms around her chest as she shivered in the cold breeze. Goose bumps covered her legs. Judging by how cold it was here, it was definitely snowing in the mountains. Got to love Wyoming weather. *Such trivial thoughts.*

The surface of the water on the small pond rolled over with the wind, turning white as it crested over. It lapped at the shoreline like it wanted to escape as much as she did. Kya stood where Mitch had placed her, not daring to move. Dirt and debris stung her skin as the wind tossed it through the air. Her eyes were gritty with it, and her ears were packed full. Kya huddled into the dirty hoodie of Mitch's she wore. She watched Mitch. He stood five feet from the edge of the water, a fishing pole in his hand. He slowly turned the reel, winding the line back up. When his lure reached the water's surface, he reeled a bit more, then drew the pole back toward the galling wind and flung it out again, letting the wind take his line even farther.

"Isn't this fun!" Mitch called back, shouting to be heard over the gale.

Kya nodded with a fake smile and stumbled forward as a powerful gust of wind tried to knock her off balance. She leaned back, counteracting the force.

Mitch gave a small glare and returned to his fishing. He talked and chatted like everything was fine. As if it was a normal day and he wasn't a psycho beater.

Kya didn't listen. None of it mattered. None. She stared at his lumpy back, burning him alive with her eyes. Her hatred for him grew with every passing speck of dirt on the wind.

She could no longer see the friend she used to know. He was dead, and she had been kidnapped by a gonna-be-convict.

His back was to her. Kya glanced around. There was no one in sight. She stepped to the side one small step. Mitch never moved. Kya made a split-second decision. She turned on the balls of her feet and started sprinting. The sandy dirt beneath her feet crunched with every step. It reminded her of track and field day in elementary school, when they ran on the old gravel track. She wasn't aware if she was breathing. She focused on her legs propelling her forward. She was fixated on nothing other than the door handle on the fugly old car. It was within feet of her. She stretched out a hand, reaching for it. A massive, heavy boulder struck her in the back. All the air fled her lungs. She tried to catch herself with her hands, but they folded beneath her and did nothing to stop her slide. She could feel the skin on her hand filleted away. Her left hand, with its tender healing flesh, was ravaged over the ground. Her face smeared across the packed earth, bloodying her from forehead to chin, and filling it with dirt. Her knees, legs, and ankles followed behind, scraping along the rough ground as she slid to a stop with the heavy boulder atop her adding to her own weight.

"Clumsy Kya. I told you not to run. Why won't you listen?" Mitch's acrid breath gagged Kya as he spoke over her shoulder.

The immense weight lifted off her, and air returned to her starved lungs. Kya rolled to her side and curled into the fetal position. She cradled her left hand gingerly to her chest. Her entire body trembled.

Mitch reached down, picked her up by the shoulders, and set her on her feet. "Oh, man, you're gonna need a band-aid when we get home," he said.

"Will I be *going* home?" she asked through chattering teeth.

A shadow washed over his face, and his voice deepened. "That depends on if you behave."

His grip cut into her arms, leaving bruises again. Fear was now a living creature inside of her. It writhed and spat. Its venom paralyzed her, numbing all her senses.

Mitch dragged her back by one arm to the edge of the water. This time she was right next to him, where he could see her. She stood on her own. She would not give up this fight. She just had to think and be smarter. But how did one outwit a psycho person with a tendency toward serial-killer-ism?

She was completely paralyzed, unable to speak. Kya wasn't sure she wanted to. She didn't want to discover more about the evil person who stood next to her. She just wanted him to stop hurting her.

Kya pulled in a shaky breath and peered down at herself to inspect the damage. Her hands looked as though she had literally put them through the meat grinder. They were all raw flesh and dripping blood. Her face stung when she moved her eyes. Blood ran down her legs and was pooling in the bottom of her worn-out flip-flops under her dirty feet. Kya looked away and concentrated on breathing.

One breath. She thought of her mom and dad getting off the bus right now, completely clueless as to the state of their daughter's brutal kidnapping. Two breaths. She thought of Tucker locked in the house, most likely holding a rifle and not knowing what to do. Three breaths. She thought of Rachel and how she wished she'd trust her, and the possibility that she might never know what was up with her. Four breaths. She thought of Jake and all his heroic glory, always rescuing her. This time was different. No one knew where she was.

Dread seeped in, trying to crush her. She shoved it back. A few scrapes would not render her dead. Yes, she was bleeding, and she hurt, and she was shaking, but she was still standing. She was going to win. She was determined now, not just determined. She was angry. She clenched her jaw, now shaking for a whole other reason. She focused on the middle space while all of these emotions washed through her, leaving her raw.

Mitch looked back and smiled a genuine smile, which scared Kya even more than the serial-killer-ism. He turned back to his fishing.

Kya released a breath and dragged a dirt-filled one back in.

Mitch yanked backward on his fishing pole, making Kya jump.

"Eh, damn it!" he muttered as he lumbered to the shore and started following the line to the cluster of weeds that snared his lure. He moved farther and farther away from Kya.

She stepped out of her sandals and quietly backpedaled

toward the car, watching Mitch the whole time. He was consumed by the snag on his line. Kya increased her speed. Knowing she had to be close, she turned and ran.

TWENTY-FOUR

KYA SKIDDED INTO THE CAR DOOR, LEAVING RED, sticky handprints on it. She ripped the door open and fell inside, slamming the door behind her. Through the window, Mitch was taking giant, speed-induced strides toward the car and her. She fumbled for the lock button. There was a loud click milliseconds before Mitch smashed into the side of the car. It rocked to the opposite side, then settled back.

Kya righted herself in the seat and froze. He pounded on the window. It reverberated like thunder, and she could feel it in her chest. The keys were in the ignition. She sprang out of her stupor and started the car. His pounding increased in tempo. Throwing it into drive, she smashed her foot on the throttle. Pound. The car threw gravel behind her. Pound. It crawled forward. Pound. Then it lurched with speed. Pound. Kya turned the wheel. Pound. A silver pickup appeared before her. Pound. She threw her weight onto the brake and skidded to a stop.

The car lurched and tossed Kya back into the seat. She glared at the pickup blocking her escape. Just as she noticed the sheriff's emblem on the side, her world exploded. Glass shattered all around her, and she covered her head with her hands.

Mitch's hand gripped her hair. It pulled tight, and Kya screamed. Her back hit the door as he pulled her by her hair through the broken window. Sharp edges of glass scraped along her shoulder and back. Her hands held onto her hair, trying to relieve the tension from her head. Then all the pressure was gone, and she fell back into the seat. At the same moment, there was a loud and heavy crash against the back door of the car. Kya scrambled as far away from the broken window as she could get. She turned in the process to see the new threat.

It was Jake. His face was dark with pure hatred and rage. It was a scary face to see, but she welcomed it then because it was directed at her assailant. Jake ducked below the edge of the window with his fist cocked back, ready to fire.

Movement caught her eye, and she turned to see the sheriff, Connor, and her little brother standing by the truck that blocked her path. She had no idea how they had found her, but she was grateful.

JAKE'S VISION FOCUSED. IN AN INSTANT, HE TOOK IN the scene before him and gathered what data he needed, which was that Mitch was hurting Kya. Nothing else mattered. He knew his purpose.

The sheriff rolled down his window. Jake reached through and had the truck door open before the sheriff could stop.

Jumping out at a dead sprint, he bulleted to his screaming woman, aiming for the beast that was attacking her. A few feet away, Jake jumped into the air, pulling back his fist, using his smaller form and agility to get the upper hand. He rocketed his fist into the side of Mitch's head. Mitch thumped into the back door of the car and rolled to the ground. Jake landed on his feet nimbly, never taking his eyes off his target. He was down, but out of pure rage, Jake pulled back his fist and pummeled Mitch's face to a pulp.

He could hear the sheriff shouting behind him, but he couldn't bring himself to care. He wanted to make this son-of-a-bitch feel pain the way he'd made Kya feel it.

The sheriff hooked him by the shoulders, and Jake stepped back, heeding the older man's caution. But, judging by the look on his face, the sheriff wanted to do anything but. However, his years of training, knowledge of the law, and self-restraint kept him from acting on those emotions.

The officer marched past Jake, heaved the unconscious Mitch onto his stomach, and cuffed his hands behind his back. Then he was on the radio to the ambulance.

Jake huffed in a short breath, staring at the lowdown piece of trash on the ground before him. One more breath and he turned away. He lifted the lock and pulled the handle to the car door. There was blood on it. Inside, Kya was huddled on the center console. One foot was in the seat, and the other was on the floor. She was shrunk into a ball and shivering. She cradled her hands to her chest. There was a wild look in her eyes.

Then he noticed her injuries. Her hands and face were

raw, the skin scraped and peeled back. She cradled her burned hand. Rivulets of blood ran down her wrist. Her legs were scraped from hip to toes. And the skin on her thighs, knees, and the top of her feet were peeled back like she'd been pulled behind a truck. Her hair was a mess of knots. Her shoes were missing. And she was wearing a gross, oily, way-too-big-hoodie.

She suddenly shivered and pulled in a shaky breath and let it out. Scooting on her butt toward Jake, she trembled and shivered all over. Jake stepped away from the door so she could climb out. Her bare feet touched the ground, and her arms wrapped around his neck in a vise. Her breathing was short, shaky, and uneven. Jake enfolded her in his arms, holding her body to his. A mantra repeated in his head, *She's alive. She's alive.*

KYA TRIED TO CONTROL HER BREATHING AS SHE drew Jake's scent in and let it restore her. He was here. She was safe. He'd rescued her. Over Jake's shoulder, Connor stood apart with a shocked and disgusted expression. Tucker still stood by the truck. He clutched the truck door in his hands like he was using it as a shield. Kya had no idea how much he'd seen already, but she didn't want to scare him more. She continued to cling to Jake to hide the blood that covered her body. If the pain she was feeling was any indication, it had to be a lot of blood.

"How did you find me?" she squeaked out.

"Your cell phone," Jake replied.

Kya settled herself back on her feet. Her head felt weird, and her hands were shaking, but she ignored it and pulled her broken phone from the band of her shorts. It was still on record. The timer read one hour, seventeen minutes and counting. Kya pressed the stop button. How much did it actually capture, if anything?

The sound of tires crunching gravel made everyone turn to see who was arriving. A white box and a light bar appeared first over the hill, followed by the rest of the ambulance truck. It drove in the ditch to get around the two pickups, and skidded to a halt adjacent to the old car Kya stood by. The team of EMTs bailed out the back. Two went to the pile of trash on the ground, and two made their way to Kya. They took her hand and asked her questions, but Kya was in a daze and didn't hear anything they said. She stumbled with them to the back of the ambulance, sitting on the end as they tended to her wounds. Everywhere they poked and prodded seemed to make her pain increase tenfold. But she endured it, knowing it had to be done to make it better.

Finally, she allowed herself to inspect the damage to her body. By the pile of red gauze next to her and the red that still coated her, she was in worse shape than after the senior party. She looked like she'd walked out of a mass murder horror movie. And worst of all, she was still wearing the disgusting hoodie.

"Cut it off!" she screamed. She couldn't bring herself to pull the infernal thing over her face, her head, her hair.

She began to panic. She couldn't breathe. "Cut it off!" she screamed until her voice broke.

Scissors appeared, and the material was cut from the neck to the hem. Kya ripped the thing off as soon as the last thread was cut and chucked it to the ground. Someone with white rubber gloves came and put it in a bag.

Kya breathed and shivered, shaking out her hands, trying to rid herself of the disgustingness of that garment.

A loud shout made Kya jump and her heart race. A commotion broke out to the side. A few more officers had apparently arrived, and the sheriff had his gun out. Mitch staggered into view. He was shouting her name, over and over, at the top of his lungs. His one eye was swollen shut and bloody. He waddled like a drunken penguin, his hands cuffed behind his back. Two officers snagged Mitch, one on each arm, and propelled him to the squad car. The vehicle dipped as he climbed into the back. All the while screaming her name.

AFTER KYA HAD GIVEN SIX RECOUNTS TO FOUR different people of the events that transpired, she sat in the passenger seat of Jake's truck. Tucker sat in the back, and neither one spoke. The sheriff had taken near hundreds of up-close, detailed, and all-inclusive pictures of her wounds. She hoped she would never have to see them again, but logic told her otherwise. The thing was there was one more fight to be fought. This one wouldn't leave her burned, bruised, and bloody, but she would certainly be raw. She would have to relive every moment, the good and the bad, when they went to court. He might have already been going to jail, but she was still going to push her case.

Kya took a deep breath. Through the windshield, Jake, Connor, and the officers milled about, pointing and waving.

"Are you okay, Kya?" Tucker's voice was small.

She turned stiffly in her seat so she could face him. "Yes, Tuck, I'm alright."

"Does it hurt a lot?"

"Yeah, yeah it does. But it will heal, and Mitch will be in prison or an insane asylum."

Tucker nodded and took a deep breath, visibly relaxing.

"I'm sorry I scared you. But thank you for calling the police."

Tucker nodded again. "I love you, Kya."

"Love you too, Tuck."

Turning back around, she saw Jake patting the sheriff's back. After they shook hands, Jake returned to the truck. Connor followed him. He walked directly to Kya's door and pulled the handle. The wind rushed in. He leaned in and gently turned Kya so she was facing him.

"It's not official, but we won't be seeing him for a very long time."

Kya nodded, a mix of emotions flowing through her. Mostly, she just wanted to sleep.

KYA DRAGGED HERSELF FROM A DEEP DREAMLESS sleep, feeling like she needed more, but her body ached, telling her she had to move. The familiar cluttered walls of her room surrounded her. Sitting up slowly, everything hurt. Her skin was like tissue paper, as if it would tear with the slightest movement. Her hands were completely encased in gauze and useless. The ambulance had taken her to the hospital. Her parents arrived about an hour after she did. The doctors had poked, prodded, and scrubbed clean every one of her injuries. They had finished their treatment by encasing her in gauze. She looked like a mummy. They gave her some heavy painkillers, and her parents were able to take her home. She'd fallen asleep in the car.

It was disorienting to wake up in a different location than where you fell asleep. She knew it was daytime, just not what time. The police had taken her phone, and she didn't have another clock. She stood and started dressing, moving about as fast as a slug. She struggled into cotton shorts and a tank top, then started shuffling her way upstairs to the kitchen.

On the landing at the bottom of the stairs, she could hear voices. Kya hobbled up the steps, forcing her body to bend and her skin to stretch in ways it didn't want to. When she reached the top, the voices stopped. She stumbled to a chair at the table and fell into it.

Both of her parents, Tucker, and Jake sat around the table.

"How are you?" her mom asked.

"I've been better."

Her mom sort of laughed. "Yes, you have... I'm so sorry."

"No, no apologies. It happened. That's it."

Everyone looked solemn, like a scolded child.

"I just want to heal and move on." Kya looked at each of them in turn. "Jake, can I talk to you outside?"

He nodded.

Kya stood ungracefully and hobbled to the door.

Outside, bright sunshine heated Kya's skin, feeling amazing and horrible at the same time as it baked her numerous scrapes.

"What's the matter, Kya?" Jake asked as he shut the door.

Kya turned to him, made a little jump, and locked her arms at the wrist around his neck, gazing into his eyes. "Thank you for saving my life. In every way and on every occasion." She paused, getting lost in his green eyes. "I... I love you."

The most glorious smile cracked his serious face, and then he was kissing her.

She kissed him back, conveying everything she felt for the man in her arms.

He pulled back and gazed at her as intently as she did him. He gently caressed her cheek. "I love you."

Kya's whole body relaxed as warm tingles flooded through her. She felt so safe in his arms. "I've faced too many battles since I met you, but I wouldn't want to fight them with anyone else."

"And you'll never have to."

Then he was kissing her again.

EPILOGUE

"YOU KNOW, I... UH... I HAVE THIS DOUBT NOW... ABOUT people. Like if the face they are showing me is authentic or if it's just the mask they hide behind." Kya paused, picking at her fingernails, trying to leave the heavy, dry, dead skin on her hands alone. "It never used to be like that. I always just trusted that people were honest and real. I never knew that it was even possible for someone to hide so much of themselves. And now every face I see, there is this small voice in the back of my head that wonders, 'What's the truth hiding behind that skin mask?' I never used to be like that, and that's changed because of you…" Kya stared at him in his hideous orange jumpsuit through the glass window. Finally, the outside reflected what was truly on the inside.

"I know, Kya, and that's what I've always loved about you most. That you always trusted unconditionally at face value." Mitch's voice was low and sounded like gravel in a blender.

"I just want you to know," Kya lifted her gaze to look him in the eye, "that I'm no longer that naïve anymore. So thank you for that. And I also wanted to tell you that you have by no means broken me. I still choose to see the honesty in people at face value. And everyone wears a mask. But if they care about you and you care about them, one day they will remove it, with the hope that you will still see the honesty underneath and love them for that too…" Kya breathed through her nose as her anger boiled to the top. "You were my friend, and I'm sorry I couldn't love you the way you wanted. But I've realized, Mitch, the only time you ever took your mask off was when you were around me.

"You see, the thing about masks is they make us feel safe and protected. They make us feel better about everything around us and who we are. What I will never understand is how hurting others, drinking, and causing pain made you feel strong."

Mitch opened his mouth like he would speak.

"I'm glad you're getting the help you need, the proper meds, and I hope that one day you can burn your bruised mask, for the sake of those around you. But I pray that I never have to see you again after this day. This very minute."

Mitch's jaw hung ajar.

Kya stood and walked out. The guard buzzed her through the doors, and she signed the checkout sheet. Stepping out of the cold, concrete building into the summer sun, she saw black clouds building on the horizon.

Jake leaned against the driver's door of his truck. His calm expression split; a wide smile stretched his lips. Kya sauntered straight to him. He placed his hands on her hips, and she wrapped her arms around his neck.

"Hey there, gorgeous." His voice was smooth as supple leather.

Kya smiled, and her toes curled in her flip-flops. Her faintly bruised and heavily scabbed skin stretched as she smiled back. "I love you." And she kissed him.

The weight she'd felt hanging on her had lifted. She saw her future before her, full of adventure and many unknowns, but teeming with hope, and life, and love.

Jake graciously escorted her into his truck and drove them to Kya's house, racing the approaching storm. She didn't speak much, just held Jake's hand in hers the whole way. The land zoomed past, her mind calm and her emotions joy-filled.

As they parked in the drive, Kya looked through the window, watching the dark thunderclouds churn overhead. Lightning split the sky, and thunder reverberated through the vehicle, making Kya jump. With the next crash of thunder and lightning, the clouds let loose, and fat, heavy rain pounded the earth.

Kya stepped out of the truck. Lightning whitened the landscape, and thunder boomed around her, crackling and echoing through the trees. The rain drenched her hair and clothes. She tipped her face to the sky, letting the rain wash over her. It was cold, near ice cold. And it was heavenly. It ran down her arms and over her healing scabs, down her legs, and around her bare feet. Kya stood there soaking in the rain with her feet planted firmly to the ground. It washed over her, leaving her a sopping-wet mess, but she felt cleaner than she had in weeks.

Her limbs shivered in the ice water. Warm arms wrapped around her and pressed her back to an extra warm and solid body.

Jake held her against him. Kya smiled up to the dripping sky. A joyful laugh bubbled through her. She reached up and placed her hands around the back of Jake's neck. He looked down to her, and her smile turned into a rib-tickling grin that had her feeling lighter than she had in weeks and euphorically happy.

Small, dime-sized, white spheres of ice began bouncing on the ground around them. One pelted Kya on the head. Three, four, five, struck her arms and shoulders.

Kya and Jake sprinted inside the house and out of the storm, shrieking and laughing as they ran.

They watched through the window as the hail grew to the size of golf balls. It hammered their vehicles and broke tree branches. A blinding white light flashed over the earth simultaneously with its deafening clap of thunder and a loud crack.

When Kya had blinked the spots from her vision, the large pine tree out front was smoking, and hundreds of pieces were scattered in every direction, blasted apart by the strike of lightning.

Kya marveled at the ferocity of the storm, its sheer powerful destruction.

Soon, the thunder only grumbled in the distance, and the rain ceased. The sky cleared of the dark clouds.

Kya and Jake strolled hand in hand back outside, turning in a circle, looking at the damage the storm had wrought.

Tree shrapnel and hail littered the ground. The sky was beautifully clear and radiantly blue. To the east, the most vibrant rainbow glittered above the trees. And the air smelled crisp with clean rain, and musky with wet dirt and grass. It was heavenly.

Kya beamed up at Jake. She had been through a hell of a thunderstorm. And what was left was a whole lot of mess to clean up. But the sky was beautifully clear, and it smelled, oh, so fresh.